M000192401

Stone Cold
MAGIC

Stone Cold MAGIC

Ella Grey Book One

JAYNE FAITH

Stone Cold Magic
Copyright © 2016 by Jayne Faith

All rights reserved as permitted under the U.S. Copyright Act of 1976. No part
of this publication may be reproduced, distributed, or transmitted in any form
or by any means, or stored in a database or retrieval system, without the prior
permission of the publisher, except in the case of brief quotations embodied in
critical reviews and certain other noncommercial uses permitted by copyright
law.

The characters and events portrayed in this book are fictitious. Any similarity
to a real person, living or dead, is coincidental and not intended by the authors.

Stone cold magic / a novel by Jayne Faith

Print Edition ISBN: 978-0-9970260-6-1

Edited by: Mary Novak
Proofread by: Tia Silverthorne Bach of Indie Books Gone Wild
Cover by: Deranged Doctor Designs
Interior Design and Formatting by:

E.M.
TIPPETTS
BOOK DESIGNS

www.emtippettsbookdesigns.com

Published in the United States of America

Books by
JAYNE FAITH

Sapient Salvation Series

The Selection

The Awakening

The Divining

The Claiming

Ella Grey Series

Stone Cold Magic

Dark Harvest Magic

Love Across Stars Novels

The Seas of Time

The Laws of Attraction

For every unknown artist or creative following a dream.

It was a pleasant summer night, but I walked with my fists stuffed deep in the pockets of my lightweight jacket and my head bent as if leaning into a stiff, chilly wind. I paused at the end of 12th Street where the mid-century bungalow houses stopped and the little shops began. Murky shapes feathered the edges of my peripheral vision, moving in a slow, curling dance like wisps of campfire smoke. There were moments, even long stretches, when the phantom shapes faded into the background of my awareness. But every time I noticed them anew, my insides chilled and gave a little lurch.

I tried to convince myself that the shadows framing my sight were meaningless. More than once, I'd sternly told myself they were just misfires of my optic nerves, artifacts of having been clinically dead for eighteen minutes. My brain had been deprived of oxygen, and there were bound to be some lingering effects. Hell, what were a few blurry dark shapes when I could have suffered serious brain damage—or not come back at all? But none of my internal cajoling had worked particularly well. Ever since I'd opened my eyes on a gurney with a sheet pulled up over my head, the shadows had been there. And as much as I wished it were otherwise, I couldn't help feeling that the smoky shapes were alive. They lurked, an ever-present reminder that sure, I may have cheated death. But I'd brought something back with me.

It was odd, knowing I'd been dead, queued up for the morgue, and yet somehow escaped the cold clutch of the grave to walk away from the hospital and return to my little apartment and the usual rhythms of life. I was like one of those drowning victims you sometimes hear about on the news, a still body with no pulse pulled from icy water and then miraculously revived. I knew I was lucky. I was beyond fortunate to be alive. Except something wasn't *right*.

I shivered and tucked my chin to my chest. Nope, not right at all.

With the dancing shadows framing my sight came horrific nightmares, jerky, unfocused visions of death that plagued my dreams when I slept and my thoughts when I woke. In the two weeks since the accident that had temporarily killed me, I'd become so sleep deprived—and, frankly, creeped out by the dreams—I'd finally decided I had to do something. I'd waited to see if my head would clear, hoping that during my forced medical leave I'd get back to normal. But it hadn't happened, and I couldn't wait any longer. Tomorrow was my first day back at my job as a Demon Patrol officer, and I needed to be fresh and clear-headed.

That was what brought me to where I stood—the hope of finding relief. The particular segment of 12th Street before me was known locally as Crystal Ball Lane. It was lined with small shops offering magical cures, a place normals came furtively seeking love potions, healing charms, and money spells. Ordinarily, most normals shunned the use of such things. They believed magic was responsible for tearing the world open twenty-nine years ago and letting in the hellish chaos of demons, the vampire virus, and the zombie virus. And, well, I couldn't blame normals for their prejudice because they weren't entirely wrong.

Those with magical ability like me—witches, or crafters as I preferred to call us—tended to see stores such as the ones on Crystal Ball Lane with disdain. They were the equivalent of magical tourist traps for the desperate and beneath the notice of crafters. But I needed something to eradicate the nightmares, to expel whatever grave-thing was clinging to me, and I didn't have enough magic ability to stir up a spell or a charm to help myself.

I pulled out my phone and pressed one of the side buttons, and it awoke with a cool white glow. It had vibrated against my hand three times since I'd left my parked truck a few blocks away, and each time the guilty little knot in my stomach tightened a touch more.

The device buzzed again as I held it, and a new text from Deb flashed.

Ella!! I'm an empath. You can't trick me. Spill it, lady. What's wrong?

There were two little frowny faces at the end.

I ruefully shoved the phone back in my pocket.

It was almost uncanny how Deb's texts had started coming through as soon as I'd hopped in my truck to seek help on Crystal Ball Lane. I'd talked to her earlier—she'd called to see how I was feeling about heading back to work—and of course Deb being

Deb she'd picked up on the fact that I was having trouble with something. I didn't possess her intuition or empathic talent, but I could tell she had her own worries. It wasn't any magical sixth sense on my part, just an instinct borne of many years of friendship. Her voice took on a particular tightness when she was having trouble with her husband Keith, and I'd be damned if I was going to add to her burden. So I'd insisted that I was fine, knowing she didn't fully believe me.

I entered the first block of the shops, eyeing the neon signs that advertised Tarot readings, herbal remedies, healing crystals, and all manner of magical cures and spells. The store I was looking for, Nature's Light, was a few blocks down. I'd checked out the website and saw the owner offered a variety of services, aura cleansing among them. I'd tried the phone number but never got an answer. Most of the businesses on the Lane kept late hours, and I hoped Nature's Light would be no different.

My phone vibrated again. I felt bad about ignoring Deb, but she didn't know the full extent of my problems, and I was hoping to eliminate them so that I could avoid telling her altogether.

She knew I'd been off since my accident. When she pressed me, I made a vague mention of insomnia. But I left out the smoky forms around the edges of my vision, the weird throbbing in my forehead. I hadn't mentioned the dreams, either, and it was partly due to my difficulty trying to describe them, even to myself, because I couldn't shake the sense that they weren't mine. They were like films shot by a camera that was held by an unknown hand, images that seemed to come through the eyes of someone—

or something—else. The *other*, as I'd begun to call it. And they weren't just visual—they were often laden with a heavy smell, a stomach-turning mix of wet leather, sulfur, and the metallic tang of blood.

Deb had given me the name of a hedge witch and made me promise I'd make an appointment. I suspected I needed a remedy stronger than a hedge witch's herbs, but Deb's suggestion had prompted the idea to look up other types of services. I wasn't convinced an aura cleansing would do the trick, either, but I had to start somewhere.

The soft sound of movement to my left brought my low-top leather boots to a scuffing halt. I sucked in a breath, and my heart thumped hard at the side of my throat. With a familiar, automatic motion, my hand instantly shifted from my pocket to my service stun gun at my hip. Some part of my mind knew that this was mostly likely perfectly normal street noise, but since my accident I'd gotten jumpy, startling so easily it was sometimes embarrassing.

As my pulse quickened, I squinted into the deeper darkness between two buildings. The center of my forehead thumped faintly, another odd post-mortem symptom that had been plaguing me on and off.

Something dark and bulky moved.

I flipped the strap on the holster with my thumb so I could draw out the gun if I needed it, and as an afterthought, I sent my senses through the bottoms of my feet and into the ground to pull up a thread of earth magic. Honestly, I probably shouldn't have even bothered. My weak-ass abilities barely even registered on the

Magic Aptitude Scale and certainly didn't give me much in the way of protection. Crystal Ball Lane was situated along a stretch of ley line, an underground vein where magic concentrated and flowed, that enhanced my abilities by a smidgeon, but not enough to properly shield myself against attack.

Movement again.

Just as I was on the verge of calling out and demanding that the lurker show himself, a large dog crept partway into the weak pallor cast by an orange neon sign across the street. We watched each other for a beat or two. The dog's tail waved back and forth, and he panted, his mouth stretching into a doggy smile. His eyes glowed like embers, reflecting the light of the signs nearby.

Assured that he wasn't going to attack me, I released the magic thread. My hand relaxed on the gun.

I nodded at the dog. "Careful of the cars, big guy. Drivers can't see you too well in the dark," I said, as if he'd understand.

Voices ahead sent him scuttling back away from the street and my attention whipping toward the new noise. *Damn*, but I was jittery these days. I shook out my hands, as if trying to fling away some of my tension, and peered ahead.

A group of boys, jostling each other and laughing, had spilled out onto the sidewalk. By their heights and builds, I guessed they were around fourteen. I grimaced. A pack of kids out this late, and right around the age when their magical aptitude, if they possessed any, would be emerging? I'd bet my paycheck they were up to no good.

The jeering voice of the biggest one confirmed my suspicion

and quickened my pace toward them.

The boys had circled around, trapping one of their own. The thin, small one in the middle had the hood of his sweatshirt up and was getting shoved around like a pinball.

My hand back on my stun gun, I sped up to a jog. "Hey . . . *hey!*"

I got closer and saw the kid they were picking on was actually a girl. Anger spiked through my chest and I yelled again, but the ring of boys was too caught up in its bullying to hear me.

When I reached the mob, I grabbed the shoulder of the nearest kid, pulling him back and breaking the circle. The boys finally looked up.

I pulled out my gun and waved it around for effect. "Go pick on someone your own size, you little apes." I drew myself up to my full five-foot-ten-plus-boot-heel and glowered down at them.

The big boy, the tallest by a few inches, shoved his hand across his snub nose and gave me a derisive once-over. He glanced at my weapon but didn't even blink. "We don't have to do what you say."

Strong currents of green earth magic swirled around his hands as he curled them into fists. The kid had a decent level of magical aptitude, but he appeared to enjoy using it for the purposes of bullying and intimidation. Great. In a depressing flash, I could practically see his future—Supernatural Crimes would eventually haul him in for gross misuse of magic, or maybe something worse, and he'd either spend time in prison or get stripped of his ability. Maybe both. One side of his upper lip lifted in a sneer that was so exaggerated I might have laughed if I wasn't so ticked off. I stared at him for a split second, surprised by how brazenly he stood his ground. Then I reached to my belt and pulled off my badge. A faint tingle of magic stirred against my palm as I tilted the charmed object so my credentials illuminated on the sidewalk:

Demon Patrol Officer
City of Boise, Idaho
Gabriella Grey
Badge #889475

One of his little henchmen sucked in a breath. "Oh shit, she's a cop."

Snub Nose snorted out a scoff. "Ooo, Gabriella Grey, demon police," he mocked in a falsetto, further raising my ire. He turned to the other kid. "She ain't real police. We ain't breaking the law anyway, don't be such a puss."

I pulled out my phone. "You're out after curfew, and that's automatic jail time. I'm going to need the names and numbers of your parents. I'll let them know where they can visit you in prison." There was a curfew law, but the other part was my own little enhancement for the purposes of getting them to scatter.

One kid shuffled back a few steps and then turned and hightailed it down the sidewalk, his arms pumping hard. Others followed. After a few seconds only Snub Nose, his victim, and I were left.

He lunged at me, and I automatically jumped back, but not far enough to elude the wad of spit he hocked. It landed with a splat on the toe of my right boot.

"Little twerp," I muttered, trying to shake the saliva off my shoe. Instead of flying off as I'd hoped, it just dribbled off the side.

With a final sneer, the ringleader jogged backward a few steps and then chased after his crew. I watched him go and allowed myself a moment of satisfaction. As I followed his progress, I caught sight of the Nature's Light sign, illuminated by tubes of blue neon, half a block away and across the street. A card in the glass door displayed the word OPEN.

I faced the girl, leaning in with concern. "You okay?" I asked, clipping my badge back on my belt. "You shouldn't be out alone at night."

She was dressed in a too-big pullover sweatshirt and the hood had fallen back, exposing wispy pale blond hair escaping from the sides of her sagging ponytail. Shaking her head once, she stepped forward, and it didn't take an empath to feel the desperation that seemed to shroud her. It gathered like two rain puddles in her soulful eyes. She took another hesitant step and then reached out as if to grasp my forearm but stopped short of touching me.

"My brother," she said, her voice already watery as tears began to pool in her eyes, causing my chest to catch in reaction. "He's in trouble, and I don't know what to do. That's why I came out here. Please, Officer Grey, you have to help me."

I glanced down the block just in time to see the blue neon Nature's Light sign extinguish. There was movement at the door, and a hand reached out and flipped the OPEN sign over.

Sorry! We're CLOSED

Even with my paltry magical aptitude, I sensed the girl was just coming into her own abilities. Not only was she strong, she also had a specialty—at least one. Curious, I mentally reached for earth energy, trying to build up enough magic in my body to help me read her specific talent, but I wasn't able to pinpoint it. I guessed she was probably fourteen, maybe fifteen, but by her small stature could pass for younger. She and I were both children of a post-Rip world where magic was no longer a secret. Magic had been around forever but had never been openly revealed by the magic community until the Rip, the catastrophic tear between dimensions that had brought hellish winged creatures into our world. It had also catalyzed the emergence of the VAMP2 and NECR2 viruses, infecting normals and turning them into blood-thirsty vampires and brain-hungry zombies. The original Rip had first opened in Manhattan in 2001, around thirty years ago. The zombie problem had been contained before I was born. Vamps weren't a huge threat anymore either, after Gregori Industries developed an implant that made them docile—taking away their bloodlust and their ability to glamor, as well as allowing them to walk safely in sunlight. That had all happened before I was born, too. These days, demons were the most imminent danger from the Rip.

"What's your name?" I asked, following her through a dingy, narrow corridor.

The stale aroma of cooked food permeated the air. It smelled like someone had browned a pound of ground beef several hours earlier. We took a left turn, putting us in a hallway that ran along the back of the building.

She glanced back at me. "Roxanne."

"I'm Ella."

Roxanne was small and thin in that waify way that was probably genetic but still made you suspect she'd never had quite enough to eat. I wasn't the motherly type, but watching the points of her shoulder blades made me want to take her home, plunk her in a chair at the little table in my kitchen, and feed her cookies.

I probed around her energy again. Her magic was definitely young. Fresh, and barely formed. She might not even be aware of the specifics of her own abilities yet, especially if she didn't have a good mentor. Something about her supernatural signature reminded me vaguely of Deb, my long-time best friend, but Roxanne's had its own unique quality, one that I'd never sensed before.

Deb was an empath and a healer, a strong Level II on the Magic Aptitude Scale. I guessed Roxanne was probably about the same as Deb strength-wise. I didn't think Roxanne was an empath, but perhaps the girl had a talent for sensing something specific in others. I barely registered at all on the scale, which put me at a low Level I and without the capacity for enough supernatural juice to have a true specialty or distinct talent. Magical aptitude level and specialized talents were fixed qualities. No one really knew if they were pre-programmed in our DNA or emerged spontaneously. Regardless, they couldn't be altered, only honed with training and practice. Because of my low level of aptitude, I'd never felt much desire to put effort toward developing my skills. I preferred to rely on my athletic stature or my stun gun if I got into a jam.

Roxanne and I passed a few doors with numbers on them, indicating there were apartments on this floor. The place wasn't dirty, but it showed signs of neglect—peeling paint here, black scuff marks there, threadbare nondescript industrial carpet lining the hallway—that gave it a depressing vibe.

Roxanne stopped at the door with a lopsided 8 on it. She pushed it open, leading me into a cramped space that served as kitchen, living room, and dining room. It was messy—dishes in the sink, crusted food on the stovetop, pillows askew on the sofa, bills and unopened envelopes covering the little table.

Continuing across the room toward a window, she pointed. "He's out there on the balcony. His name's Nathan."

The window sash was raised a foot, the glass fogged with dirt and age. I glanced around, counting three doorways leading out of the main room. Two bedrooms and a bathroom.

"Where are your parents?"

Roxanne sighed a sad, quick little reflex of a noise. "Gone."

"Is your brother a crafter, too?"

"Yeah, he's a high Level I."

No surprise. If one sibling had magical ability, then in most cases the rest did too.

I tried to peer through the window, as I had no idea what I was going to find out there. If Nathan were possessed by a demon, he already would have been wreaking havoc. Apprehension pulled my insides tight as I approached the open window. Roxanne hovered behind me. It was dark on this side of the building, which faced the alley, and I couldn't see much of anything outside. My pulse tapped, every swift beat seeming to emphasize the uncertainty of the situation I'd walked into.

"Nathan?" I called. "My name is Ella Grey. Your sister says you could use some help."

"He can't answer," she said behind me.

I forgot my weapon and moved forward more hastily. "If he's unconscious, we need to call an ambulance."

I shoved the window sash up as far as it would go. It protested my efforts with a loud scrape and only budged about six inches.

Leaning out, I expected to see a fire escape landing. Roxanne had called it a balcony, but proper balconies had doors, not rusty old windows you had to climb through to get to them. Instead of a fire escape, there actually was a tiny balcony, but it wasn't meant to be used as such. It was a sort of decorative architectural flourish, a well of concrete under the window.

The only thing on the balcony was a garish-looking stone statue about three and a half feet tall. It faced outward like a frozen sentinel keeping watch.

I pulled my head inside and twisted around to shoot a questioning look at Roxanne.

"He went out there for a smoke." She spoke breathlessly, and she was tearing up again. "I heard flapping noises and sounds like rocks hitting together. He hollered, and when I ran over he'd turned into a gargoyle."

A wave of vertigo began to sweep over me, and dread curdled through my gut like a dirty, dark tide.

Oh no, not now.

It couldn't be happening. Not while I was wide awake.

I squeezed my eyelids closed, and there was a bright flash across the screen of my mind. My heart skipped a beat as an arch-demon the size of a horse flew straight at me. Even though I knew it was in my head, I flinched back. The scene swung and jerked nauseatingly as if I watched a home video made by an unsteady camera operator. I opened my eyes, blinking hard a couple of times. Cool relief rushed through my veins when I saw Roxanne peering at me. For the moment, at least, the strange foreign images in my head had subsided.

I cleared my throat as if that would also clear the residual fog of the brief vision. "This is probably just a gargoyle that came to roost here for the night. People don't turn into statues. Don't you think it's more likely he just went somewhere else, maybe took off for a while?"

She planted her hands on her hips, and her pale cheeks reddened with irritation. "He did *not* leave me! Nathan was out there. No gargoyle. And now there's a gargoyle and no Nathan. My brother is in that statue."

She looked at me with her brows raised, her face turned at an angle, as if it should all be perfectly obvious. I knew that look. It was teenager for "adults are *such* morons." I felt my defenses rise. I was only twenty-four, for cripes sake. Surely not old enough to be considered the enemy by someone her age.

She extended an arm and pointed toward the balcony. "That's my *brother*. It *is*." Her expression dissolved back to desperation, and I realized it wasn't just about the disappearance of her brother. She needed me to believe her. She came over beside me. "Here, touch it. It's warm."

She leaned through the window to place her hand on the statue's, well, neck, I guess it was. From this angle the stone figure appeared to be a crouching mythical creature—big pointed ears, narrow feline face, bulging eyes, and folded wings.

Roxanne looked back at me, waiting.

I stepped forward, reached out, and pressed my fingertips against the stone surface. It was smoother than I thought, more like marble than the textured concrete it appeared to be. As soon as I made contact, the shadowy shapes in my periphery began to swirl like curtains whipping in a storm. My heart slammed against my ribcage as I tried to fight, but an image crowded into my vision, replacing Roxanne, the apartment, and the gargoyle. As in my recent dreams, it was colored only in yellows and blues, as if the eyes that saw it had a strange sort of colorblindness.

I sucked in a gasp and blinked, trying to force the image away, but it persisted. Edges sharpened into objects, and then into recognizable human forms. The off-color scene clarified, and I was no longer standing in a dingy little apartment, but in an unfamiliar room. I could make out the faces. At first, the people lounging on tattered sofas and curled up on the floor looked too still, and my chest clenched with the sudden fear that they were all dead. Then one of them, a teenage girl who lay in a heap against the sofa like a forgotten rag doll, with her legs splayed at awkward angles, shifted her shoulders. I caught a glimpse of the two puncture wounds on her neck and smear of what had to be blood. Most of the others had visible double puncture wounds, too. One round-faced boy had scarring that traced from his collarbone up to the edge of his jaw. Somehow, through the vision I could *smell* the blood, stale and metallic in the air, and my throat constricted as bile tried to rise up with a sickening roll of my stomach.

It was a vampire feeder den with people subdued by glamor and drunk on the high brought on by the vampire saliva in their systems. My mouth twisted in disgust, and I squinted, willing the vision to disappear and wishing I could turn away. But a shift of movement drew my eye to a young man.

He changed position, rolling to his side, and his head lolled, revealing in profile long lashes over a slant of cheekbone and a slightly protruding lower lip that was full enough to give the impression of a pout.

My chest seized. I knew his face.

I gasped, reflexively jerked my hand off the hard surface of the statue, and the vision dissolved, replaced by the window, the balcony, the gargoyle, and the darkened summer sky above. My pulse sped, each beat of my heart chasing the one before it so there was barely any space between.

The young man . . . he'd looked so much like my brother, Evan, but more angular and mature than the last time I'd seen him. The young man in the vision had to be around the age Evan would be today. If he were alive.

I'd been clinging to that *if* for five years. I didn't know whether the vision was someone else's memory that inexplicably found its way into my head, or maybe a complete fabrication of my own imagination, but my heart and my mind clutched at it and cradled it like a kid with her teddy bear, willing it to be true. Willing my brother to still be alive somewhere.

"Are you okay, Officer Grey?" Roxanne asked.

I jumped at the sound of her voice. She stood next to me, looking up into my face with concern etched in faint lines across her forehead. I drew a sharp breath in through my nose and nodded, but my hands shook. I clenched them into fists to hide the trembling.

She looked at the statue. "You felt it, didn't you? It's warm."

I fought to focus on her, on the present. I peered at the stone figure. She was right—when I'd touched the gargoyle it was warmer than my own skin. I reached out and placed my fingertips on it again, nearly breathless with hope that I'd get another glimpse of the young man who looked like Evan. The shadows framing my visual field churned . . . but the image didn't return.

I was about to ask Roxanne if she could remember anything else that happened before the gargoyle appeared, but the words died in my throat.

I heard it before I saw it—the leathery flapping sound of wings above. Adrenaline surged through me as I leaned my upper

went still.

I looked over at Roxanne and shook the trap like it was a can of spray paint. There was a faraway but angry-sounding squeal from within it, and a few little thumps against the inside walls.

"Contained and under control." I gave her what I hoped was a reassuring smile.

Actually, we were damn lucky the demon wasn't any bigger, and it was alone. The trap wasn't graded to contain much more demonic energy than what was in it, and certainly wouldn't have held two arch-demons.

"That was a close one," Roxanne said, shakily returning my smile. The encounter had obviously rattled her, and she was giving me some bravado. I looked down, reattaching the can to my belt and giving her a few seconds to collect herself. I heard her take a deep breath. "Officer Grey, can you get my brother out? I don't know how much longer he can survive in there."

"I'm going to call a friend of mine," I said, pulling out my phone. "I think he might be able to help us."

There was definitely something odd about the statue—gargoyles were cold-blooded creatures, and this one was much warmer than my own body temperature—but I wasn't convinced there was actually a human trapped in it because, well, I was pretty sure that was impossible. I knew someone who'd be able to tell me if Roxanne's story had any merit.

I scrolled to Johnny Beemer's number and tapped it. Johnny was a freelance supernatural P.I. and he'd developed a slew of devices that could detect all manner of phenomena. He did private jobs, but also was often called in as a consultant when the police suspected supernatural involvement in a crime. That was how we'd first met a couple of years back. It was on a messy case involving an idiot who'd managed to summon and cage an arch-demon with the intention of domesticating it, his pissed-off witch neighbors, and some not-so-neighborly hexes.

Johnny often showed up at the drinking hole where Demon Patrol officers tended to gather after shifts. We sometimes ended up at the same table or knot of people around the bar, and though we'd always greeted each other by name, we'd never had much more than casual conversations peppered with his flirty little gestures and phrases, which I'd always deflected. Johnny seemed like an okay guy, but I'd watched him flit from woman to woman too many times to take his advances seriously.

"Ella Grey," came Johnny's smooth voice though the phone. "I knew you'd give in eventually. Your place or mine, sugar?"

I snorted. "Nice try, but this isn't a booty call. I've got a . . . *situation*. Any chance you could bring your toys and meet me?"

"Okay, I'll bite. Just for you." I could hear the faint smile in his voice. "Where am I going?"

"Crystal Ball Lane. I'll text you the address."

"I'll be there in ten," Johnny said.

"Great, thanks."

I disconnected the call, asked Roxanne for the building's address, and then sent it to Johnny.

While Roxanne righted the lamp, I went to the window. We needed to get the thing closed before any other winged creatures of Hell showed up because I didn't have any more large demon traps on me.

I jumped up to the sill, standing on it so I could put my full weight into shoving the window sash down.

I glanced at Roxanne, who'd moved to the kitchen area to clean up the broken mug.

"You okay?" I asked, grunting with effort. I hopped a little, dropping all the force I could onto the stubborn window. It gave a few inches.

"Yeah." She didn't look up.

"You've got to keep the windows closed," I said. "It's not safe to leave them open."

By law, all structures were infused with magical wards against demons so they couldn't shatter a window or bust in through a door. The protection worked as long as doors and windows weren't left open. But there wasn't any known magic to prevent the spontaneous rips that dumped hell-spawn into random locations, as had happened during the Demon Patrol call that had killed me.

"I know, I just . . . I thought if Nathan turned back into himself, I wanted him to be able to get inside," she said. "You know, he'll probably be weak from not having any water or food, and I was afraid he wouldn't be able to open the window."

The stupid window finally gave in to my efforts. I slammed the sash closed and dropped to the floor.

"That's thoughtful of you," I said quietly. I wasn't maternal like Deb, but even I could see how distraught the girl was. "How long has the statue been there?" I just couldn't quite bring myself to call the thing "Nathan."

She pulled her phone from the pouch of her hoodie and looked at it. "It's just after ten o'clock, so . . . an hour and a half?"

"Why didn't you call the police?"

She lifted one shoulder and let it drop. "Nathan is seventeen. We're not supposed to be living on our own."

The familiar ache sprang around my heart, gripping it like a fist with such swiftness it nearly took my breath away. My brother Evan and I had been alone like this. After Grandma Barbara died, we'd stayed in her house until the bank repossessed it. A few months later we were forced out, and shortly after that, Evan had disappeared. He was only fourteen, and I'd just turned nineteen.

I held my breath, letting the pressure build up in my lungs, pushing back against the pain of loss blooming through me. My mind pulled at the vision of the young man, the one who looked like he could be nineteen-year-old Evan, but I held it off. I'd save that for later examination.

"Did you see anything strange when you touched the gargoyle?" I asked.

"Like what?" she cocked her head.

I shrugged. "Anything supernatural . . . visions . . ."

She peered at me. "Huh uh. Why, did you?"

"I thought I saw something, but it was probably just my imagination," I said. For a second I'd hoped the visions weren't just my own personal phenomenon, but I wasn't surprised at her answer. I gave her a thoughtful look. "You knew when you asked for my help that I was Demon Patrol. Weren't you afraid I'd tell someone about you and Nathan living here on your own?"

"Nope. Not after I saw how you handled those stupid boys. Even though you said you were going to throw them in jail, I knew you were just trying to scare them off, and you wouldn't really do it. I knew I could trust you. I've always been really good at knowing the good eggs from the rotten ones. That's what Nathan says." Her wide blue eyes projected such sincerity it was actually difficult for me to keep my gaze on her face.

I cleared my throat, a little embarrassed at the unexpected compliment. I looked around. "Your brother must work hard to afford a place like this for the two of you."

She nodded solemnly. "He works two jobs. Nights at the kitchen in the Crescent Moon Pub, and part-time in the produce department at Albertson's on State Street. I do random jobs, mostly babysitting and cleaning houses."

When she spoke of her own contribution, the pride on her face chiseled a crack through the middle of my heart. A kid her age shouldn't have to worry about contributing to the household income.

Footfalls in the hallway drew our attention. I went to open the door, and Johnny stood there hefting two big nondescript black suitcases with metal latches. The cases looked like the things you might see a band's roadie hoisting around, but I knew they contained a bunch of supernatural detection and diagnostic instruments.

He flashed a perfect white-toothed grin that seemed to gleam in his tanned face, and out of the corner of my eye I watched

Roxanne swoon.

Yeah, Johnny Beemer had that effect on women.

He set the cases down near the end of the sofa and then clapped his hands and rubbed them together briskly. "So, ladies, what do you have for Johnny?"

"Over here. A demon paid us a visit, so we had to shut it." I led Johnny to the window. "This is why Roxanne brought me up here. She says her brother is trapped in that statue."

Johnny stood close to the pane and cupped his hands around his eyes so he could see outside.

I glanced over at Roxanne. "I wasn't so sure about her story, but the thing is warm," I whispered to Johnny. "Too hot for a cold-blooded gargoyle."

He backed away with a nod and a purposeful purse of his mouth. He took off his leather jacket and put it over the back of one of the dining chairs. It was way too warm out for leather, but I couldn't recall ever seeing him without his jacket.

He strode to the window and his biceps flexed momentarily as he forced the sash up. I couldn't help a little zing of appreciation, and I saw Roxanne take note, too.

"I need it open so the scanner has an unobstructed view. Give a holler if you notice any more winged visitors out there." He reached out to place a hand on the statue and glanced back at me. "Huh, it is warm."

Roxanne grinned, clearly pleased at the confirmation of her story, but her expression quickly faded to worry. "Is he okay?"

Johnny had gone to one of his cases and laid it flat. He squatted in front of it with the lid tipped back. "Give me just a sec, and I'll see if I can figure out what happened."

Roxanne and I watched him pull a tablet out of its little nook in the molded foam that filled the case's interior. The device looked like a modified iPad with handles attached to both ends and some extra electronic doohickeys plugged into the ports. Johnny was a normal, but one of the few who seemed completely at ease around crafters. He was so knowledgeable about the supernatural sometimes I actually forgot that he had no magical aptitude himself.

He stood and positioned himself square to the window, powered on the tablet, and held it up by the handles. An image of the window frame and the dark shape of the statue outside filled the tablet's screen. Johnny tapped through a couple of menus, and the image changed. It showed blobs of bright colors, reminiscent of a heat map, with faint ghosts of lines like an X-ray.

"Oh yeah, there's something interesting going on," Johnny murmured, enlarging different sections of the image. "I'm detecting . . . three different life forms?"

I stepped closer to peer over his shoulder, but I didn't have a clue how to read the image. "Do you know what they are?"

Johnny's eyes flicked to Roxanne and then back to me. He gave me a pointed look.

"One of them is definitely human," he said. The brightness in his voice was a little too forced. "And his vitals are within the normal range. I need to consult with Officer Grey for just a moment." He powered off the tablet and lowered it to his side, holding it by one of the handles, and with his other hand he pulled down the window sash. A tilt of his head at me indicated he wanted us to move out of Roxanne's earshot.

We huddled near one of the bedroom doors. A waft of his clean-smelling aftershave filled my nostrils, and I resisted the temptation to lean in for a deeper whiff. I wasn't interested in Johnny, not like that, but I wasn't made of marble. He was handsome and he smelled good, and that was all . . . was what I told myself sternly.

With a hard blink, I forced my focus from his expressive lips back up to his eyes. "What is it?" I whispered, glancing at the tablet he still held.

He gave his head a little shake. "I think her brother is okay, but there's a demonic life form in there. I've actually never seen three life forms in one entity. This is really strange, Ella. We should call Supernatural Crimes and turn this over to them. It's going to require multiple separations. Whatever gets Nathan and the demon out of the gargoyle, followed by a standard exorcism. Honestly, I have no idea how this could have happened in the first place."

My surprise registered on my face, and he saw it. Johnny wasn't an outlaw exactly, but I didn't expect him to be the one to suggest following protocol.

"But Nathan is safe, more or less, right?" I asked, and waited for him to nod. "She doesn't want to involve the authorities. Her brother's underage. They're not supposed to be living here alone."

With a pained look he tucked the tablet under his arm and pushed one fist into the other palm, popping his knuckles. His dark eyes roved the room. "I really don't think we should be going rogue on this, Ella."

I scoffed, brushing off his suggestion. "Johnny, I know you of all people can handle this without getting the authorities involved. You know everybody. There's gotta be someone in your contacts list who has the skills we need. And I'm here to help. Come on, we can do it." It was a thinly veiled challenge, but I hoped my appeal to his ego would work.

His mouth thinned to a hard line, bringing out his dimple. Then he scrubbed a hand through the tousled waves of his dark hair. When his gaze leveled on mine, I knew I had him.

With an amused twitch of his lips, his eyes narrowed, flicking down to the badge on my belt. "Aren't *you* the authorities?"

"Not tonight. I'm rogueing it." Another subtle challenge.

"I bet it's not the first time, Officer Grey."

His comment gave me a split second of pause. We didn't know each other particularly well, and I wouldn't have pegged him for subtle insights. Maybe it was just a lucky guess on his part, or maybe the remark was simply meant to be flirtatious. Either way, he was right—I did have a tendency for bending the rules.

I allowed myself a full-on smile of triumph, which I imagined would just encourage the steady stream of his advances, the little hooks he'd been tossing my way since we'd met. But at the moment I didn't care.

"Please tell me you know how to get him out." Roxanne called, breaking up our little exchange. She was gazing at Johnny with an adorable mix of hero worship and infatuation.

He went to her with a warm smile. "Unfortunately, darlin', that's beyond my skillset. But I do know someone who might be able handle this sort of challenge. I'm going to make a call."

Roxanne blushed, looking up at him with stars in her eyes, and nodded.

He pulled his phone from a front pocket of his jeans, tapped it a couple of times, and then put it up to his ear, holding it there with a raised shoulder.

"Lynnette, how are you, gorgeous?" he said into the phone. While he spoke, he knelt to tuck the tablet back into its case. "Right, right. Same here. Listen, I've got a little supernatural puzzle, and I do believe you're the only woman in the world who can solve it."

I rolled my eyes.

"Oh, you are?" Johnny's smile sagged. "Damn. When do you get back? Okay . . . sure. The sooner the better. Will do. Safe travels. Talk to you soon. Bye."

He let the phone drop into his hand, tapped it with his thumb, and slipped it back into his pocket.

"What did she say?" Roxanne had pulled her hands into the sleeves of her oversized hoodie, and she was pressing her two sleeved fists together in front of her chest in an unconscious prayer.

"She's outta town right now, but she's returning tomorrow." He faced Roxanne. "I promise I'll come back with her tomorrow night, and we'll get this sorted out."

Roxanne's eyes filled with disappointment, but she nodded.

"Do you have someone you can stay with tonight?" I asked. She was probably old enough to spend a night alone, and had likely done so many times while her brother worked late, but I didn't want to leave her on her own.

"Mrs. Johnson, down the hall. She comes over sometimes if Nathan has to be gone all night." Roxanne looked out the window and then turned her blue-eyed gaze on Johnny. "Are you sure he's not going to suffocate before you come back?"

"I swear on my favorite crystal that he'll be okay until then." With a flourish, Johnny pulled a polished, faceted stone from a small leather pouch clipped to his belt. He held it out. "Keep it as collateral until tomorrow night."

She took the clear crystal, rotating it in her fingers, and then she looked up at him. "You're one of the good ones. I can tell."

He gave her a little grin.

"Are all the other windows closed?" I asked, eyeing the doors to the bedrooms.

Roxanne nodded.

"Good," I said. "Don't open them for any reason, okay?"

"I won't, I promise." She took a couple of quick steps toward me and slipped her arms around my waist. "Thank you, Officer Grey."

After a surprised pause, I awkwardly embraced her thin shoulders. She wouldn't normally do this. I always recognized another non-hugger. But her relief and gratitude were palpable.

"I'm glad I could help. And you can call me Ella."

She moved back, looked at the floor between us, and nodded again, obviously self-conscious.

"Here, let me put my number into your phone in case you

need anything. Give me yours, too."

We traded phones and entered our info while Johnny finished packing up. He lifted both cases by the handles.

"Stay safe, darlin'," he said to Roxanne, winking at her. "We'll see you soon."

I fought the urge to roll my eyes again, knowing I should cut him some slack. He'd shown up at a moment's notice, and he'd been extremely helpful after all.

Johnny and I left the apartment. As soon as Roxanne closed the door behind us, I turned to him.

"Are you sure he'll be okay in the gargoyle?" I asked.

"*You're* the one who didn't want to call Supernatural Crimes." He cocked a sidelong look at me. "But yeah, if he's okay right now, I think he'll be just as okay tomorrow. He certainly isn't going anywhere."

"So you've never heard of a double possession?"

He shook his head. "Before tonight, I would've said it wasn't possible for a demon to possess a gargoyle. And with a human mixed up in there, too . . . just bizarre."

I groaned.

"But the good news is, being locked in there is keeping the demon from hurting anyone."

We exited the building to the staircase I'd come up with Roxanne. I inhaled a welcome breath of night air, glad to be out of the stuffy apartment.

"When I get home, I'm going to do some research." His voice dropped in register and turned buttery smooth. "You're welcome to come with me. Be my sexy assistant. And after, you could show me your badge, and I'll show you how my plasma probe works."

"Terribly tempting, but I'll pass," I said with slow sarcasm. I dug my fists deeper into my jacket pockets. I remembered what Roxanne had said about Johnny being one of the good ones. I shot him a glance. "But seriously, thank you for coming. I didn't know who else to call."

"Aw, it's no problem." He shrugged and gave me a half-smile.

At the opening of the alley, I made a right turn at the sidewalk and paused to see if Johnny was going that way. He stayed with me.

"Who did you call, anyway?" I asked.

"A witch who specializes in exorcisms."

"You think Nathan is locked inside the gargoyle and also possessed?" I asked.

"Possibly. The fact is, there are three species that need to be separated. Species separation is essentially the definition of exorcism, though we usually only hear about it in terms of demon-human separation. Regardless of the exact configuration, Lynnette should be able to perform the separations. She's one of the best. If she can't do it, we're pretty much screwed."

I pursed my lips into a grim line and let that sink in. After a second or two, I looked over at him. He was tall, but my five feet ten inches plus an inch of boot heel put me slightly above eye-to-eye with him.

"Johnny, I don't expect you to work for free . . ."

He gave me a playful grin. "Don't worry about it, sugar. I'll find some way for you to repay me."

I rolled my eyes. "Good luck with that, Romeo," I said with a good-natured laugh. There was nothing menacing in his words—it was more flirtation.

He slowed, and I spotted his Mustang parked on a side street. We stopped on the corner.

"Will you text me if you make any breakthroughs in your research?" I asked.

"Yep, will do."

I jogged the rest of the way to my pickup. Weariness washed over me as I got in, started it, and headed home. I was just considering allowing my brain to return to the vision of the vampire den and the guy who looked like my brother, when I happened to glance in the rearview mirror.

Two orange eyes stared at me from the bed of the truck.

I started, accidentally jerking the wheel and crossing the yellow line with the left front tire.

"Shit!" I yanked the wheel the other way, correcting.

I pulled to a stop at a red light, gripping the wheel hard with both hands, and twisted around.

My heart hammered as a dark furry face stared back at me. It was the dog from before. His tail wagged, and his panting breath made a little patch of fog on the glass. I listened to my pulse beat in my head for a few seconds and then let out an unexpected laugh.

I considered turning around and dropping him off but didn't want to risk him getting hit by a car as he wandered Crystal Ball Lane. With only a few more blocks to home, an old house on Hays Street that had been converted into a four-plex, I decided to continue on with the dog in the back. The house where I lived had two apartments upstairs and two on the main floor. The two upper ones were occupied by couples—one in college and the other a newly-married man and woman in their early 30s. Mine was the ground level one on the right. The apartment on the left was the home of a crotchety middle-aged witch named Simone. Her familiar—a very clichéd black cat—sometimes watched me out the front window, its yellow eyes radiating uppity feline disapproval.

I parked in my usual spot on the street. The slam of the truck's door seemed unusually loud in the quiet night. By day, a steady stream of traffic flowed up and down Hays. Not a main artery, but it was a well-used street at the north edge of downtown.

I went to the back of the truck and leaned on the side rail.

"So, you think you're spending the night with me, huh?" I reached out a hand and the dog came over to give it a sniff. No collar, of course. Apparently liking what he smelled, he swiped his tongue across my knuckles. He had strange eyes, reflective like a cat's. He had unusually long legs, a wide chest, and a dark, short, curly coat. Definitely a mutt, though I didn't know dog breeds well enough to even begin to identify his make-up. But he looked healthy, like he'd been cared for and fed regularly. Though he'd been a little skittish on Crystal Ball Lane, he seemed at ease around humans. "Okay, big guy, just for tonight. Tomorrow we'll figure out who's missing you."

I moved toward the back of the truck to open the gate for him, but before I could release the latch, he leapt over the rail and onto the strip of grass between the sidewalk and the curb, landing on silent feet.

He followed me up the steps to my little porch where the lamp next to my door bathed us in wan yellow light. I unlocked the door, walked in, and flipped on a light switch, holding the door for the dog.

He followed me through the living room and into the tiny and underused kitchen, where I pulled two ceramic bowls from a cupboard. I filled one from the faucet and set it on the floor, and piled Cheerios in the other bowl.

The dog gave the Cheerios a sniff and then crunched a few. He looked up at me.

"Sorry, this is the best I've got in the way of dog chow." I left the kitchen, pulling my t-shirt off over my head on the way to the bathroom.

I dropped the shirt in the hamper, turned on the shower, and finished undressing.

"Don't shred anything or poop on the carpet," I called to the dog and then stepped into the shower.

I quickly washed, shampooed, and conditioned my hair, rinsed it all off, and then shut off the water.

With one towel turbaned on my head and another wrapped around my body, I poked my head into the living room, expecting to see the dog curled up on the slightly worn but still cool retro low-backed sofa I'd bought at the Idaho Youth Ranch thrift store. When I didn't see him, I leaned through the doorway to look into the kitchen. No dog there, either.

The only possible place left was the bedroom. I flipped on

the light and snorted a laugh. He'd pulled down the quilt that was usually folded on the end of my bed, dragged it over to the wall, and bunched it into a little nest on the floor. He was curled in a tight circle in the middle of it.

When he saw me, he raised his head, and the tip of his tail flipped up and down.

"Don't get too comfortable, big guy." I watched him for a second or two. I wasn't a dog person, but the intelligence in his eyes was unmistakable.

I pulled on an old Demon Patrol Recruit t-shirt and boy shorts-style underwear, and switched off the overhead light.

I held my phone and typed out a text to Deb, telling her I was sorry I didn't get back earlier. I hit send, knowing she'd already be in bed and sound asleep. She was teaching summer school for another couple of days and had to get up at some ungodly hour.

I set the phone on its charging pad and swung my legs up and under the covers.

Once my damp head hit the pillow, the vision swam back into the forefront of my mind.

I tried to remember as much detail as I could. Over and over, my mind's eye focused on the young man's face. I tried to look at it with objectivity, but failed. I wanted it to be Evan—my brother as he was now, at age nineteen—even if he was mired in a vampire's den, because that could mean he was alive.

I had no idea how or why the vision came to me, but it had the same distorted, strangely-colored quality as the dreams that had haunted me since my accident. The dreams, the images, the

shadows that accompanied me like a swarm of silent dark spirits .
. . they were all somehow related. They had to be. They'd all shown
up after the accident, when I'd revived eighteen minutes after my
pulse and respiration had stopped.

I'd set out for Crystal Ball Lane looking for relief. Hoping
for something that would rid me of the smoky swirls and the
disturbing dreams—the *other*. I'd gone in search of a remedy that
would bring back the Ella Grey from before.

But whatever clung to me now, whatever Dark Thing had
followed me back from death and given me the visions, it had
shown me my brother. It had gifted me with the first possible clue
I'd had in years that Evan might still be alive.

I had to figure out how to make the *other* reveal more.

My phone buzzed with an incoming text, jolting me from my
sinister musings. I reached for it and saw it was almost 11:00. The
message was from Deb.

*I'm out back, going to use the hidden key to let myself in. If you
see this, don't get up. We'll talk in the morning.*

I texted back: *I'm up.*

The dog raised his head, his attention drawn to the kitchen.
He jumped up and silently followed me to the back door as the
deadbolt clicked. I switched on the light above the stove.

The door swung open, and Deb stood there. My best friend
looked terrible, her strawberry blond hair swept back into a messy
ponytail, her eyes puffy, and her nose red.

Deb's backpack, the one I thought of as her escape bag, was hanging from the crook of her elbow. I knew it held a change of clothes, a toothbrush, and some shampoo and makeup.

"What happened?" I asked.

She shook her head, her eyes welling. "It's just me and Keith. I promise I won't stay long, just a night or two."

I took her arm and pulled her over to one of the two chairs at my tiny breakfast nook table. She sank down and then heavily propped her elbows on the chipped tabletop. The dog's head was just tall enough for him to rest it on the table. His tail drooped as he gave her an unblinking gaze that I would almost swear was sympathetic.

"Of course you can stay as long as you like."

"Thanks," she said, her attention sliding over to the dog. "Who's this?"

"A stray. He followed me." I watched her, trying to assess how bad it was. "Okay, what'd the idiot do this time?"

She gave a weary sigh. "The usual stuff."

I moved to the stove, turning to my rarely-used tea kettle that sat on one of the burners, so I could hide my irritation from Deb. This happened every few months, going back almost since the start of Deb and Keith's relationship. There was some blow-up about something that was always Keith's fault. I tried to be a good friend, but it was difficult not to throw my hands up and ask why the hell she didn't leave him. Sure, they were happy some of the time, but it wasn't enough. Deb deserved more.

I filled the kettle and put it on the stove, then pulled out two mugs and found a box of herbal tea. I thought herbal tea tasted like wilted flowers and smelled like a combo of dried grass clippings and an old lady's house, but it always seemed to soothe Deb.

Deb's lips twisted unhappily. "We had some money saved, you know, for when I would eventually take maternity leave. Keith used it."

I felt my face cloud over. "On what?"

Her eyes pooled with tears again. "Does it even matter?" She pulled a tissue from her pocket and dabbed at her lower lids.

"I'm so sorry, Deb. That royally sucks. He had no right to do it behind your back."

"He had good intentions. He was investing it. He said he was sure he could double it. But . . ." She looked down at the tabletop.

She didn't have to finish. I knew the money was gone.

"Well, at least you can build it up again?" I ventured, trying to find some hope in the situation. I sat back down across from her. "And this time get a separate account, one that he doesn't have access to."

When she raised her eyes to mine, the look of misery on her face hollowed out my chest.

"I don't have time," she whispered. "I'm six weeks pregnant."

My mouth fell open. I snapped it shut as surprise and then anger coursed through me. This was what Deb had wanted her entire life, but instead of radiating joy like she should have, she'd never looked more unhappy. All because she'd married an irresponsible knucklehead.

"Uhh, congratulations?" I said, wincing.

She started to laugh, softly at first, but pretty soon she had both hands clamped over her mouth. It was contagious, and we looked at each other across the table as our shoulders shook. The kettle made the whooshing sound that comes right before the whistle, and I sprang to the stove to pull it off the burner. When I returned to Deb with two steaming mugs, she was wiping her eyes again, but there was a faint smile on her lips.

She sipped her tea and then looked down into the mug. "I haven't told Keith yet."

I tilted my head. "How come?"

With another sigh, she slouched a little lower. "I guess . . . I guess I'm not completely sure I want do this with him." Her eyes took on a dazed, glassy sheen. "Wow, that's the first time I've really admitted that."

My chest stirred with a storm of emotions—hope that she'd finally seen the light, fear for what it meant, and a little ray of happiness at the knowledge that she was going to be a mom. Something she'd wanted more than anything.

"Then don't," I said firmly. "We can get a place together, just like old times. I'll help, you know, do the diapers and bottles and stuff. Whatever you need."

The image of the clock displaying the wee hours of the night while a red-faced baby howled its tiny lungs out made me want to writhe, but I tamped it down and managed to control myself.

She gave me a teary but grateful smile. "I know you would. I just don't know yet what I'm going to do."

"Well, you probably need some sleep. You're sleeping for two now." I glanced pointedly at her belly with an exaggerated, wide-eyed expression.

She giggled, but exhaustion pulled at her features.

"Take my bed so you can get some rest. I'll sleep on the foldout."

I stood, but she reached for my wrist, stopping me. "Are you okay, Ella?"

"Yeah, why?"

Her gaze roamed all around me, and I knew her empath senses had kicked in. "Your energy feels . . . tangly. Did you go see that hedge witch I recommended?"

"Not yet," I said. "Let's talk about it later, okay?"

Normally she would have pressed me, but she was running on empty.

After I got Deb settled in my room, I moved the living room furniture so I could pull out the sofa bed. I expected to toss and turn for a while, after the eventful evening, but my eyelids grew heavy and I dropped off quickly.

The next morning I was up early, even before Deb who had to rise at still-dark-o'clock to get to her summer school teaching job. I'd fallen asleep hoping to see more images of Evan, but the night had passed with only regular dreams.

While the dog was doing his business in my postage-stamp yard, I called the Humane Society and the pound to report my late-night hitchhiker. Neither one had any record of someone looking for a dog like him, but maybe his owner didn't know yet that he was missing. I couldn't imagine he was a stray—he was well behaved and clearly comfortable inside a home.

Three days ago the doctor who'd been monitoring me since my accident—my *death*—had reluctantly cleared me to return to work after my two-week leave. When he'd taken my vitals and everything checked out normal, he'd actually seemed annoyed that I wasn't showing obvious physical effects from my ordeal. He forbade me from resuming my daily runs or any other extended cardio until after my next checkup, but I couldn't start a workday without some sort of physical exertion.

Out on the tiny square of patio in the yard, I did fifteen minutes with the jump rope and then set out a rubber mat and went through my usual 50 pushups, crunches, and leg lifts.

I let the dog in and then hopped in my truck and drove to the grocery store for a collar, leash, and small bag of dog food.

Back home, I filled the Cheerio bowl with kibble and refreshed the water.

Deb appeared in the kitchen doorway. She rubbed one red-rimmed eye with the heel of her hand, but overall she looked much better than when she'd shown up last night.

"Morning. Want to shower first?" I asked.

"No, that's okay, I don't have time. I've got to get dressed and head to work."

"Are you sure? Maybe you should just call in sick today."

She shook her head. "I'll be all right."

She went into my room, and I headed to the bathroom. "Check in later?" I hollered down the hallway at her.

"Yeah, I will," she said. "Thanks again for letting me stay."

I quickly used the restroom to freshen up, and by the time I emerged, Deb was gone.

In my room, I dressed in my Demon Patrol uniform: royal blue button-down shirt with the patrol emblem patches on the sleeves and over the left breast pocket. It would be over 80 degrees by afternoon, so choosing the short-sleeve summer version of the shirt was a no-brainer. Gray fitted pants with cargo-style pockets. Service utility belt with stun gun, guided net launcher, flashlight, badge, and a pouch for brimstone burners. Black leather low-top boots.

I secured the cylinder-shaped demon trap from last night, the one containing the arch-demon that had invaded Roxanne's, onto a band on my belt. I pulled my shirt over it to hide it the best I could. I wasn't actually supposed to have this type of trap, but I disagreed with the policy that forbade Demon Patrol from carrying higher-level traps. I'd swiped the can from the supply room at work, and it wasn't the first time I'd done so.

I swept my dark hair back into a long ponytail, put on my black patrol visor, and slipped sunglasses into a shirt pocket.

My patrol precinct was about seven blocks from home, so I walked. When I arrived and saw how full the lot was, my stomach dropped a couple of inches.

It was my first day back after two weeks mandatory leave, and I'd intended to get there earlier to beat the crowd and take a seat in the back for briefing. I really preferred not to make an entrance in front of an audience.

And there was one other thing I was dreading: the absence of my partner, Terrence.

He'd been injured in the demon attack that had me on the way to the morgue until I miraculously revived. Supernatural Crimes, the arm that oversaw Demon Patrol, had given him an extended medical leave that would transition into retirement. He was set to retire in less than a year, anyway, and the accident had ensured he'd probably never walk without a limp. It was a generous move on the part of the division, and I knew it was the right thing for him.

But I'd get a new partner. Terrence and I were practically family, we'd been together since I started on patrol, and the idea of walking the beat with anyone else felt disloyal.

I let out a long sigh as I passed Terrence's parking spot. A late-model Lexus stood where his old Jeep used to be. I snorted. What self-respecting Demon Patrol officer drove a fricking *Lexus*? I was half-tempted to take a picture of it and send it to Terrence for a laugh.

"Grey!"

I turned at the sound of my name to see Brady Chancellor, dressed in Supernatural Strike Team dark gray, crossing the parking lot with a few of his Strike buddies.

"I see the rumors of your death were greatly exaggerated," he said.

The guys walking with him peered at me with curiosity. I stifled a groan. Just call me Sideshow Ella.

Brady and I had a thing back when we were both recruits going through training. It was short-lived, and a mistake on my part. He had a huge mouth and thought he was hot shit due to his Level III magic aptitude and Strike Team position.

With a nonchalant shrug, I cast him a cool glance. "Taking on an arch-demon without all your fancy-ass Strike weapons, all in a day's work."

He answered with a smile that looked more like a smirk and jogged a few steps to beat me to the door. He opened it and swung his arm out in an exaggerated invitation to walk inside. "After you."

He wasn't being a gentleman, I was sure of that. He probably just wanted to look at my ass.

I headed toward the Patrol briefing room while the Strike guys turned toward their wing. I exchanged greetings with the other officers, genuinely glad to be back. But suddenly feeling self-conscious under the curious looks, I didn't pause to chat. As I approached the briefing room, the din of chatter indicated it was already nearly full. When I entered, I tried to sidle toward the back. But the officers near the door noticed me right away, and made loud noises of greeting.

I felt my face heat as I walked through the gauntlet of people clapping me on the shoulders and welcoming me back. Most of the officers were good people, and I appreciated their concern, but Terrence was the only one I'd truly been close to. Sure, groups of us would go out for drinks after work once a week or so, but it wasn't like we had deep, personal discussions.

I tried to blend into the crowd, but Andy Briggs, an old-timer like Terrence, cupped his hands around his mouth and hollered, "Speak, speak! She's gotta say something so we know she's not a zombie! *Speak!*" A few others took up the call.

I batted a hand in the air but couldn't help a good-natured grin. "If I were a zombie, I wouldn't eat your sorry brains if you paid me, Briggs."

That brought a round of guffaws, and internally I loosened a little. I found a chair next to Sasha Bowers. We'd graduated from patrol training together. She'd visited me right after the accident and called a couple of times to see how I was doing. As I sat, she reached over and wrapped one of her toned arms around my shoulders in a side hug.

"Glad you're back, girl."

I took a deep breath. "Thanks, Sash, me too."

Sergeant Devereux and Captain Morrow appeared in the doorway, and everyone settled as our superiors strode to the front of the room.

I sat and automatically angled my body to hide the demon can on my belt, the one holding the Rip spawn I'd captured at Roxanne's. It was the final of three Strike Team cans I'd swiped years ago, back when I was new on Demon Patrol. The arch-demon capacity traps were equipment that as a Patrol officer I wasn't allowed to have. Back then I still had hope of finding Evan. I wasn't there when he disappeared, but according to the people he'd been with, he was carried off by a large demon. True, most of those eyewitnesses were junkies I wouldn't trust to remember their own birthdays, but it was all I had to go on.

In any case, Patrol was supposed to leave the big catches to Strike. And if it was too much for Strike to handle, they'd evacuate the area and call in Supernatural Special Forces. Demon Patrol only took care of minor demons, which looked like ugly, leathery bats and didn't carry enough demonic power to possess humans, though their pointed claws could do some damage. On Patrol we used brimstone burners, baited discs that attracted the minor demon and then fried it with a strong magical charge like a moth in a bug zapper. Minor demons were fairly easy to kill. Arch-demons, on the other hand, had so far eluded death at the hands of humans. Because no one had figured out how to kill them, they had to be trapped and permanently contained instead.

The day of my accident, I'd had a Strike can with me, but the trap alone simply hadn't been adequate. Terrence and I only had our net launchers and stun guns, neither of which was enough to force the arch-demon within range of the trap.

My insides chilled at the memory. I'd thought that the higher-level trap was all I needed to beat an arch-demon. I'd trapped one of them before using a Strike can. It wasn't until after the accident that I realized how lucky I'd been that first time. Last night at Roxanne's, too. The demon in her apartment had been hesitant to get too close to me for some reason, and that had likely saved our bacon.

I'd kept my shirt partway untucked to cover most of the contraband can, and I'd meant to arrive early enough to dispose of it unseen, but the calls on behalf of the dog and my trip to the store had delayed things.

I knew my fellow Patrol officers wouldn't rat me out for taking a Strike can—many of them shared my opinion that Demon Patrol should at least be allowed to carry one for emergencies—but my sergeant had already written me up twice for the same offense. One more and I'd face a job review, which could lead to suspension without pay or possibly firing.

The Strike can felt like a lead weight. I was glad I'd had it at Roxanne's, but in the rational light of day, I recognized how brash it had been to take on that demon alone. I'd been too bold the day of the accident and not much better last night. If I'd been more cautious, maybe Terrence would be sitting next to me instead, and I wouldn't be trying to figure out how to deal with the *other* swimming around in my head. But then, I also wouldn't have hope that my brother was still alive out there somewhere.

Sergeant Devereux stood behind the podium, with Captain Morrow next to him.

The captain smiled as she nodded at us. "Good morning."

The room answered.

"I'm here to present a commendation to one of our own." As she zeroed in on me, my eyes widened. "Officer Gabriella Grey and her partner Terrence Willingham responded to a routine patrol call that turned out to be anything but routine. After disposing of two minor demons in the basement of a residence in the North End, they were attacked by an arch-demon that entered the basement through a spontaneous dimensional rip. Officer Grey saved the life of her partner. On behalf of the entire division and a grateful city, I thank you for your bravery, and I present you with the pin of valor."

She conveniently left out the part about how I'd died between the time I'd saved Terrence and Strike stormed in. The sudden tear between dimensions had sent out a ripple of force that toppled a heavy bookcase onto Terrence. It hadn't knocked him out, though, and he'd managed to call for backup. I remembered shooting my net at the demon's head and seeing it hit its mark, though it didn't do much more than irritate the creature. I'd thrown myself across Terrence and then a couple of seconds later screamed at the sudden, excruciating pain that ripped at every nerve in my body. I suspected the demon tried to possess me, and for whatever reason, it failed and killed me instead.

When Captain Morrow looked at me again and I felt the attention of the room trained on me, my heart dropped straight down through my guts.

"Officer Grey, please step forward."

My hand snuck back to my belt to unhook the can. I set it on my seat before I stood and then made my way up the center aisle to the podium.

Feeling a little stunned, I watched Captain Morrow reach out to attach a silver V overlaid with the Demon Patrol insignia onto my lapel. Facing the room and the swell of applause, I waited a beat and then ducked my head and beelined back to my seat. I sat forward a little, hiding the demon can that was still on the seat.

Captain Morrow left, and the sergeant took her place at the

podium. To my enormous relief, he launched into the briefing as a map illuminated on the screen behind him.

"We've had several bubble-ups around the city in the past few days. Most of them are clustered around the Foothills ley line and the ley line that runs down Capitol Boulevard. Minor demons only, so far."

The line in the Foothills was out of my beat, but the northernmost three blocks of Capitol Boulevard, including the Capitol Building itself, were my territory. Normally I would have looked forward to a bit of action, but with a new partner, I'd been hoping for an easy first day back.

Remembering I still didn't know who was replacing Terrence, I straightened and peered around, searching for a new face. There were nearly seventy officers on this shift, and the room was crowded. I craned my neck, trying to see to the far front corner. If my new partner was present, he or she was hiding.

"Special Forces is still manning the Boise Rip," Sergeant Devereux continued in his faint Louisiana accent. "And it's been over two weeks since anything bigger than a minor demon came through it."

"Any updates from New York?" Sasha Bowers called out.

The original Rip—a tear between this dimension and another that allowed demons to spill into this world—was centered in lower Manhattan. Supernatural Special Forces kept it under control most of the time, but last week there'd been a breach. It was the largest one in the past five years, and if I remembered the news report correctly, it made the Top 20 in magnitude since the Rip first broke open in 2001.

This recent large breach had resulted in several deaths. Tragic, but nothing compared to the many thousands when the Rip first appeared between the twin towers of the World Trade Center and spilled the VAMP2 and NECR2 vampire and zombie viruses, along with a plague of demons, into an unprepared city. People of my parents' generation and older still spoke of that day in 2001 with a mix of deep grief and echoes of the disbelief they must have felt back then. But for me it was part of the fabric of history, a fact of everyday life, and an event that today in 2030 continued to shape the world.

"They've got the breach under control, last I heard," Sergeant Devereux said. "There were twelve citizen deaths and about two hundred injured. A few officer injuries, but nothing serious."

He updated us with a few more local incident reports and then closed the cover on his tablet. "Be safe. Good hunting." His gray-green eyes found me, and he pointed and then crooked his finger in a beckoning motion.

My stomach soured. I was forced to leave the contraband— and occupied—demon can on the seat. Walking against the flow of officers heading out, I spotted someone standing next to the sergeant, a bookish-looking blond guy, late 20s. He had fine features and neatly-combed hair. His trim build, and patrician face made him look like he belonged on a yacht off Martha's Vineyard. Something about him gave the impression of breeding and money. I could easily imagine him in khaki and seersucker, but he looked out of place in a Demon Patrol uniform.

My sergeant drilled me with his piercing squint. He always looked at me as if he'd just caught me picking my nose.

"Officer Grey," he said. His Southern accent gave an impression of warmth, but there was nothing cuddly about Devereux as far as I'd ever discerned.

"Sergeant." I saluted, even though it really wasn't necessary. Demon Patrol wasn't as formal as the regular police force, though we tended to follow a lot of the organizational formats they used. Things were tighter and more militant in the Supernatural Strike Team and Special Forces divisions.

Devereux lifted his chin at blondie. "Meet your new partner, Damien Stein."

The blond guy shifted a thick leather-bound notebook and a bulky little drawstring sack to his left hand and stuck out his right. "It's a pleasure to meet you. Congratulations on your commendation." His voice was steady with an upper East Coast edge to his pronunciation, which didn't surprise me. His sky blue eyes were wary under my scrutiny.

After hesitating *almost* long enough to make me look like an ass to the sergeant, I grasped Stein's hand. "Welcome to the force," I said evenly.

This guy just did not seem like Demon Patrol material. And there was something else. Supernatural power practically oozed off him. Even with my low-level aptitude I could actually *see* a faint corona around him, like a shaft of sunlight that hung in the air an inch or two away from his skin. If he didn't register at the tippy-top edge of Level III aptitude, I'd eat a bowl of dog chow.

What the hell was a Level III doing on Demon Patrol? Level I aptitude was the magical requirement for the job, and rarely did any IIs end up on Patrol. I couldn't recall ever seeing a III here. This guy could be doing a thousand other jobs. And frankly, he just didn't appear to be suited to this one at all.

Devereux was giving Stein a little background on my history with the force. Graduated near the top of my recruit class, nearly five years' service, same downtown beat since I started, blah, blah . . . He left us alone without offering anything about Stein.

Stein and I were the last two people remaining in the briefing room. I folded my arms and peered at him.

"You related to one of the higher-ups?" I asked.

He frowned and then caught himself, but not before I read his expression. It was only a flash, but it clearly said no he did not come from a Force family, *heaven forbid such a thing.*

He shook his head. "No connections. And no one handed me this job. I went through training the same as you did."

I gave him a withering look. "That's not what I mean. You're a high III. Is this job some kind of punishment or something?"

"No, I just thought demon catching would be an interesting job, that's all."

I didn't buy it. But I was stuck with the guy for at least six months—that was the breaking-in period for new partners. If the pairing didn't work, at the end of the six months either of us could apply for reassignment.

I tipped my head toward the door, and we headed that way.

"Well, we'll have plenty of time together for you to explain to me in great detail why a Level III out-of-towner would take a job on Demon Patrol in Boise, Idaho. Because no offense, but you in that uniform makes zero sense."

To my surprise, he let out a rumbling laugh. It was low and warmer than I would have expected. "I'll do my best."

I paused, my eyes sliding back to the briefing room.

"Gotta grab something, I'll meet you over there." I pointed down the hall, waited until he turned away, and then ducked back through the doorway.

The can had gotten knocked off my chair and had rolled over to the wall. I let out a breath of relief when I spotted it. I attached it to my belt and bloused my shirt out and over it as well as I could.

I jogged to catch up with Stein.

"You haven't been issued a belt and a weapon yet?" I asked.

"Sergeant Devereux said I should ask you about that. He only gave me my badge, phone, and earpiece."

"The armory should have the rest of your stuff."

We descended to the basement where Herb, my favorite armory sergeant, was on duty. He was an older guy with an asthmatic wheeze and a gut that hung over the waist of his pants, completely obscuring his belt.

"Welcome back, Officer Grey." Herb gave me a broad smile, his rheumy eyes lighting up. "Very happy to see you upright and in one piece. I'm surprised you returned to active duty so soon."

I shrugged. "Ah, you know. Being clinically dead for a few minutes was all the rest I needed." I pointed a thumb at Stein, who stood a step behind me. "Do you have Officer Stein's things back there?"

Peering at my new partner sidelong, Herb pressed his hands to the counter to heave himself to his feet. I knew what he was thinking: the same thing I'd thought when I realized Stein was a Level III—*why* Demon Patrol?

The sergeant went back among the shelves and returned with a stiff new belt loaded with the usual accoutrements identical to the ones I carried—stun gun, net launcher, flashlight, brimstone burner pouch. Herb also held out a slim backpack. The pack was Force-issue—we were allowed to carry them if we had personal things we wanted to have on us while working our beats—but I could only think of a couple officers who used them regularly.

"You sure you need that?" I asked. "Most of us don't use them."

"I requested it."

Something about the way he replied made me want to stick out my tongue and pull a juvenile face while he wasn't looking. I watched him place his leather-bound notebook, a few pens, and the drawstring bag full of unknown items into the pack. No self-respecting Patrol officer needed all that stuff on the beat. He slung it around onto his back and then reached for the belt and cinched it around his waist.

He checked the charge on the stun gun, just like we were taught in training, and then holstered it. Reaching into a pants pocket, he produced his badge and clipped it onto his belt.

I nodded. "Okay, we're off to get a few brimstone burners. Thanks, Herb."

He waved at us. "Good hunting."

We headed back to the stairs.

"Clip your phone onto your shoulder, like this." I turned to show Stein mine. Our service phones had a walkie-talkie function that we activated while we were on duty. "And turn on your earpiece and put it in your left ear."

"You don't seem the Force type either, you know," Stein said once we were back on the main level.

"Oh yeah? How's that?" I challenged. I didn't disagree with his observation, but I wanted to hear how he'd respond. Whether he'd inadvertently insult me, try to kiss my ass, or something in between.

"You're independent. Not the type to seek out institutions. And you don't like authority figures."

I pursed my lips and tipped my head at an angle, an acknowledgement but not necessarily an agreement.

"Why did you join?" he asked.

"Oh, no," I said, wagging my finger. "You're going to explain why *you're* here before you get an answer to that."

I took him to the window of the supply room. "Four brimstone burners for each of us," I said to the clerk.

She passed us the fat plates, each fitted with a lid. A burner was about the size of a medium pancake and with a solid heft, and Stein and I stuck them into the plate pouches on our belts.

"Let's go." I pointed to the exit.

Once outside, he started to veer toward the navy patrol cars.

I shook my head. "Our beat starts three blocks from here. We walk." Then I stopped short, pretending I'd forgotten something.

"Wait here, I'll be right back."

I jogged around the side of the building to an unmarked door in the alley. It was an emergency exit at the back of the supply room, and as usual it was propped open. Some of the clerks came out to smoke and often left the door ajar.

I took the Strike can from my belt, palming it against my thigh as I slipped inside. The demon trap disposal drums were at the back of the supply room. I darted around rows of shelves, avoiding the clerks, and reached a drum undetected.

My hand was on the drum's release latch when an irritated voice made me jump clear off the floor. "Officer Grey!"

I squeezed my eyes closed, cursing silently, and slowly turned around to face Sergeant Devereux.

He folded his arms and looked at the canister in my hand for a long moment.

I opened my mouth and took a breath, trying to formulate my excuse, when he held up a palm.

"I don't want to deal with the paperwork today, Grey." He jerked his head toward the drum. "Just get rid of it. If I catch you in here again, your job will be in serious jeopardy."

I jammed the can into the hatch and scurried away before he could change his mind.

I rejoined Stein outside.

"Everything okay?" he asked.

"Yep, fine." I stared straight ahead. I knew I'd been lucky that Devereux had let me escape, but at the same time I was pissed I'd missed my chance to grab another Strike level demon trap.

We crossed Washington, and I looked over at Stein. "Okay, it's time for you to explain what you're doing here. Spill."

He chewed his lower lip for a moment. "Have you ever heard of the Stein family of mages?"

My mouth dropped open and my boots scuffed along the sidewalk as shock brought me to a halt.

"You're one of *those* Steins?" I gaped at him.

He nodded. And he didn't look happy about it.

Faint red blotches formed on my new partner's cheeks as I continued my dumbfounded gawping.

I closed my mouth with a click of my teeth and forced my feet back into motion.

"Okay. So. You're one of the famous Steins."

That explained the well-bred appearance. The Lexus. The not-from-around-here accent.

"Yep. I'm one of them." He slid a sidelong look at me. "But I'm not really *one of them*."

It finally clicked home. "Ohhh. You're not a mage."

I couldn't help staring. He'd grown up in a family of mages. Magically, he was one of the most powerful people I'd ever met, but mages could out-magic Level IIIs in their sleep. Most of them were back East, and they were deeply secretive about their lives and their magic. If they chose, they had the ability to shield themselves so thoroughly that they could pass for normals. They could also alter their appearances—not just hair color and face shape like a standard obfuscation spell could do, but things like height and voice. No one outside of mage society knew exactly how many living mages there were in the world. It had always been rumored that they occupied high positions in government, and that many actors, models, tycoons, and other famous and powerful types were actually mages. After the Rip, mages had come into the public eye, as they'd aided the authorities in many different ways. In Patrol training, I'd learned that it was mage magic that made the demon traps and brimstone burners work.

With a shake of his head, Stein hooked his thumbs around the straps of his pack and hunched forward. "Nope. I'm not a mage."

"Did they—" I dropped my voice to a stage whisper. "Did they disown you?"

Cracking a smile, he gave a short burst of that low, warm laugh again. "No. I just wanted some distance. You know, to go someplace where there aren't any Steins."

"Why here?"

His shoulders moved under the backpack straps in a little shrug. "It's almost as far from New York as I could get without leaving the U.S. Plus, this is an interesting area, magically speaking. It's a sort of conflux. All the ley lines, a huge concentration of people with magic aptitude for an area this size, the large population of vampires, all the shifter packs in the surrounding mountains. And then there's the Boise Rip, of course. Second largest interdimensional tear in the world. There are other factors, too, that give this area a heightened magical vibe. You might not think of the ore and gemstone deposits, for example."

His words were picking up speed, his enthusiasm obvious. Everything he said was true, but I sensed an underlying reason for his fascination.

A voice spoke via the walkie function on our phones,

interrupting Stein's mini-lecture. It was dispatch. Report of a minor demon in a residence two blocks away.

I touched my earpiece, stated our location, and told dispatch to show us responding.

We increased our pace to an easy jog and turned right at the next corner. Minor demons weren't dangerous, in that they didn't have enough hell-power to possess a human. But they did tend to scare folks, sometimes killed small pets, and could be a general nuisance. If they got pissed off, they could scratch a human to shreds. And more important, if small demons were allowed to flock, they could trigger spontaneous small rips that would let through the larger, much more dangerous arch-demons.

"This isn't a bubble-up, is it?" Stein asked.

"Nah, Headquarters would have told us if Strike Team was responding, too. It's not classified as a bubble unless there's at least half a dozen minors or an arch-demon. This is more of a dimensional burp."

Was it my imagination, or did he seem relieved? Again, I wondered why he'd wanted this job. And I hoped he was at least well suited enough to the work to have my back. He wasn't Terrence, never would be. But Stein was all I had now.

"Who was your training officer?" I asked.

"Robertson, out at the Meridian facility. Real militant, by-the-book hard ass."

I nodded, remembering Robertson.

Stein seemed in good condition, at least, catching his breath as quickly as I did when we reached the address dispatch gave us.

The Victorian-style house was one of the last remaining residences in the immediate area. Most of the houses had been turned into businesses, or torn down completely to make room for office buildings.

I went up the half-dozen steps and knocked firmly on the door. "Demon Patrol responding to a call!" I bellowed.

I flipped off the strap over my stun gun.

When a woman with a salt-and-pepper bob opened the door, I pulled my badge from my belt and held it up. The charm, a relatively simple one, alternately displayed my headshot and my name and badge number, slowly switching back and forth between the two screens so she could get a good look. "Good morning, ma'am. I'm Officer Grey, and this is Officer Stein. Can you show us where the demon is?"

One of her hands fluttered around her face in agitation. She opened the door wider to let us in but gave us a narrow-eyed look. She wore a flowered housecoat and terrycloth slippers. "At first I thought it was squirrels. They keep getting in under the eaves, and then they make nests up there. I had to bring in an exterminator last year."

I nodded but cut to the chase. "How do we get to your attic, ma'am?"

She led us down the hallway away from the front entrance and then stopped and pointed at a closed door. "The stairs are there."

She kept well away from us, as if afraid we'd brush up against her. Normals often reacted to us with suspicion even as they were relieved that we were there to take care of their problem. It was typical for normals to fear and shun people with magical aptitude, though they knew they needed us.

I reached for the knob. "Keep the door shut while we're up there," I said. "Wait here for us to come back down. Is there a light?"

She nodded and flipped the switch on the wall next to the attic door.

When I opened the door, a musty scent of stale air and old, forgotten stuff greeted me. I drew my stun gun with my right hand and my flashlight with my left. I sensed the presence of demonic energy as a faint, heated prickle under my skin. Stein followed me up the steep, narrow staircase. A naked light bulb glared above us.

At the top of the stairs, I made room for Stein.

"See it?" I asked, swinging my flashlight and gun around.

There were stacks of sagging boxes, a few rickety high-back chairs, a big trunk with leather straps—the usual attic stuff.

"There."

I looked to where Stein was pointing. Sure enough, a demon about the size of a large crow perched on the crossbar of an empty clothing rack. Its head was narrow and sleek, its eyes illuminated and beady. Most minor demons looked like the deformed offspring of a pterodactyl and a bat, and this one was no exception.

"I'll cover you," I said, raising my gun arm. "Pull the top off one of your traps and set it on the floor under the demon and then get out of the way."

Keeping my eyes and flashlight trained on the creature, I heard the soft snap of a brimstone burner opening, and caught a whiff of a scent reminiscent of a struck match.

Stein moved toward the rack but stopped about eight feet away and bent at the waist to set the disc on the floor.

"No, that's too far away to—"

I started to tell him the trap needed to be closer to pull the demon in but forgot my words as a halo of magic formed around Stein.

The tingling across my face and bare arms was like the brush of wind, but nothing stirred. It wasn't the shift of air that caused the sensation, but the movement of magic.

Stein raised the index finger of his right hand and a stream of green earth magic shot out. He moved it in a clockwise circle, and the magic made a ring that quickly spread to form a sphere, capturing the creature. The demon freaked out and tried to take flight but just banged into the walls of the energetic enclosure Stein had created.

He lowered his arm, directing the sphere down to the disc with his finger until it hovered right above the trap, and then flicked his hand. The green bubble dissipated and the trap activated. I turned my face away to protect my eyes from the flash. There was a sizzle and then a smell of sulphur and cooked meat.

Okay, so maybe I'd underestimated his suitability for Demon Patrol detail.

When I opened my eyes, Stein was squatting down to retrieve the disc. The charred remains of the demon stuck to the disc in a tarry residue. He slapped the lid on it, stood, and turned to me.

"Was that cheating?" he asked, perfectly deadpan.

Half-laughing, half-coughing as the smoke from the trapping

process billowed around me, I shook my head. "Whatever gets the job done."

Stein's little trick was beyond my abilities, and he didn't even break a sweat. A low Level III would have at least needed a pause to catch their breath after that sort of energetic expenditure. A Level II would have required a chair and a couple of minutes to recover.

I checked in to report the demon contained, and Stein and I went back downstairs where the homeowner was waiting.

"All taken care of, ma'am," I said.

"Oh my goodness, thank you!" She clasped her hands over her large bosom. In her relief, she seemed to be warming up to the thought of having crafters in her home. "They can make such a mess, and I have a neighbor who was scratched up something awful last year when a trio of demons appeared in her pantry."

"You're welcome." I headed for the front door, where I turned and gave her a little wave. "Have a nice day."

It was best not to get too chatty, especially with the retired folks who called in, or you could get stuck in their house for an hour as they tried to show you a bazillion pictures of their grandchildren. Demon Patrol officers were graded partly on how much time we spent on each call. More time wasn't better.

Back on the sidewalk, I looked over at Stein with new curiosity.

"So. Even though you're the most powerful Level III I've ever seen, you're the black sheep of the family, huh?"

He gave me a wry smile, but his eyes were guarded. "In the Stein family, anything less than a mage doesn't really count."

Mages had magic abilities that were literally off the charts.

They had their own social and political structures, though they worked with mainstream government and had their fingers in various sectors of industry. Even before the Rip and magic became known to the world of normals, mages had always kept to themselves within the magic community. They were a breed apart—a club with an exclusive membership. And there was only one requirement to get in. If you didn't have mage-level ability, you were an outsider.

I tried to imagine a young Damien Stein at home with parents and siblings who were all mages. Surrounded by people who could freeze him with a look. Compel him with a wave of a hand. It was no wonder he'd fled a couple thousand miles to escape them.

"Your family helped to contain the original Rip," I said, my voice lifting a little in question.

It wasn't an actual question—everyone knew the Steins had played a key role in rallying the mage community to respond to the New York Rip. The death toll would have been much higher if the mages hadn't stepped in. I didn't need Stein to confirm the fact, really, I was just interested in his family's lore.

He nodded. "It was right before I was born, so obviously I have no memory of it, but yeah."

That made him around twenty-seven or twenty-eight. Another member of Generation Post-Rip.

I aimed us back toward the center of my beat—*our* beat, my grudging mind corrected—toward Capitol Boulevard.

My head was doing its offbeat throb, and the shadows seemed to be stirring. Reminders that I'd yet to manage a truly good night's sleep since I'd died.

I stifled a yawn with the back of my hand. "There's a coffee place a block from the capitol building, let's head there before another call comes in."

Before Stein could answer, my phone jangled. I pulled it off its shoulder mount.

My insides gave a little twist when I looked at the screen. It was Roxanne calling. Maybe it was good news. Maybe the statue cracked open and her brother popped out, whole and unharmed. And unpossessed.

Yeah, it probably wasn't good news.

"Hello?" I answered.

"Officer Grey, they're taking Nathan!" Roxanne's voice was shrill with panic.

"Who's trying to take him?" I stopped walking, considering whether I should try to book it on foot to Crystal Ball Lane, or run to my place and take my truck.

"Men. Big men! They're going to put the statue on a wheelie thing and take him away. They said it's their property and they have the right to claim him."

"Okay, try to stall them," I said, talking fast. "I'll be there in a flash."

I took off, running toward home.

Stein caught up with me. "What's going on?"

"I need to help a friend. It's an emergency."

"Is this part of the job?"

"No."

His footfalls faltered a little, and then he sped up to draw even with me again. "We're not supposed to leave our beat without notifying our sergeant first."

I glanced over at him. "You don't have to come."

On the force, leaving your partner was a cardinal sin. But Stein was new, and I was obviously going to break the rules. I wouldn't have held it against him if he didn't stick with me. Besides, with my luck, I'd probably get caught and end up in deep shit. Stein didn't need to get mixed up in my tainted reputation with Devereux.

We were almost to my block. I lifted the flap on one of my pockets, awkwardly digging for my keys as I ran.

I skidded to a stop at my truck, threw open the driver's side door, got in, and jammed the key in the ignition. The passenger door slammed, and I looked over to see Stein with his mouth open, panting, as he shoved his pack down next to his legs and reached for the seat belt.

I pulled away from the curb with a faint whine of rubber on asphalt.

We reached Roxanne's building in four minutes flat. There was a white truck double-parked there with its hazard lights on, one of the long movers with a ramp that extended out the back. Unremarkable except for the logo. My hands convulsively clenched into fists, and my head whipped in a double-take when I spotted it—a navy letter G enclosed in a circle, like a copyright symbol but with a G instead of a C.

Gregori Industries.

Shit.

Gregori was a global dark horse in industry, a company that pushed the boundaries of genetic engineering, technology, and magic. It'd been around since long before the Rip, but it wasn't until after the catastrophe that the corporation's magical enterprises were exposed to the general public. Many blamed Gregori Industries for the Rip, though the courts hadn't managed to pin responsibility on the company or its owners. The Gregori logo always made me clench up inside, but this wasn't the moment to entertain my personal issues.

I pounded up the stairs with Stein right behind me.

The door to Roxanne's apartment was open.

Inside, three beefy goons dressed in navy onesie janitor-type uniforms were wrestling the statue through the window. An oversized hand truck and a tangle of bungee cords and straps waited near the sofa.

When Roxanne spotted me, her red eyes welled up. With a hoarse cry she rushed to me and grabbed my arm, pulling me toward the men. "Tell them they can't take Nathan!"

"Hey! You're in a private residence, and that's private property," I bellowed, anger fueling the force behind my words. All three goons paused their grunting efforts and looked around at me. I planted my feet and hooked my thumbs over the top of my service belt. "Get out now, or I'll have you arrested for trespassing, unlawful entry, attempted burglary, and whatever the hell else I can come up with."

Two of the men resumed what they were doing, and the one nearest me reached for something in his back pocket. Without a word, he handed me a bundle of papers folded lengthwise.

I flipped through them, noting the official Gregori letterhead and logo on all of them. The logo shone off the page, literally rising up in three dimensions off the paper, in holographic "ink"—a techno-magical material that Gregori had developed—and I knew the paperwork was legit. The holographic seals were impossible to forge.

Stein had come to peer over my shoulder. "That's not a warrant, is it?"

"No. It's documentation showing Gregori Industries owns that gargoyle," I ground out through clenched teeth.

"*What?*" Roxanne's voice broke, and her pale face contorted in horror.

Dammit. Dammit. Dammit.

I should have listened to Johnny and called the authorities. Not the regular police, but someone in Supernatural Crimes and Public Safety, like he'd suggested. SCPS would have claimed the gargoyle, but it would have been a hell of a lot more accessible than it was going to be once Gregori had it. Johnny's instincts had been right. But had I listened? Nooo. Of course not. I was so sure I could handle it, so I'd batted my eyelashes at him and convinced him to do it my way.

"Tag number is right here," Head Goon said. With a sausage of an index finger, he pointed at the side of the statue's base. Next to the tag number was an animated seal of authenticity, another Gregori techno-magical invention.

I whipped my phone off its mount and snapped a picture. But my stomach was dropping like a faulty parachute. Embossed into the stone were the words "PROPERTY OF GREGORI INDUSTRIES. SPECIMEN #G5996613-06B" along with the company logo.

I shoved the paperwork at Stein. "Take pictures of all of these."

Then I tapped Head Goon on the back and folded my arms, waiting until he turned around. "Explain to me how Gregori came to own this rare creature."

"Sorry, can't disclose that info."

"Then tell us how it ended up on that balcony," I demanded.

"Classified."

I squeezed my eyes closed and pinched my temples between

my thumb and middle finger.

Think.

I turned to my phone, finding Johnny in my contacts. He picked up on the second ring.

"I'm at Roxanne's," I said. "Gregori Industries has claimed the gargoyle as their property, and they're currently in the process of hauling it away. It's got their name and serial number on it. They've got paperwork." With each word, misery deepened in the pit of my stomach.

Johnny let loose an impressive concentration of four-letter words.

The twisting sensation in my guts pulled tighter.

"When they get that thing onto Gregori property—" Johnny started.

"I know," I cut in. "Then we're officially screwed."

The Gregori Industries campus, situated just outside Boise city limits, was practically its own sovereign nation. I never understood how Jacob Gregori had pulled it off, but anything on that property was more or less exempt from police search warrants or entry by law enforcement.

There was a dull bump that shook the floor, and I looked up to see that the goons had worked the statue inside the apartment. One of them manned the hand truck while the other two tipped the statue, lifting one edge of its base so the flat plate of the hand truck could be slid under it.

"You could call the cops, try to stall them," Johnny said.

I looked at the ceiling and blew out a harsh breath. "You know how the police are when it comes to Gregori Industries. The cops will conveniently wait a couple of hours and then respond to the call after the gargoyle is long gone."

Johnny sighed. "I don't have any bright ideas. I'm sorry, Ella."

"Please, don't apologize. I should have listened to you in the first place. But I'm not going to let this drop," I said. "I may need your help again."

"You know I'm here, sugar."

Good old Johnny.

I pulled my lips in between my teeth and clamped down. There *was* something I could do. The prospect of it made me about as happy as the thought of eating a chocolate covered piece of dog poop, but . . . I looked over at Roxanne. She stood in the same hoodie she'd worn the night before with her arms wrapped around her body, shivering in spite of the stuffy air as tears rolled down her cheeks.

"Hey," I said to Head Goon, drawing out the word and aiming for a genial tone. I gestured to Roxanne, and he glanced over at her. I warmed my voice to the extent I was capable. "Can you guarantee no harm will come to it? At least until we have a chance to free him?"

With my eyes wide and upturned, I stepped close to Head Goon and touched his sweaty, hair-covered forearm. He was slightly shorter than me, so it was a real challenge to try to angle my head to make it seem like I was looking up at him with doe eyes.

"Pleeease?" I crooned. BO and stale coffee breath drifted up my nose.

I wasn't a fan of this type of manipulation, and I knew I wasn't good at it. But I could see him softening.

He actually smiled, showing me a row of stained teeth that looked like corn kernels. "The statue won't be harmed. Not right away, anyway. It'll be quarantined and under observation for the first twenty-four hours."

I returned his smile and gave his arm a squeeze. "Oh, thank you!"

Allowing the saccharine expression to fall off my face, I went to Roxanne, purposely blocking her view of the men, and put my hands on her shoulders. I waited until she looked up at me.

"This isn't over." I pitched my voice low so only she would hear. "I can't stop them from taking the statue, but I'm going to find a way to get your brother back."

She nodded, but her eyes were far away and void of hope.

"Do you want to hang out at my place the rest of the day?" I asked, feeling weird about leaving her, even though she was clearly used to being home alone.

"No, that's okay. I have a babysitting job in fifteen minutes." The corners of her mouth drooped.

"When my shift ends, I'll call you and tell you what we're doing next. Johnny wants to help, too. Hang tight, Roxanne. Okay?"

Not even the mention of Johnny's name elicited any spark. "Yeah," she said, her voice tiny and flat.

I went to Stein and took the papers from him. "You got all of them?"

He nodded. Then he flicked a look at Roxanne. "Why isn't she in school?"

She heard him and pulled a face as if she'd just smelled something spoiled. "Because it's like the *middle* of *summer*?" There was that adults-are-morons curl of her lip.

My mouth twitched with the beginnings of a grin. Roxanne still had some fight in her.

"Oh, right." Stein gave me a sheepish look.

"Officers Stein and Grey, report your status immediately," came a voice through our earpieces.

Cursing silently, I puffed my cheeks and blew out a harsh breath. We'd missed our check-in. And we were away from our beat.

I pressed and held the walkie button on my earpiece. "Stein and Grey checking in. We were, uh, responding to a direct call for aid. All clear, no demon activity. Current location Twelfth Street, returning to Capitol Boulevard now."

There was no point in lying about where we were. The station's communication center constantly showed our position.

"Stein and Grey, you have orders to report to your Sergeant at the end of shift."

I closed my eyes, slumping with defeat. Not only had I failed Roxanne, I'd gotten Stein in trouble his first day on the job.

"I'm sorry, we have to get back to work," I said to Roxanne. "I'll call you this evening."

Stein and I hurried from the apartment and down to my truck.

"I'll tell Devereux this was all my fault," I said as I drove us toward our beat. "I'm already a troublemaker in his mind, so it won't take much to convince him. I'm sorry about this." I glanced over at him.

The tension on his face was obvious. "You were trying to do something good. It was my choice to go with you."

"Thanks for that, but I wouldn't take offense if you want to request another partner. They'd probably grant it, given the circumstances."

He blew out an annoyed breath. "Then I'd look like an ass. Who decides they can't deal with shit their first day on duty?"

He had a point. He *would* look like a first class wuss if he asked to switch to someone else right now. A large part of me wished he'd do it anyway, but it was a selfish desire. I wanted it only to help relieve my own guilt.

With a furtive look out of the corners of my eyes, I tried to get a read on just how upset he was. He stared straight ahead, his jaw muscles flexing as he ground his teeth.

"I'll, uh, make it up to you," I said, all too aware of my own awkwardness and hating it. "Whatever you want, just tell me. I want to make this right."

Hell's bells, I sucked at contrition.

He tilted his head slightly, his eyes cast upward. "Okay," he finally said, nodding.

I waited for more, but he remained silent as I found a parking spot at the edge of the green that fronted the capitol building.

Great, he was going to dangle it over me a while. I supposed I deserved it.

"So that girl thinks her brother is trapped in the gargoyle?" Stein asked, clearly dubious.

"Yeah, I know how it sounds, but she actually may be right."

"How do you explain that?"

I lifted a shoulder. "I can't. We have no idea how it could have happened."

The doubt on Stein's face said he wasn't completely buying it.

I pulled out my debit card and waved it at the meter, even though I'd probably end up with a parking ticket anyway. The spots around the capitol were one hour max, and I couldn't go running back every hour to feed the meter or move my truck. The alternative would have been to park at home and walk the handful of blocks to our beat, but that would have delayed us getting back to our territory and made it look like we were purposely dawdling, which only would have incurred more wrath from Devereux. I preferred a ticket.

A crowd was gathering on the green. The shadows framing the edges of my vision took notice, too, gyrating like dark smoke stirred by a breeze. A dull ache thumped between my eyes.

"Rally or something?" I asked Stein, mostly just for something to say.

"That guy looks familiar." Stein was squinting at someone in the crowd.

I followed his gaze, and my eyes jumped right to the man who, despite standing at one edge of the people milling around, gave off the impression of being at the center of things.

"Rafael St. James," I said.

"Why do I know that name?"

"He's in the news every so often. Activist for equal treatment of vampires and other causes."

"That's right, I remember. He lives around here, doesn't he?" Stein asked enthusiastically, as if he'd just realized we were in the presence of a celebrity, which wasn't far from the truth, actually.

Glad that he seemed to be thawing, I nodded and quickly tried to dredge up anything I could think of about Rafael St. James. Some of the things I knew about Raf weren't appropriate for polite conversation, but I'd leave that revelation for another time. "Yeah, he grew up here. Comes from money, but instead of following in his father's footsteps, he dedicated his life to humanitarian causes. His father was a rich farmer and his mother was an illegal from Central America. Both are gone now, and he must be sitting on a fortune, but for the most part you'd never know it. Let's make a loop and see what's going on."

We'd reached an intersection, but instead of crossing, we angled around to continue following the sidewalk that bordered the green. Now that we were back on our beat, we could take our time until another call came in from dispatch. As we neared Rafael and his people, I spotted a news van parking across the street.

I glanced at Stein, wondering what he sensed from the vampires in the crowd. I saw several—recognizable by their ethereal, ageless faces and the way they seemed to glide rather than walk—but I identified them by sight, as my magic wasn't strong enough for me to sense what little magical signature they emitted. If there was a rogue vampire nearby, I'd feel the presence, but these were all dociles, treated with a special implant that released a continuous low-level dose of silver and other proprietary ingredients. The treatment allowed the vamps to walk in sunlight without burning and suppressed their bloodlust. It also made them much less detectable by people with magical aptitude.

The implants had been invented by none other than Gregori Industries not long after the New York City Rip and the subsequent emergence of the VAMP2 virus. All vampires were required by law to get the implant. The federal government claimed compliance was over 99%, but many believed that was an overestimation to diminish public fear and discrimination against vampires. Independent groups estimated compliance was quite a bit lower.

Rogue vamps were out there, but they were stealthy and smart. They tended to pick their victims from the fringes of society, and once they had their human feeders drunk on glamor and the high that came from vampire saliva, they usually didn't worry about their prey trying to escape.

My chest clenched as the image of Evan flashed through my mind, his body slack and surrounded by others like him in a vamp feeder den. I'd had no sign where it was located, whether it was in real-time or a memory inserted into my brain, but one thing was certain—if the vision was real, there was a blood-hungry, impossibly strong and lightning quick rogue vamp keeping my brother there. I squeezed my eyelids closed, willing away the hurt that accompanied the thought of Evan serving as a helpless feeder.

"Are you okay?" Stein asked.

I drew a breath. "Yeah, fine." I forced my focus to my partner and our present surroundings.

By the way Stein was staring at a porcelain-skinned vampire with corn silk hair down to her waist, I guessed this was a novelty for him. It made sense. Before the implants came along, vampires in New York and the surrounding areas were massacred. It wasn't a place they tended to want to live.

Manhattan wasn't just ground zero for the Rip, it was also the birthplace of modern vampires. In vamp culture, it was sort of holy ground, but not the type of landmark they wanted to visit. Once the implants became widespread and proved effective, vampires were allowed to live anywhere they chose. Vamps fled the Northeast, where the prejudice against them was strongest. It was possible that Stein, having grown up back East, had never even seen one in person before.

"What do you think about vampire rights?" Stein asked, his eyes still glued to the vamps.

"I think it's a worthy cause. The dociles shouldn't be discriminated against. It's not their fault they're infected, and they pose no harm to society as long as their implants are working. They have the right to death, liberty, pursuit of happiness, et cetera."

"Do you know any?"

"Yeah, I've known a few, but they tend to keep to themselves. There are a ton of them out west off Hill Road," I said, naming a long, winding road that began not far from my apartment and stretched westward at the base of the foothills. "There's a big neighborhood that was built about twenty years ago. Sunshine Valley. Other pockets of vamp communities live farther west."

"It's interesting. The different attitudes about vampires, I mean." Stein glanced at me, but I couldn't read his eyes. "Back home, there are too many who lost loved ones to the virus. Others whose loved ones disappeared into feeder dens. It's too fresh."

In the early days of VAMP2, SWAT teams shot vampires on sight using rounds infused with oak filaments and silver—a sort of vampire stake in bullet form. Citizens killed a fair number, too. It was considered acceptable self-defense back then in the midst of the panic, so no one was ever charged with murder of a vampire. Today, the fear of even the docile vampires was still heavy and public in some places. In general, the farther west you went, away from the East Coast and the original Rip, the greater the acceptance of docile vamps.

It was an uncomfortable topic. I wasn't born yet when it all went down, but I knew enough from old footage on the web, media references, and what I'd learned in school to understand that out here, so far from New York, people had been incredibly lucky to suffer only a few deaths at the hands of a relatively small number of rogue vamps that made it this far west immediately after the Rip.

By the time I was born, the implants had been around for a few years. The prejudice against vamps, however, still lived on.

We slowed and then stopped at the edge of the crowd. Rafael's people were setting up a little fold-out platform. A few were handing out pre-printed signs from the back of a pickup. I caught a look at some of the signs. One read, "EQUAL HEALTH CARE FOR ALL." Another read, "VOTE AGAINST LEGAL DESCRIMINATION."

Some of the people arriving on the green carried their own

homemade signs.

Vampires are people too!

I'm a vampire, and I pay my taxes.

Rafael hopped onto the platform, and there was a little smattering of applause and cheers. He flashed a smile at the crowd and then looked down to switch on the megaphone in his hand. There was a brief screech of feedback, and he winced good-naturedly.

I'd read somewhere that he used old-school megaphones at his rallies instead of modern PA systems because he liked the way megaphones played in media photos. It wasn't vanity, though. Despite his rock-god looks—tall, broad-shouldered, tousled dark hair, a wide mouth with an easy smile, pale green eyes the color of sea glass that stood out starkly against his Latin coloring—Rafael was always about the cause. His rallies might look like spontaneous, grassroots gatherings, but everything he did was carefully orchestrated for the greatest effect.

"I'd like to meet him," Stein said. "Seems like an interesting character."

"He is."

He turned to me. "You know him?"

"We've crossed paths a few times," I said mildly. Just then, Rafael's gaze swung my way. The corner of his mouth lifted in a little half-smile of recognition.

I couldn't help smiling back. No heterosexual female could resist the attention of Rafael St. James.

"What kind of shifter is he? I don't remember ever seeing

mention of it."

My head swiveled to Stein so fast everything blurred for a split second. "*What?*"

"He's not a wolf." Stein's brow creased, his eyes still on Rafael. "I don't know the signature, but then I've only ever been exposed to wolf shifters."

"Rafael St. James isn't a shifter."

Stein finally looked at me. He barked a little laugh. "Yes, he is. There's a hefty veil of impressive magic concealing it, though. An extremely powerful mage did that."

I squinted at Rafael, but of course I didn't have enough magical juice to even sense a mage-level obfuscation spell, let alone see what it was hiding.

"I just . . . that's extremely hard to believe," I sputtered, shaking my head. "You're really seeing *shifter*?"

"Yep. One hundred percent positive."

"It can't be. There's no way something like that would stay secret. He doesn't run in a pack or—or spend any time in the wilderness. Not with his schedule and high profile. And if you can see through the spell, then others could, too. If he had to shift at least once a month, it wouldn't stay secret," I repeated. "There's just no way."

"Mages are bound to secrecy about their work if the subject requests it, so they wouldn't tell. And I'm probably the only non-mage in the world who'd be able to pick up on it." He gave me a wry look. "You don't grow up in a family of mages without learning a few advanced tricks."

There had to be some other explanation for whatever Stein was sensing from Rafael, but given that I'd already gotten Stein in trouble, I didn't feel like I had the right to launch a heated argument. Besides, how could I prove I was right? Magically speaking, Stein was about a bazillion times more powerful than me.

"We're going to get started in just a few, folks," Rafael's voice projected through the megaphone. "There's a big group coming over. We don't want them to miss out on the fun."

Stein had pulled his phone from its mount and had been busily tapping away on it for the past several minutes. "I'm trying to figure out what they're rallying for. Or against."

I spotted a vamp guy with a stack of papers near Rafael. I gestured. "Let's go find out."

I threaded through the loose crowd and approached a vamp guy who was handing out flyers.

"Hello, officers." His poreless vampire skin looked like golden-tan porcelain in the sunlight. Both wrists were tattooed with a thin band of proprietary neon blue ink—another Gregori Industries product—that indicated he had an implant.

"Hi there." I pointed to the stack in his hands. "Is that literature on your cause?"

"Sure is. Here, let me fold one for you." His honey-smooth voice gave me an involuntary shiver. Even the dociles, stripped of the ability to glamour, had magnetic appeal. He quickly tri-folded the piece of paper into a pamphlet and then handed it to Stein with a little wink.

"Nice of you to pay us a visit, officers," came a rich, deep voice from off to the side.

Rafael.

"Are you here for work or as concerned citizens?" he asked.

I tried to scrutinize his handsome face without being too obvious about it. I detected nothing that indicated he was a shifter. If anything, he emitted charm worthy of a vampire, not the rough-edged wildness of a shifter. He definitely wasn't a vamp—he wouldn't be able to conceal that. "No demon activity reported. We're just patrolling our beat."

Rafael planted his hands loosely on his hips, somehow making it a gesture of relaxed attentiveness.

Remembering Stein's interest in Rafael, I gestured to my partner. "This is Officer Stein. It's his first day on the job."

Rafael nodded at Stein but didn't offer a hand to shake. "Nice to meet you."

"You as well," Stein said.

"It's been a while, Ella," Rafael said mildly, but his eyes were unblinking and intent.

I knew better than to allow myself to get drawn in—Rafael looked at everyone with that steady intensity—but in spite of my brain knowing better, my body temperature climbed slightly under his gaze.

"It has." I imitated his mild tone. "How was DC?"

"Productive. But I'm glad to be home for a while." A couple of his people were hovering a few feet away, clearly waiting to get his attention.

I half turned away. "Well, we should get back to work. It's good to see you, Raf."

The corners of his generous mouth turned up. "You too. We should get a drink."

I gave him a nod and a little wave of my hand, which he could take as agreement to his not-quite-ask if he so chose.

As we walked away, Stein laughed, a soft noise low in his throat. "So the two of you have a thing, huh?"

"No." I tipped my phone on its shoulder mount so I could see the time. "We should try to grab lunch before another call comes in."

I aimed us toward Eighth Street, which ran parallel to Capitol Boulevard, intending to head to the deli that was within our beat.

"What do you mean no? There's clearly something between the two of you," Stein ribbed.

I gave him a cynical look. "Trust me, I'm not special. Rafael St. James gives that smoky look to a lot of women."

"He was surrounded by women, and he wasn't looking at any of them like that."

"Yeah, he did. You just missed it." I heaved a long-suffering sigh. "Let's just get lunch, okay?"

"Fine. But I'm calling in part of your debt. Over lunch, I want to know why you joined Demon Patrol."

I rolled my eyes. "*Part* of my debt? How long do you get to string this out?"

"Depends on how much trouble we're in with Devereux."

That shut me up.

We grabbed sandwiches at Blossom's Deli and sat down on a

bench outside.

"You may begin." Stein made a rolling motion with his index finger.

Shooting him a withering look, I took a giant bite of turkey on sourdough, which allowed me to stall for a minute while I chewed.

"I joined Demon Patrol because I wanted a job where I wouldn't be pinned to a desk or stuck inside all day. I wanted something with a little bit of excitement," I said. "And seeing as how I'm barely Level I on the Scale, and not some kind of Level III wizard prodigy like you, I didn't have the option to go for Strike or Special Forces."

"Do you come from a police family?"

I shook my head and took a long pull of iced tea through the straw.

"I didn't think so. But there are lots of jobs where you could work outside. Judging by what I saw of the dynamic between you and Devereux, I'd guess our diversion today isn't the first time you've gotten in trouble with him. I'm also guessing you're not interested in advancing to a higher position. The old-school hierarchy of the Force seems counter to your nature, and I think it grates on you. So . . . there's a deeper reason for you choosing this job."

I took another bite and looked off down the street. He was right, of course. I didn't really want to talk about it, but I owed him. Plus, he was my partner, and some amount of confiding between partners was good for the working relationship.

I swallowed, took a breath and held it for a moment, and then let it out.

"My younger brother, Evan, disappeared about five years ago. Originally when I joined the Force, I thought it would give me a chance to search for him. I had no money, so I didn't have the luxury of traipsing all over to try to find him, especially when I had no idea where to begin. I figured on Patrol I'd be out all day, and I could show his picture around and try to figure out what happened to him. And I think I expected to have more access to, I don't know, police tools. Something that would help me search for him."

Stein set his sandwich down on its butcher paper wrapper and went still, intent on what I was saying.

"Looking back now, it seems pretty naïve. I quickly learned that there's not actually a whole lot of freedom on the job, and we don't get access to much of anything except the gear we have on our belts," I continued. "I did what I could. I picked up a bit of information here and there, and of course kept searching on my off days, but all the leads went cold."

"What were the circumstances of his disappearance?"

I moistened my lips, hesitating. "An arch-demon grabbed him and took off."

Stein's dark blond brows pulled together. "Grabbed him?"

"I know it sounds weird, but multiple eye witnesses swore to it."

"I've never heard of a demon behaving that way. The arch-demons go straight for possession. They don't play around. And they don't haul off their victims."

"It's the only instance I know about," I agreed.

"I'm so sorry, Ella. Carrying this around for so many years . . . it's got to be really hard."

I stared down at the sidewalk, but in my mind I saw the older Evan from my vision. "Yeah, it is."

Whether the vision was real or not, it was the only thing I had to cling to, and the *other* had given it to me. I wanted more, something, anything. I'd take the headaches and the death dreams and the dancing shadows. I'd gladly sublet part of my brain to the *other* if it led me to Evan.

Suddenly, I knew what I needed to do. If I could induce a deep sleep, maybe the thing in my head would show me more. I needed to get back to Crystal Ball Lane for a sleep charm.

But first, I'd have to face the music back at the station at the end of shift and then figure out how to rescue Roxanne's brother.

"So you'd better count yourself lucky that with your commendation today you happen to be the golden girl of the Force. Enjoy the fifteen minutes' reprieve it's getting you, Officer Grey," Sergeant Devereux said. After five straight minutes of lecturing and threatening me, his face had reddened to a hue that was somewhere between a strawberry and a red delicious apple. For some reason the fruit comparison made me want to burst out laughing. But I did my damnedest to look deeply repentant. Like a girl who'd learned her lesson, by darn, and moreover sincerely appreciated the lambasting her righteous boss was bestowing upon her.

Inside, I was just relieved that Devereux wasn't going to bring down the hammer. Toward the end of his tirade he'd told us he was adding a note to my file and letting my partner off with only a verbal warning.

I knew I'd likely used up my get-out-of-jail-free cards.

Devereux turned his face away like he could no longer stand the sight of us, flapped his hand back and forth through the air as if waving away something smelly. "Go home, both off you. And stay off my radar, Grey."

All too happy to comply, I scooted out of the Sergeant's

cramped office, practically stepping on Stein's heels in my haste to escape.

"Again, I'm *so* sorry," I mumbled to him in a low voice once we were well down the hallway.

He gave a nonchalant shrug. "Eh, that was kind of exciting. I've never been screamed at by a boss like that. Makes me feel like a real renegade."

He was doing his best to be lighthearted, which I appreciated, but I could tell the reprimand had rattled him a little. Stein didn't seem like the type to break the rules and he wasn't used to getting in trouble.

He looked down at his service belt as we headed toward the exit for the parking lot. "What do I do with this? Do I have to turn in the stun gun?"

"Nah. If it were a more powerful weapon, like the ones Strike Team carries, you'd have to lock it up before you leave. But on Demon Patrol we keep our belts and all our toys. Wear it into work. It's considered amateur to show up in uniform but without the service belt on."

"Got it." He pushed open one of the double doors and held it so I could walk out ahead of him. "If you're going back to Roxanne's now, I'll come with."

"Thanks for the offer, but I can handle it."

"Ella, I just got sprayed with my Sergeant's spit for the sake of the girl. I'm invested now. I think I have a right. Plus, I'd like to know more about how a human could have ended up inside a gargoyle."

I held in a withering sigh. How had I come to owe all these debts? Stein, Roxanne, Johnny . . . twenty-four hours ago, I was footloose and fancy free, just me and the creepy shadows and the nightmares. I didn't owe anyone anything, and I could do as I pleased. I should have appreciated it more.

"Okay," I said, trying not to sound grudging about it. "We need to make a stop at my house first, though."

The poor dog had been cooped up inside all day, and I just realized I'd received no calls from the Humane Society on behalf of a worried owner.

"Come on, I'll give you a ride back to your truck," Stein said, jangling the set of keys he'd pulled from his backpack's pocket.

The Lexus I'd spotted earlier was indeed his ride. I almost felt guilty sliding onto the pristine storm-gray leather seat, afraid I'd scratch it or leave a smudge. The vehicle's motor made a quiet, smooth hum, nothing like the throaty rumble of my truck. The fresh-off-the-lot scent still clung to the car's interior.

Stein dropped me at the green, and I gave him my address so he could meet me at home. Rafael's gathering was long gone. It seemed an odd time of year to stage such an event, as the local legislature was on break for the summer, but I didn't pay a whole lot of attention to politics.

The Lexus was parked in front of the four-plex by the time I got there. I pulled up to the curb on the side street, and Stein followed me up to my porch. Suddenly a little nervous about the state of my place, I unlocked and opened the door. I wasn't messy by nature, but I wasn't used to having people I barely knew in my home.

"Where are you, big guy?" I called the dog.

I heard paws drop to the wood floor in the bedroom, and he emerged, bounding toward me with a happy loll of his tongue. I caught his paws as he jumped up to greet me, and he swiped my chin with his tongue. I couldn't help returning his doggy smile.

"Come on, I'm sure you need to go out." He followed into the kitchen and then trotted through the doorway that led to the back yard.

"Interesting dog," Stein remarked from the kitchen doorway. "What's his name?"

"I'm not sure. He followed me home last night."

"Followed your truck?"

"Hitched a ride in the bed, actually. I didn't see him until I was nearly home. He didn't have a collar on."

The buzzer sounded, and my head whipped to the front of the apartment. I hardly ever had visitors.

I passed Stein to go see who it was.

Johnny. I opened the door.

"Hey," I said, beckoning him inside after a moment's hesitation. In the two years I'd lived in this apartment, I couldn't recall having two people in my home at the same time.

"I was going to stop by Roxanne's, but when I saw your truck, I thought I'd see if you were home," Johnny said.

I didn't recall ever giving him my address, but I supposed I shouldn't have been surprised he knew where I lived. After all, he was a private investigator.

"Hi, Johnny Beemer," Johnny said to Stein.

"This is my new partner, Stein," I said by way of introduction. "Stein, meet Johnny Beemer, supernatural PI."

"Stein? Interesting name." Johnny said.

"Last name, actually. It's Damien." Stein crossed the small living room to shake Johnny's hand.

Suddenly unsure about my obligations, I briefly wondered if I should offer the guys something to drink. I didn't really want to do anything hostess-y. I preferred to get down to the business of helping Roxanne.

The dog bounded in, saving me from my silly dilemma.

"Whoa, who's this?" Johnny asked. The dog went over and bumped Johnny's hand, asking for some petting.

"He hitched a ride in the back of my truck. I called the pound and the Humane Society and gave his description, but no one seems to be looking for him."

Johnny dropped to one knee and took the dog's face in his hands. The dog didn't seem to mind. He tried to lick Johnny's nose.

"What?" I asked, moving closer. Johnny had that focused look in his eyes, the one he got when he was concentrating on one of his gadgets.

"Any idea what kind of dog this is?"

"None at all," I said. "Why?"

Johnny rose, stepped back, and crossed his arms. He tilted his head to the side, peering at the dog. "Definitely a mixed breed. But there's something odd . . . If I had to guess, I'd say labradoodle hellhound."

I burst out laughing, but a thin line of apprehension threaded through me. This dog didn't seem malicious at all, but "*What*? The only living hellhounds are owned by Gregori Industries."

Hellhounds had come through the original Rip along with demons, but all except a few had been killed. Jacob Gregori had somehow managed to pick up some, and the authorities couldn't do a thing about it because the hell-spawned beasts were on the Gregori Industries campus.

"Maybe one escaped and mated with a local dog," Stein suggested.

"That seems unlikely. Hellhounds aren't exactly friendly," I said. That was an understatement. Before the situation was brought under control in Manhattan, packs of hellhounds worked in concert with demons, herding people into the open where the demons could swoop in for easy possession.

"Hang on, I'm going to get my scanner," Johnny said.

He went out to his car and returned a moment later with the tablet he'd used at Roxanne's. He powered it on and aimed the camera at the dog, who'd jumped up onto the sofa to sit next to Stein. Both Stein and the dog were captured in the image on the tablet's screen.

Johnny glanced up. "*Damn*, Stein. You're leaking magic all over the place." Looking back down at the image, he gave a low whistle.

"He's an extreme Level III," I supplied.

"Yeah, I'd say so," Johnny said.

Sometimes I forgot that Johnny didn't have any magical

aptitude, which meant he wouldn't have sensed my partner's abilities. Johnny was so immersed in the supernatural world through his job—and his passion for using technology to "quantify magic," as he put it—he was practically an honorary supernatural.

I glanced at Stein and then looked harder. His eyes were intent on Johnny, and the look in them was, well . . . *appreciative*. I filed that away for the moment.

"What about the dog?" I asked.

Johnny pointed to the screen, tracing a purple aura that shimmered around the dog. "See that? Indicates hellspawn." He snapped a still of the image. The screen froze for a second and then returned to the live picture. "I'll do some more analysis, but I'd say my original guess was right."

We all peered at the dog, who lay with his head resting on his paws.

"Is he dangerous?" I asked Johnny.

I watched him scroll down his tablet and then back up before he met my gaze. "If he were driven by hellhound instincts, he definitely wouldn't be hanging out on your couch like this. He'd be aggressive, calling to his demon master, and herding us. I'd say you're safe."

A shiver spread through me as I recalled the baying of hellhounds. I'd never witnessed it personally, but I'd seen footage. Even on video, the sound was bone chilling and terrifying.

Stein reached over and scratched the back of the dog's neck. His tail thumped, and he rolled over to his side in a submissive posture.

"You know what that means, don't you?" Stein asked.

I looked at him out of the corners of my eyes. "What?"

A faint smile played on Stein's face. "He's yours. Or more properly, you're *his*."

I glanced at Johnny, wondering if he had any idea what Stein meant.

"Hellhounds, full-blooded ones, imprint on their demon masters," Stein said. "A dog will follow only his demon master, and the hound is loyal to the death."

"Nah." I shook my head. I eyed the dog as he shifted again and began licking the back of his paw. The faint maroon glint in his eyes shifted to orange, yellow, and then faded. "That's just urban legend. Besides, Johnny said he doesn't have hellhound instincts."

"I think Damien's probably right," Johnny said, looking down at his data again.

Stein had stood and moved over to us to get a closer look at Johnny's tablet. My partner's eyes shone like he was a little kid and Johnny held the biggest candy bar Stein had ever seen.

I planted my hands on my hips and looked back and forth between the two guys, suddenly getting the sense that they were ganging up on me and enjoying it *way* too much.

"Seriously, Ella, I think this dog has claimed you," Johnny said. "And I don't think you're going to hear from an owner. This hella-doodle is sticking around."

I snorted. *Hella-doodle*. The next wave in designer dog breeds.

For a moment I allowed myself to consider that the guys were right, that the dog had imprinted on me—but why? Hellhounds were not of this world. Perhaps he recognized that I'd recently spent a bit of time elsewhere, too. People always said that dogs could sense things.

I looked at the dog, who still sat on the sofa. For a moment I could have sworn I saw the flicker of orange flames deep in his eyes. His lips stretched wide, and he panted a little. Then he turned in a couple of tight circles and curled up against one corner of the sofa. He seemed like a good dog. Would it be so bad if he stayed?

I let my arms drop. "I guess we'll just have to see. How about we focus on Roxanne now?"

"Right," Johnny said. He took a breath, but then hesitated, glancing at Stein.

"It's okay," I said with a small sigh. "He was over there with me today, and we got into trouble with the Sergeant. Stein's part of this now, so whatever you have to say about the case, he can hear it too."

Johnny nodded and then pulled out the old blue leather ottoman from its place in front of the matching chair and sat down. I sat between Stein and the hellhound-doodle on the sofa.

While we waited for Johnny to tap and swipe at his screen, I filled Stein in.

"Johnny detected three life forms in the statue," I said. "Human, presumably Roxanne's brother, plus a demon and a gargoyle."

Surprise registered on Stein's face. When Johnny set his tablet on the coffee table, it displayed a chart with a bunch of numbers. Stein reached down to unzip his backpack, which sat at his feet, and pulled out his notebook. He flipped to a blank page and started scribbling some numbers.

"I ran a deeper analysis on the scan I took." Johnny pointed at a column of numbers on the tablet, but before I could discern what they meant, he swiped to a different screen.

I gave up on trying to decipher the numbers and peered at Johnny. "What does it say?"

"Looks like the demon possessed both of the other life forms." Stein said. He glanced at Johnny for confirmation.

Johnny nodded once. "Yep."

Stein was clearly struggling to wrap his brain around the news. "So, the scenario with the statue . . . a demon possessed Roxanne's brother, and what, then the gargoyle ate him and also became possessed?"

Johnny tilted his head. "Maybe."

"The statue is stamped Gregori property," Stein said. "Gregori must have captured some gargoyles in the wild and then started breeding them."

"Poor things." Johnny shook his head. "Gargoyles are shy creatures and have never been known to harm humans unless people are threatening their nests. They need space, large habitats to hunt and roost."

"Is it even legal to keep them in captivity?" I asked.

"Probably not, but compared to the other things that go on behind the walls of Gregori Industries, this is nothing," Johnny said. He grimaced. "Lucky for the gargoyles that Phillip Zarella isn't around anymore."

The mention of the madman sent a chill winding up my

spine. As long as I could remember, there'd been rumors that it was actually Zarella who'd caused the Rip. He was one of the most brilliant scientists of the 21st century, but his experiments on supernaturals—including docile vampires—made the Nazis look like choirboys. If Gregori Industries thumbed its nose at the law, Zarella put it on a chopping block and gleefully sawed off its head. Zarella and Gregori had never been officially linked, but the madman's lab had been located near the original Gregori headquarters in New York. To add to his creep factor, he was one of the world's few necromancers—able to take command of and steer death-touched creatures, including vampires, zombies, and demons.

Zarella had finally been tried and convicted for his long list of atrocities when I was a teenager and had sat in prison while his team of lawyers went through appeals of his death sentence. Until last year, when in an escape attempt he'd been gunned down.

"Lucky for the world in general that the bastard is dead," I said.

We had a moment of silent mutual agreement.

"Gregori has literally stamped its ownership on the creature," Stein said. "Knowing Jacob Gregori, he's probably found a way to patent his gargoyles."

His mention of Jacob reminded me of my earlier resolution to make one last-ditch effort on behalf of Roxanne. My stomach flipped over with a nauseating lurch. I rubbed my damp palms across the tops of my thighs.

Johnny pulled a hand down the side of his face and then slumped against the back of the sofa. "What the hell are we going to do?"

"I, uh . . ." I cleared my throat and started again. "I'm going to, uh, try to talk to Jacob Gregori."

Johnny squinted at me. "Huh? That's a nice idea, but you can't exactly go knock on his door. Even if you could get in touch with him, he's refused meetings with the *president*."

"I sort of . . . know him." Ugh, I *so* did not want to be having this conversation.

"Ella," Johnny said my name slowly, the pitch of his voice rising at the end, as if he'd just caught me stealing a dollar from his wallet. "What do you mean, you *know* Jacob Gregori?"

I closed my eyes and let out a long breath. When I raised my eyelids, I looked at Johnny and Stein in turn. "What I'm about to tell you cannot ever leave this room. I'm absolutely dead serious."

"Okay." Johnny was looking at me with concern, his brows raised. "You have my word."

"Mine, too," Stein said.

I moistened my dry lips. "I have personal ties to Jacob Gregori. Trust me, he'll take my call."

For several seconds the only sound in the room was the faint whuff of the dog's measured breathing.

Johnny's mouth had dropped open. Stein's face was frozen in a wide-eyed stare.

Johnny snapped out of it first, snorting a laugh. "You're joking. You're trying to get back at us for telling you you're stuck with the hellhound-doodle. Which, by the way, I think you'll find out is the truth."

I gave him a hard glare. "Do I look like I'm kidding?"

Discomfort and dread did a nauseating tango in my stomach. Terrence and Deb were the only people who knew my secret: Jacob Gregori was my uncle, my father's brother. My mother and father never married. They met in New York, and I believed they had a relationship for many years. She loved him, she'd always been open with me about that, but considering the controversy around the Gregori name, my mother thought it best not to saddle me with it. She legally changed her own last name to Grey right before I was born, so that's the one I was given. I think Grey was a kind of homage to my father, a name that was similar to Gregori but generic enough that no one would make the connection.

Johnny's deep brown eyes were wide and intent on me. He

was curious, but I also read concern on his face. "Are you going to elaborate?" he asked softly.

I filled my lungs and held the breath for a moment before letting it out. I appreciated that Johnny and Stein both wanted to help free Roxanne's brother, but I didn't feel the need to reveal the entire truth.

"No," I said. "Sorry."

"What year were you born?" Johnny asked suddenly.

I hesitated, looking at him. He was trying to deduce my connection with Jacob. He might have already guessed the truth, or something close to it, but I didn't owe him or anyone else confirmation.

"Two thousand five," I said. "Four years after the Rip."

He seemed to consider that for a moment. "Ella, it just doesn't seem like a good idea."

"I was just about to say the same thing," Stein chimed in.

I knew what the guys were thinking. At the time of the Rip, Gregori Industries had been headquartered in the New York area. The company was on the forefront of an emerging area of technology that sat at the cross-section of disciplines like genetic engineering, artificial intelligence, and the magic arts, among others. The general public didn't know about the magic part of Gregori's dabblings, of course. Not until after the Rip. But even before the Rip, many people protested Gregori's work. Back then the laws didn't even acknowledge technologies that utilized magic, let alone try to regulate them, and Gregori had free license to do whatever it pleased. After the Rip, anti-Gregori sentiments exploded and grew into a worldwide movement. New laws were passed, but it was too late—the company had already somehow managed to establish itself in a way that it was practically untouchable.

It was never proved in court that Gregori Industries was responsible for opening the tear between this world and the hellish one of the demons and the outbreak of the VAMP2 and NECR2 viruses, but Gregori Industries was like the O.J. Simpson of the industrial world—everyone knew they did it, but somehow the corporation escaped responsibility.

The thing was, even if Gregori Industries was responsible for the Rip, it was also responsible for the technologies that helped to clean up the aftermath. If the corporation was indeed a villain in human history, it had also positioned itself as a necessary evil.

When I was seven, my mother moved us out here to Boise to be close to her mother. In an odd twist, Gregori Industries followed not long after, moving their headquarters from New York to its campus just outside Boise city limits, a piece of land the company had purchased decades before. I didn't believe in coincidences, and always suspected that before his death my father had a hand in the decision purchase of the Gregori property in Idaho. Maybe even because of my mother's ties to the area. The move was obviously part of a larger rebranding plan, an attempt to try to reform the company's image. Thanks to developments like the vampire implant and a handful of later inventions, it partially worked.

By the time Mom relocated us to Boise, my father was dead, claimed in an accident during an exploratory research trip with

Jacob somewhere in Europe. I had a few wispy memories of my father from when Mom and I still lived back East. But after so many years, I couldn't say if the hazy images were real or partial inventions of a child's wishful imagination.

"Are you on good terms with Jacob?" Johnny asked.

I wrinkled my nose. "Eh, I'd say neutral terms."

In truth, Jacob had tried a handful of times to get in touch when I was a kid, but my mother blocked it. She didn't trust him, and she blamed him for my father's death. After Mom died he tried again, but Grandma Barbara had the same opinion about him Mom did.

Actually, the last time he'd reached out was shortly after Grandma Barbara died. Before Evan disappeared. He'd offered help for Evan, which I'd declined, believing I had things under control. In retrospect, I realized that Evan wouldn't have accepted it anyway. He carried Mom's suspicion of Jacob, as well as the soul-deep anger at having been abandoned by our father. He knew that Dad had died in an accident, but that didn't keep Evan from having some serious abandonment issues. The familiar cramping ache of guilt around my heart began to form, but before its darkness could consume me, I firmly pushed away thoughts of that time.

I dropped my palms onto the tops of my thighs with a soft *whap*. "Anyway, enough about me. Let's go check on Roxanne. I'm sure she could use some cheering up." I stood.

The guys followed my lead, seeming to get my cue that I was done answering questions on the topic of my link to Jacob Gregori. I sent Roxanne a text, telling her we were heading over.

The dog jumped up, too, and followed us to the front door. He looked up at me expectantly.

"Stay here, boy, I'll be back soon," I said.

The dog whined and started circling me, bumping Stein and Johnny aside as he moved.

"You'll be fine." I tried to speak in a soothing tone. It didn't work. The dog added some yips to the whining.

I grabbed and held his collar, trying to get him to settle. "You guys go ahead, I'll be right out."

I exited and closed the door behind me, and the yips turned to barks and scratching noises against the door.

"Shit," I muttered. I couldn't leave him if he was going to bark up a storm and shred the door with his nails. He'd seemed like such a well-behaved dog before, but maybe I'd made my assessment too quickly

I looked at Stein and Johnny, who were waiting on the sidewalk. I gave them a wide-eyed exaggerated shrug.

"Bring him," Johnny said. "Kids like dogs, right?"

Grumbling, I opened the door and went back in. The dog bounded around me in delight as I went to the kitchen to grab the leash from the counter. I hooked it to his collar. "Okay, you win."

I got him situated in the back of my truck while Stein and Johnny started their cars and pulled away.

At Crystal Ball Lane, I took hold of the dog's leash and gave him a stern look. "Best behavior, big guy," I said. "Don't scare the girl."

We went up to Roxanne's apartment, where she'd already let in

Stein and Johnny.

Her face brightened at the sight of the dog, and she came over to pet him. I looked across at Johnny, and he gave me a little told-you-so grin.

"What's his name?" Roxanne looked up at me.

"Uh . . . Loki," I said. "After the Norse god of fire and mischief."

Stein gave an appreciative laugh.

"Hi, Loki. Are you still working?" she asked, glancing at my uniform. "I don't want to get you in trouble."

"Nah, I'm off duty now, I just didn't have time to change." I looked toward the window. "No more demons or visitors or other . . . strange stuff?"

She straightened and shook her head.

"Everything went okay last night, and your neighbor kept you company?"

"Yeah." She looked so forlorn, I felt like a total ass even thinking about leaving her alone here again.

"How about if you pack some things and come with us back to my place?" I said, managing a smile. I didn't want to host a party, and I hated houseguests, but I forced myself to keep saying words. "We'll order pizza, and then you can stay the night with me."

The corners of her mouth started to lift, but then a conflicted look took over. "But what if Nathan comes home and I'm not here?"

"Let's leave him a note in a place he'll see it, and also let your neighbor know where you'll be."

"Ummm . . . okay." She gave me a wavering smile.

Roxanne went into her room to get her things together.

I gave the guys a rueful look. "You up for pizza and beer?" I asked with zero enthusiasm.

"Gee, how could I turn down such an enticing invitation," Johnny said sarcastically, and Stein snorted a laugh, but Johnny's eyes sparked with warmth.

"Sorry." I wrinkled my nose. "The thought of so many people in my place makes me twitchy."

"I'll pick up pizza and meet you back there," Stein volunteered.

I gave him a look that was equal parts relief and gratitude. "Awesome, thank you."

He left, and I turned to Johnny. "Would you mind waiting for her and bringing her back with you? I need to run a quick errand. It will make her week to get to ride alone with you," I added in a whisper.

He gave me an amused roll of his eyes. "Sure."

"Thanks, Johnny." I squeezed his forearm—he really had been a champ the past couple days—and went to tell Roxanne I was taking off.

The dog—*Loki*—and I set off down the street. I peered at the signs as I passed, looking for a shop that offered charms.

I slowed at a door that read "Discount Spells and Charms" but then decided I wasn't too keen on the "discount" part. What did that mean, anyway? Crappy spells produced in bulk? Charms that didn't always function as advertised? No thanks.

A sign across the street caught my eye: Personalized Magic. In the little window stenciled words read "Drop-ins welcome – Custom spells – Results guaranteed." And underneath: "Fully

Licensed and Insured."

I angled toward it. When I pushed open the door, little tinkling bells attached to the inside announced my arrival. The owner's license to sell magic was posted at eye level.

A woman dressed in a flowy boho skirt and peasant top rose from a chair behind the counter. Her pale blue eyes sparked with a genuine smile. Her face was smooth, but her hair was nearly all gray, making it difficult to guess her age.

"Good evening," she said. "What can I provide you with?"

"Oh, um. I need a charm that will induce a deep sleep." I glanced down at Loki. "I can tie him up outside if you prefer."

"He's welcome here." She reached out and patted his head, and Loki panted happily. She peered up at me, and I was pretty sure I knew what was passing through her mind—she was assessing my level of magic aptitude and probably thinking something pitying. "What you want is a spell rather than a charm. A charm is a magic-infused object you carry with you. Something for luck or courage or protection, for example. A sleep charm would make you perpetually sleepy."

I scratched my cheek, a little embarrassed that I'd exposed myself as a magical dunce. "Ah, yeah, you're right. I should have said spell. Single-use, something I can use tonight." I hesitated. "And if there's a way to make me, um, open to visions while I'm asleep, I'll pay extra."

"Sure, I can do that. It will be forty-five dollars plus a fifteen percent surcharge for the insurance. If that's okay, I'll go to the back to create your spell."

I nodded, and she disappeared through a batik curtain hung in the doorway behind the counter.

I looked around the shop. There wasn't much actual merchandise—a rack with a couple dozen different types of incense. Another rack full of different colored spell candles. A shelf with little bottles of essential oils. I picked up the peppermint oil bottle that had a red "Sample" label on the top, unscrewed the lid, and took a whiff. The pungent, refreshing scent seemed to perk me up and sharpen my mind.

I'd been in magic supply stores with Deb, but I'd never had much interest in witchy rituals and supplies. She was a full-on practitioner of the craft and self-identified witch, with an altar set up at home and a Book of Shadows she'd started when she was a teenager, and like many witches, she celebrated the pagan holidays. I knew she'd been vying for months to get into a specific coven, but I didn't really know the details. The world of witches and covens never held any attraction for me, even though Deb had tried more than once to get me interested. She kept telling me that magical aptitude didn't matter—even people with no detectible magic could have an altar and celebrate the pagan holidays—but I just wasn't the type to burn herbs, chant under a full moon, and talk to Mother Earth or Universal Wisdom or whatever was out there supposedly listening. I understood that nature was the source of magical energy, but I'd just never really identified with the spiritual aspects of magic that most witches seemed to embrace.

The curtain stirred, and the woman emerged with a few items in her hands. I sensed she was probably a high Level II, like Deb.

The woman set the items on the counter next to the register. She held up a printed piece of paper. "Here are your instructions." Then she pointed to a white spell candle and a little white muslin drawstring bag. "The candle has been anointed with oil and carved with some runes. The bag contains some crystals and herbs for under your pillow. Just follow the sheet, it outlines what to do."

I glanced at the printout. "Okay, sounds good."

She placed all the items into a small paper sack. "Would you like to start a punch card? Tenth spell is free."

"Nah, that's okay." She'd been helpful and I was grateful, but I doubted I'd be returning here nine more times. "Thanks for the offer, though, and thank you for the spell."

I paid and left with my spell.

Loki and I went back home and found that in addition to Johnny and Stein's cars, Deb's Honda stood out front.

When I pushed the door open and found four people making themselves at home in my tiny living room, I nearly backed away.

"Ella!" Deb jumped to her feet, her long strawberry blond hair swinging, and ran over to throw her arms around my neck. At barely five-foot-four, she practically had to hop clear off the floor to make it happen. She laughed at my startled expression. "Don't freak out. I told everyone to speak softly and not make any sudden movements or you'd clear the room."

As usual, Deb had accurately read my emotional state. I relaxed a little when I caught the familiar scent of her floral-woodsy perfume, and actually felt a smile lifting the corners of my mouth.

"How are things at home?" I asked in a low voice.

For the briefest of moments, her face clouded. But then she blinked, and her usual contented expression returned. "Eh, it'll be fine. I just wanted to check on you after your first day back at work." She gave a tiny shrug as her eyes grew a little misty.

My initial reaction was to brush off her concern, but I'd died on the job, and I supposed that gave her the right to hover and get a little bit emotional. My throat thickened, not at the thought of my own death but at the thought of what it would have done to Deb. What it *had* done to her for about twenty minutes. I turned my head to look around the room, partially to cover my own unexpected emotions.

"You got here just in time for the party, I guess," I said, not quite keeping the rueful tone from my voice. "Want to help me get some beer?"

She rolled her eyes at my less-than-enthusiastic expression and followed me into the kitchen.

I pulled glasses from the cupboard to the right of the sink, noting with an amused chuckle that I actually only owned six proper drinking glasses, one of them a random lone pint glass. Fortunately, five of them were clean. I filled one with ice and water for Roxanne. Deb found my bottle opener in a drawer, pulled a bunch of paper towels from the roll on the counter, grabbed a six-pack of local lager from the fridge, and helped me carry everything to the living room.

I sat between Roxanne and Johnny on the sofa, and Deb took a patch of floor across the coffee table from me. To my relief, they'd all done introductions before I'd arrived, saving me that little hostess job.

As we ate, we kept the conversation light, with Johnny taking the lead for most of it. He entertained us with stories from his work as a supernatural PI. I'd always found it interesting that he was so at ease around self-proclaimed crafters. Most normals had some level of discomfort around magic users, vamps, shifters, and anything supernatural. And the magic and supernatural communities generally kept to themselves partly due to a long pre-Rip history of secrecy. So, social stratification tended to split people into two groups: normals and everyone else. Johnny's equipment gave him the ability to see and detect the magical world through technology, which made him unique among normals. I watched with warm satisfaction as Roxanne giggled at Johnny's antics and blushed every time he leaned her way. For the moment, at least, she seemed to have forgotten her troubles.

While everyone seemed to be relaxed and having a good time, I rose and slipped away to my bedroom, where I closed the door and pulled out my phone. With my heart tapping a nervous rhythm and an uncomfortable prickle creeping up the back of my neck, I found Jacob Gregori in my contacts and tapped the phone number. I'd never actually made a call to the number, and had no idea if it would go directly to his personal phone or to an assistant or what. Considering the hour, if it wasn't a personal line, I'd probably just get voicemail.

After four or five rings I fully expected to end up leaving a message, but then a man's voice answered.

My heart stuttered. "Is this Jacob?" I asked.

"Gabriella Grey, I presume?"

I sat down on my bed, my legs suddenly shaky. I'd changed my phone number the previous summer. Considering Jacob's wealth and resources, I probably shouldn't have been surprised he knew my new number, but it creeped me out all the same.

"Yeah, this is Ella."

"Has something happened? I imagine you would only contact me under extreme circumstances." He sounded genuinely concerned, but I couldn't help recalling my mother's and grandmother's deep distrust of him.

"Yes, something has happened. Not to me," I added quickly. "I'm trying to help a friend. Your men came to her home today and took a statue. A Gregori-bred gargoyle that has her brother, still alive last time we checked, trapped inside. I need access to that statue."

I didn't really have any leverage or grounds for threats, but I wanted him to know that I wasn't totally ignorant about what he was doing. I was almost positive that whatever gargoyle-breeding scheme Gregori Industries was playing around with was illegal. At the very least, it was unethical, and as far as I'd been able to discern it was still secret.

Jacob made a little *tsk* sound. "Ah yes, one of our prototypes failed to find its way back home."

His mild tone sent a spark of indignation shooting up through my chest, though I did feel some satisfaction that he'd more or less confirmed our suspicions about the gargoyle breeding. "Can you at least tell me if Nathan is still *alive*?" I gripped the phone hard against my ear, trying to control the irritation in my voice.

"Of course he is. We would never purposely hurt a human being. Our entire mission is centered around protecting humanity. But the situation is delicate, and the specimen is under observation."

"His sister is only thirteen years old, she's now living alone, and she's terrified she's never going to see her only family member again," I said. My voice cracked and I struggled to keep it under control. "Exactly when do you plan to release her brother?"

"I understand your concern," he said, but instead of reassuring me, his words only pissed me off more. "How about this? You come to the Gregori campus tomorrow after your shift and we can discuss it in person. I'll be able to let you know when the young man may be freed."

"You know there's a human trapped in that statue, and you're knowingly risking his life. It seems pretty obvious that the best thing to do, the *right* thing to do, is to release him immediately."

"If you'll meet with me, I can explain the situation. It's a sensitive matter that I can't discuss over the phone. But once we've spoken, you'll understand why we haven't released him yet."

My nostrils flared as my breath came faster, but for Roxanne's sake I couldn't lose my temper. "Can you swear to me that Nathan is being monitored and nothing will happen to him?"

"I swear on the name of your dear departed father."

"Okay," I relented.

"Instructions will be sent to you in the morning," he said. "Good night, Ella."

I hung up and sat on my bed for a long moment, holding my

phone and staring blankly at the closet door. I'd achieved what I'd set out to do—contact Jacob to try to get Nathan free—but cold apprehension settled low in my stomach. I couldn't pinpoint why, but the whole thing made me uneasy. I pushed myself to my feet, trying to shake off the inexplicable film of ick the conversation had left me with. Perhaps I was being unfair, allowing my mother's and grandmother's prejudices to so strongly slant my feelings about Jacob. After all, he did seem to want to help.

I blew out a harsh breath and then went back into the living room to rejoin the others. I wasn't going to let Roxanne know the specifics, but I planned to text Johnny and Stein about my impending meeting with Jacob.

Deb was the first to leave, and I walked her out. She'd gone quiet several times, with a drawn look on her face. I paused at the sidewalk, and she stopped too.

"I don't have your empathic skills," I said softly. "But if I had to guess, I'd say things are still rough with Keith?"

She hesitated for a moment before responding, which partially answered my question. I loved Deb like a sister, but I'd never been a fan of the man she chose to marry. During the seven-ish years they'd been together, married for the past year, they'd had more ups and downs than I would have wanted for her.

She forced a smile and reached up to gather her strawberry blond hair at the nape of her neck. "Oh, we'll figure it out." She kept fiddling with her hair, pulling it around to the front of one shoulder and worrying a strand between her fingers, another sign that things weren't okay.

"Is there something I can do?" I asked.

She let out a little sigh and looked off down the street. "No, but thanks. You know Keith, always chasing the rainbow for the pot of gold." Her gaze returned to me, and she gave a short laugh that held no actual amusement.

I shook my head, trying not to appear too judgmental but knowing I wasn't doing a great job at hiding my irritation. Keith and Deb had been together since Deb was seventeen and he was eighteen, and he'd always been searching for the next sure-fire get-rich-quick shortcut. Over the years, she'd tolerated more pyramid schemes and crazy-ass business ideas than I cared to tally. I had no doubt that he loved her, but all Deb had ever wanted was to have lots of kids and immerse herself in being a stay-at-home wife and mother. She needed—and deserved—someone who was steady and supportive and wanted the same life she did. I suspected that Keith was okay with having children only because he knew Deb would do the heavy lifting. He didn't seem to have any real aim or plan to support a family financially, though, and I hated the thought of Deb having to work full-time when her deepest heart's desire was to stay home and care for her babies. And gain a place in the coven of her choice, of course. She'd been talking about coven life almost as long as she'd been dreaming of a big family, and both of those dreams were born of an obvious desire to be part of a close community and family. Deb was a former foster kid, so it was no surprise.

"Do you need some space?" I asked. "You're welcome to stay here more than just a night."

She smiled, and this time it was genuine. "I know. Thank you."

I pulled her in for a hug—Deb was the only person in the world I hugged willingly and without any internal cringing—and didn't really want to let her go. On the surface we didn't seem to have much in common, but we'd been tight since the start of junior high. I was a loner who preferred to devote my social energy to one or two people, and she had always longed for closeness. My focused loyalty to her seemed to fulfill something she deeply desired, and in turn her genuine warmth had been a bright point through my difficult years of losing one family member after another.

I went back up to the porch and watched her pull away. The sounds of Roxanne's laughter and Johnny's deep voice drew me back inside. The two of them were sitting on the floor facing each other with their phones out. It looked like they were engaged in some sort of game. Stein was sitting on the old navy leather chair with a notebook spread on his lap and his backpack sagging open on the floor next to him. His brows were drawn low in concentration as he scribbled on a page.

Through the doorway into the kitchen, I saw Loki standing at the back door. I let him out and then tiptoed up behind Stein to try to get a peek at what had him so intent. His handwriting was almost annoyingly neat, and it looked like he was making notes about moon phases. There were also some symbols I recognized as representations of the zodiac signs.

"I didn't take you for an astrology buff, Stein," I said.

He jolted and snapped the notebook closed, twisting to shoot me a look that was half-irritation and half-chagrin.

"Why don't you call me by my name?" he asked.

"Um, Stein *is* your name." I reached for the last beer, popped the cap with the opener, and plunked down on the ottoman.

"You use last names for people you don't like. Devereux, for instance."

I took a swig of beer, considering. "Huh. I guess you're right."

"Do you have something against me?" He crossed one arm over his stomach to grip his other elbow in his palm, his gaze ticking down and away before coming back to rest on my eyes.

I lowered my lids partway and gave him a wry look. "I'm not sure yet."

His mouth tightened.

I shifted a little, remembering how he'd looked at Johnny earlier, and suddenly suspected I knew why Stein was getting closed off all of a sudden.

"So Damien Stein, are you—?"

"A Virgo?" He cut in, giving me a wry, unblinking look.

"Gay, I was going to say."

"I know you were. And yes, I am." His eyes tensed the slightest bit.

"Gay or a Virgo?"

"Both."

"Good. I don't have to worry about you checking out my ass all day long." I gave an exaggerated sigh of relief.

A small smile broke over his face, and he seemed to relax.

"Well, since we have to work together, how about if you make a leap of faith and call me Damien?" he asked, hardly missing a beat as he returned to our previous topic. "At least until you've completed your assessment and know for sure whether I'm first name worthy?"

I laughed. "Fine. Damien it is. For now, anyway." I jutted my chin at the closed notebook in his lap. "What's that, your diary?"

"*No*," he said emphatically, accompanied by a withering look. He shifted a little on the seat, obviously reluctant to discuss the contents of the notebook.

"Come on," I cajoled. "You don't have to let me read it, but at least tell me what you're so interested in. You know, in the name of partner bonding or whatever. Or do we need to go back to Stein?"

He brushed one hand over the cover of the notebook in a gesture that was almost a caress. Whatever was inside was meaningful for him, I suddenly realized.

"I'm collecting data," he said at a near-whisper, clearly not wanting Johnny or Roxanne to overhear. "Observations about things that seem to influence magic."

"Huh." I peered at him. "You went to college, didn't you?"

He nodded. "Two degrees."

"In?"

"Bachelor of Modern Magic Arts and Sciences with an emphasis in research. Master's in the same."

The look on his face was so sincere and solemn, I couldn't bring myself to rib him about being a high-minded academic in a blue-collar job.

"Sounds interesting," I said, and actually kind of meant it. I wasn't the bookish type and always felt antsy and trapped in a classroom. "Is this independent research you're doing?"

"Yeah. An extension of something I worked on for my master's, you could say."

I wanted to probe more, less due to any academic interest on my part as suspicion that his presence in Boise somehow related to his project, but Johnny had stood and was making motions to head out.

I reached for my phone to check the time, and my eyes bugged—it was past eleven. "Yikes, I didn't realize how late it was." I pointed at Roxanne with a mock-stern look. "You need to get to bed, young lady."

Johnny gave Roxanne's arm a squeeze and moved toward the door. "I need to get going, but give me a ring if anything comes up, okay?" he said to me.

"Will do, thanks for everything." I lifted my hand in a little wave.

Stein—no, *Damien*—was packing up his things. "I'll get out of your hair, too. See you at work," he said to me. He turned to Roxanne. "Sleep tight."

"Thanks for the pizza!" she chirped.

I went to the door with him, digging into my pocket. "Here, let me give you some cash for the food."

He waved off my offer. "It's on me. You can get it next time."

I nodded. "Thanks. See you in the morning."

I locked the door behind him and then showed Roxanne to the bathroom so she could brush her teeth and change into her pajamas. While I was waiting for her, I let Loki in and moved the living room furniture around so I could pull out the hide-a-bed in the sofa.

She came out in baggy cut-off sweatpants that looked like they might have been her brother's at some point, and an oversized t-shirt. I pulled an extra set of sheets and a fleece blanket from the built-in cupboard next to the bathroom, and she helped me make the bed. After she climbed in, I shut off the overhead lights, leaving on only the lamp next to the sofa, and sat down next to her. I scratched at the back of my neck, suddenly feeling awkward. Did someone her age want to be tucked in? What was the protocol here?

She saved me by pulling a hardback book stamped with "Boise Public Library" on the edges from her bag and scooting down under the covers. "I like to read for a while before I go to sleep." She clutched the book and glanced around the room with a slightly forlorn look on her face.

I nodded. "I want you to know I'll be talking to someone at Gregori about your brother tomorrow. And in the meantime, I've been assured that he's okay and nothing bad is going to happen to him. I'm going to take a quick shower and then turn in. You know where to find me if you need anything during the night."

She managed a small smile. "Thank you for helping me, Ella. I know you'll get him back."

I patted her leg and then stood. I hoped I could live up to her faith in me. I was well aware of why I was so invested—I saw enough of myself and Evan in her situation with her brother—but knowing why I felt the tugs on my heartstrings didn't seem to matter. I genuinely wanted to see things work out okay for her, and some part of me felt that if I could help it might redeem my failure with Evan just a smidge.

In the bathroom, I turned on the hot water and then typed out a text to Damien and Johnny.

I have a meeting with Jacob at the G campus tomorrow after work. He seems to want to help, but I'm not so sure. Claims the boy is safe. More tomorrow.

I hit send, stripped out of my uniform, and stepped under the water. As I scrubbed off the day, weariness seeped into my bones and settled there. I heard a series of pings as texts came in. After I shut off the water and dried with a towel, I picked up my phone to check them.

From Johnny: *I'll go with you. Even if I can't go in, someone should be there waiting to make sure you come back out.*

Another one from Johnny, this one sent only to me: *'Night, sugar.* Followed by winky-face and kissy-lips emojis. I rolled my eyes.

The text from Damien read: *I wouldn't trust Gregori. You're right to be on guard. I hope you can sway him.*

Wrapped in a towel, I tiptoed out of the bathroom. Roxanne's book had fallen to the floor, and she was sound asleep. Loki was curled up next to her, and his head rose when I came over to put the book on the side table and turn out the lamp.

"'Night, boy," I whispered.

In my bedroom, I closed the door and switched on the bedside light. Once in my old Demon Patrol Recruit shirt, I pulled out the bag from Nature's Light that I'd stashed in the nightstand drawer. I glanced at the door, hesitating. The spell should put me into a solid sleep, but not an all-out coma. If Roxanne needed me, she'd be able to rouse me.

The lady had included a cheap aluminum holder for the spell candle, as well as a book of matches printed with the store's name and logo. I fitted the candle in the holder, and set it on the nightstand.

Scanning quickly through the instructions, I realized I needed to move the candle to the dresser so it was on the east side of the room. I did so and struck a match, lit it, and then climbed in bed. As instructed, I sat for a moment with my eyes closed, clearing my mind and pulling in my focus. It was the same little exercise I did whenever I tried to draw up some magic—every crafter had his or her own way of preparing the mind—and I took more time than usual to make sure I was centered and could feel the tingle of receptivity in my hands and feet, the signal that I'd mentally cleared the way. It's akin to placing a finger on a light switch but not yet flipping it.

Still holding my focus, I clutched the muslin bag in my left hand, drew up a thin wisp of magic from the earth, and whispered the words of the spell the woman had written for me. I sealed my intent by releasing my connection to the earth magic. Further worn out from expelling energy for magic and already feeling the pull of sleep from the spell, I put the muslin bag under my pillow, dropped the piece of paper on the bedside table, and turned out the light. I passed out within seconds.

Some indeterminate amount of time later, I jolted awake. With my heart pounding in my throat, I blinked in the darkness of my bedroom. Something had pulled me from sleep. My first thought was Roxanne, but I could see by the weak street light coming in through the window that I was alone.

I tried to sink back and lay down, but my muscles refused to obey. I sat there rigidly, wanting to move but unable to.

I forced my breathing to slow, trying to calm the panic and adrenaline that rushed through me. The spell must have misfired. Maybe it had brought on sleep paralysis. If I could just relax, it would probably subside.

I waited, listening to the sound of my breath, as a few seconds ticked by. But instead of regaining control of my body, my limbs began to shift in ways that I was not commanding them to. I gasped and tried to scream but produced only a weak exhalation.

Something had taken control of me.

My terror deepened as I watched my hand push back the covers, and my feet swing to the floor. Like a puppet with no will of its own, I moved under the power of an unseen influence. It forced me to walk to the bedroom door and out into the living room. It brought me to a pause near Roxanne, who was still sleeping. Loki's eyes shone orange in the darkness, and his rumbling growl swelled as he jumped from the bed.

With every fiber of my being, I tried to fight what was happening, but my efforts failed to halt my progress toward the front door and only brought a sheen of sweat to slick my skin. I stared in horror as I watched my own fingers fumble with the deadbolt. My hand unlocked the door and then opened it. My feet carried me outside, across the porch, and down the steps to the sidewalk.

I was powerless, and I had no idea where the invisible force was taking me.

Hays street was dark and dead silent. I supposed that was good because even if there were people around I couldn't form words to ask for help. If anyone saw me clomping zombie-like down the sidewalk in my pajamas and bare feet, I'd probably just get picked up by the police. Possibly committed. Or worst case, mistaken for an actual zombie, though these days the only remaining zombies were kept in containment for study.

I was going to have to ride this out. Whatever had assumed control of me couldn't hold on forever. At least, that's what hoped. I wished like hell I'd told someone I was going to use a sleeping spell. For the second time in two days, my assumption that I could manage everything on my own had backfired massively.

Only my pounding heart and my near-hyperventilating breaths seemed to be still under my power, so I focused on trying to calm them. The shadows were writhing in my periphery, like wraiths performing a furious, fevered dance of glee. I couldn't explain how, but I was sure the shadows were celebrating, happy that I was forced to move under the control of something that wasn't me. My gut told me that the *something* was connected to the shadows, and to the thing that had pounded in my temples and fed me nightmare visions since my accident. Somehow I knew it was the *other*, now no longer occupying just a corner of my mind but out full-force and in charge.

Wincing internally as my bare feet plunked onto pebbles, I hoped there wasn't any broken glass on the sidewalk. I was heading west on Hays, passing old houses that had been divided into apartments like mine and homes that had been converted to small businesses. Only a couple of windows were illuminated from within, either night owls still up or lights that had been left on. No one looked out, and no cars passed. I half wondered what would happen if someone approached me. Would the *other* carry me away on my own running feet? Attack somehow? Force words out of my mouth?

At the intersection of Fifteenth and Hays, it turned me left. We were heading toward State Street and a stretch of businesses.

We. I shuddered internally.

There would be street lights and likely at least a little traffic. Albertsons came into view up ahead to my right. I knew the grocery store was closed at this late hour, but there was a gas station across from it that was lit up like Christmas twenty-four hours a day. And yes, up ahead on State, I saw a couple of cars motor past. When I got half a block away from State Street, a white SUV pulled into the gas station. The driver, a man with glasses, peered through the windshield at me. He stepped out, watching me for a moment.

"Hey, are you okay?" he called out. "Do you need help?"

I lost sight of him, as the *other* didn't allow me to turn my head to look at the man or respond. A car whizzed past ahead of me on State, and a scruffy-haired dude leaned out of a back window to whistle and holler at me. I caught a glimpse of his leering face and suddenly it hit me in a new way just how vulnerable I was.

I heard the SUV's door slam, and strained in vain to turn and see if the man at the gas station would try to approach me. But a moment later the rhythmic sound of the gas pump filling his vehicle told me he wasn't coming after me. I forgot about him as I faced a new concern. I'd come to State Street, and the light ahead was red with a solid don't-walk sign illuminated. My feet weren't stopping. The *other* wasn't going to wait for a green light.

My heart hammered as I became aware of multiple sets of headlights out both sides of my periphery. Unsure exactly how far away the approaching cars were, I held my breath as my right foot moved off the curb and into the road. I reached the midpoint across the four-lane street, my skin slicked with cold sweat. I strained to send signals to my legs, but it was as if the connection had been snipped. My brain tried to command my muscles, but they didn't get the message. Was this how it felt to be paralyzed? The disconnect was maddening in how deeply wrong it felt, and a new wave of nauseous fear rose up through me.

A horn blared to my left as a car swerved and passed behind me. The car approaching on the right didn't seem to be slowing. A soft, long squeak escaped my lips as I continued helplessly, unable to even brace for an impact. Tires squealed against asphalt and headlights glared. The driver leaned on the horn and cursed at me and then swerved around me and sped away.

By the time I reached the curb and my feet carried me back onto the sidewalk, my chest heaved with shaking breaths. With the danger of State Street behind me, I noticed the stinging on the bottoms of my feet. My soles were probably bleeding.

Then there was a noise behind me, a scuff of feet. I was away from the street lights and standing next to a building that housed a real estate company. The parking lot was empty, and the building was dark. The sounds of quick footfalls sent my heart jumping into my throat. My own feet slowed, and I gasped as the unseen force swiveled me around, presumably to see who'd followed me.

A dog stood a dozen feet away. Not just a dog—*my* dog, Loki. I tried to say his name, but of course I couldn't. Even in the dark I could see his hackles spiked along his spine. His growl rumbled louder and louder, like a fast-approaching train, and his eyes flared into two burning coals. The growling deepened into snarls, and dread washed through me. What if he attacked me? He'd seemed friendly, but I'd only had him for a day.

I felt my arm lift and dropped my gaze to my outstretched fist. My entire body began to tremble, and I swayed a little as something began to fill me. I felt the first tiny tendrils of relief, thinking that the new sensation meant I was regaining control. But I still couldn't move, and I realized that whatever was happening now was even worse than before. It was a sensation I'd never felt, and it was horrifying, as if death and horror had liquefied and replaced the blood in my veins. It throbbed and hurt and made me wish I could shed my own skin and run away screaming. The feeling bubbled through me and seemed to pour into my outstretched arm, concentrating in my closed fist. My hand sprang open, my fingers splayed, and the air rippled outward like waves over the surface of a pond.

The ripple slammed Loki hard, blowing him back ass over teakettle, and his snarls turned to high-pitched whimpers and then went quiet. I didn't get a chance to see whether he was still alive before the *other* steered me back around and forced my feet to march.

Drained of whatever dark power I'd just expelled, terror mixed with nausea. My knees wanted to buckle and my stomach tried to retch, but the *other* didn't allow either. It pushed me onward toward the deeper darkness of a block with ramshackle houses that were mostly abandoned, some deteriorated past the point of any salvage effort. It was one of those blocks that you passed on the way to somewhere else without looking around too hard because the houses were depressing shells of gaping windows and peeling paint.

A ten-foot high chain-link fence with "keep out" signs surrounded one of them, and that was where my feet halted. The *other* turned me to face the house, a three-story structure with a steep roof. From my vantage point it looked as if part of the house had burned. It was hard to tell in the dark, but one side of the top story appeared to have a charred hole through the roof, and dark burn stains smeared upward from the broken-out windows on that side. Other than the fire damage, it didn't look as bad as some of the other houses nearby. As I peered at the abandoned house, the nauseous dark magic began to fill me again. My eyes rolled back, and for a moment I thought I might pass out—and actually kind of hoped I would. I swayed and blinked several times, and when I focused again my breath snagged in my throat.

I was seeing the house through the dream eyes, the ones that gave me visions hued in yellows and blues. And through the eyes of the *other*, I saw that the house wasn't vacant. A pale yellow glow of light shifted around inside. A human form with a sallow face suddenly appeared at one of the windows. I sucked in a breath and tried to take a step back, but my feet moved me forward instead. Against my will, I stepped closer to the fence, my arms lifting to push my palms against the chain link.

More shapes passed behind the windows. I tried to understand what I was seeing, but there was nothing familiar about it. I had no context for the yellow and blue flickering images lighting up the house that had appeared empty only a moment ago. But one thing was certain: the *other* wanted to get in there. I was moving along the fence, my hands trailing across it as my feet shuffled sideways. I knew the *other* was looking for a way in. There was no gate, not on the street side at least. It lifted my hands from the fence and planted them higher, curling my fingers to grip the criss-cross links.

Oh *shit*, it wanted to make me climb.

It didn't seem to have a great grasp on my body mechanics, at first trying to flex my arms to dead-lift my body upward. One hand slipped and my chin hit the fence, scraping painfully as I dropped several inches. It tried again, and again I slipped, this time ripping a couple of nails. My hands rattled the fence, displaying the *other's* frustration.

Again, it forced my hands into a tight grip on the chain link. Then my right foot lifted, and I winced as it jammed forward into the fence, finding a partial foothold. My other foot lifted and did the same, and then my hands moved higher one at a time. It was slow going, but to my horror I was actually moving upward. I watched the flickers and movements inside the house. It reminded me of a haunted Halloween house . . . and all at once I *knew*. The things inside were ghosts. I'd never seen them myself, but witches with grave talents could see ghosts.

My foot slipped mid-step, and suddenly I was dangling by my hands several feet off the ground. My knees scraped the chain link as the *other* tried to find purchase with my feet. A burst of snarling barks behind me caused the *other* to freeze my movements, bringing my progress to a halt and literally leaving me hanging.

It was Loki. I couldn't see him, but I knew it was him. I felt growing heat at my back, and Loki's bark seemed to deepen and distort, but I couldn't turn to see what was happening.

Then a rushing roar filled my ears as the heat intensified, and my entire body went rigid. I lost my grip, and for a moment it felt as if I hung in mid-air. The ground rushed up to slam me, knocking the wind from my lungs and snapping against the back of my head.

Darkness consumed me.

When i came to, I felt like I'd spent the night inside a rock tumbler. My feet, hands, knees and chin stung with cuts and scrapes. And my head . . . I could only lie there and moan. My temples, my entire skull, throbbed like the worst hangover in history. I flopped over to my side, and it hit me: I was moving under my own power. My second thought was that whatever had happened after I cast the spell, it wasn't what I'd expected. I'd intended a deep sleep that I hoped would prompt the *other* to give me more images of Evan. But it hadn't delivered a single glimpse of my brother. Instead, the spell had made me vulnerable to the *other's* control, and it had taken over.

A furry face filled my vision, and Loki's tongue lapped my cheek. My eyes misted as I reached up weakly to touch his head. He'd scared the *other* or done something to momentarily disrupt its control, I remembered now. He'd saved me. He pushed his head under my arm, nudging me to sit up. Exhausted, drained, and sick to my stomach, I looked around. I was at the base of the chain link fence, but the house behind it was dark and still. I closed my eyelids and pushed the heels of my hands into my eyes, groaning, and then dropped my hands to my lap. Maybe I'd actually been sleepwalking, maybe that stupid spell had caused me to hallucinate, and my weird dreams had mixed with reality and—

Wait. What the hell?

I raised my right arm, bringing it close to my face. Early morning light was beginning to leak into the sky, just enough to allow me to see the pale lines on my skin. The lines formed shapes in faint pearl-white. They didn't glow, exactly, but seemed to have a subtle shimmer. I lifted my other arm and found the exact same design. The shapes looked like sigils—simple geometric designs that expressed an intent, symbols that held magical power—but I had no idea what these ones meant.

I was pretty sure I would have remembered getting inked. Except these didn't look like regular tattoos. They couldn't be. A tattoo needle would have left some swelling, but my skin was completely smooth as if the lines had always been there. I licked the pad of my index finger and rubbed at one of the lines, but it didn't come away.

Loki yipped, drawing my attention. I wasn't sure of the time, but it was going to be morning soon and regardless of what had happened in the night I needed to haul my ass back home. Roxanne was there alone, and I was pretty sure I'd left the front door wide open.

I stumbled toward Hays, keeping to patches of grass where I could to give my damaged soles a break, and hiding in the shadows whenever the odd car approached. When I finally reached my porch I was lightheaded and reeling. Loki and I went inside and I crept past Roxanne who was remarkably still fast asleep. In the bathroom, I flipped on the light and winced at the sudden brightness. When I looked down, I let out a low groan. I was an absolute mess—bloody, dirty, and scraped up like I'd tried to use a chunk of asphalt as a loofah. I had to shower, even if it meant waking Roxanne. I turned on the hot water and then bent to dig around under the sink for a first aid kit.

While I waited for the shower to heat up, I stripped down and examined my injuries. After a quick evaluation I let out a relieved breath. There was plenty of damage, but none of it required stitches. In the shower I scrubbed myself clean, biting my lips against the pain as the soap hit my cuts. I rubbed at the marks on my arms, too, but I wasn't surprised to find they didn't wash off. I turned the water off, tried to dry myself without causing additional bleeding, and then wrapped a clean towel around my body. Sitting on the toilet, I went to work with the first aid kit, disinfecting and bandaging my skin until I looked like a patchwork of Band-Aids and gauze. I dry-swallowed four Advil from the medicine cabinet, and then with a weary sigh I flipped the light off and quietly opened the bathroom door. The cooler air of the living room hit my skin, raising goosebumps up my limbs and bringing an involuntary shiver. I clamped my arms against my sides, trying to ward off the chill but too tired to really care that I was cold.

Loki was curled in a tight circle on the floor next to where Roxanne was miraculously still asleep, and his tail thumped when he saw me. Hobbling over on sore, scraped up feet, I knelt next to him and held his furry face in both hands. As I peered into his eyes, I thought I caught a flicker of flaming orange deep in his pupils.

"I don't know where you came from, but I'm glad you're here. Thank you," I whispered. "I hope you know it wasn't really me that zapped you with magic, but I'm sorry just the same."

A sudden swell of emotion warmed some of my chill away. What would have happened if Loki hadn't followed me and done . . . whatever it was he did to save me? He poked his head forward to lick my cheek.

In my room with the door closed, I collapsed face-down onto my bed with the towel still wrapped around me, and groaned into my pillow. Everything hurt. Fatigue battled pain for a few minutes until the Advil kicked in. Exhaustion delivered a knockout punch, and I slept.

Too soon, my phone alarm was sounding. I hadn't checked the time when I went to bed—the second time—but it felt like I'd only slept about twenty minutes. Blinking at my phone, my eyelids felt like sandpaper. I caught sight of the spell sheet on my nightstand and flipped it the finger. Some fricking spell. The thing had nearly killed me. "Results guaranteed," the store's window had said. Well, in the witch's defense, she didn't know about the *other* when she created the spell for me. It probably wasn't entirely her fault.

There was a knock on my door. "Ella?" Roxanne called.

"Uh, just a sec, I'll be right out."

I dropped the towel and put on the plaid flannel bathrobe that hung on the back of the door. I limped into the living room and followed the sounds of cupboards and drawers opening and closing. When I rolled my shoulders and flexed my back I had to choke back a cry. There would be no pushups, situps, or "ups" of any kind this morning. Roxanne was in the kitchen with Loki. I opened the back door to let him out into the yard.

"How did you sleep?" My voice rasped like I'd smoked half a pack overnight.

Roxanne paused with her hand in the silverware drawer and looked up at me. "Really good. That sofa bed is better than my futon at home." Her wispy blond bangs stuck out at an odd angle that was kind of adorable, but her chipper smile faded as she looked me up and down. "Are you okay?"

"Yeah, just had kind of a rough night. Uh, sleepwalking. Sometimes I do that." I cleared my throat, but it didn't improve my scratchy voice. "I see you're finding your way around. You're welcome to whatever you can dig up. Sorry there's not much to eat, but I'll leave you some cash and you can walk to the store and pick up a few things, if you'd like. I gotta change for work."

I turned to hobble back toward my bedroom.

"Okay, thanks. I'm going to fix you some breakfast to go!" she hollered. Then to herself, "And coffee, right? Yeah, I'll make coffee."

There was more clanking and cupboard slamming. In spite of how crappy I felt, I cracked a tiny smile. Didn't most teenagers spend summer vacation sleeping until noon and then waking up all hormone-addled and grumpy? That basically described me at fourteen. But go figure, apparently Roxanne was a morning person.

I pulled out a fresh Patrol shirt and got dressed, clamping my teeth together to keep from screeching in pain when I pushed my feet into my boots. In the bathroom, I stuck a few Advil in my mouth and lowered my head to the faucet to gulp some water and wash them down. Not the classiest move, but I wasn't exactly in a classy state of mind. I raked my hair back into a ponytail and then twisted it around itself and pinned the bun in place, trying to ignore my throbbing feet. Walking the beat today was going to be hell. My chin was red and raw where I'd skinned it on the fence. I leaned close to the mirror, trying to decide whether concealer would do any good. Probably not, and I didn't have time to fiddle with makeup anyway. I looked down at my forearms, exposed in short sleeves. The pearly white sigils had faded until they were only visible if you got really close and knew where to look. A little thread of relief twined through my various aches. I'd melt in the summer heat if I had to wear a long sleeved shirt, and probably would have drawn even more attention than just leaving the tattoos exposed. Maybe the marks would disappear altogether and I could forget they'd ever been there. Sure, that would happen, because all *kinds* of things were going my way lately.

When I emerged, dressed and as ready for work as I was gonna get, Roxanne came out of the kitchen. She held a travel mug with a faint line of steam curling from the sippy hole in the lid, and what appeared to be a sandwich wrapped in a paper towel.

With her thin arms outstretched, she offered both items to me. "I couldn't really find any portable breakfast foods, so I made you a toast sandwich with jelly, peanut butter, and Cheerios in it. Oh, and the coffee has some of the creamer that's in the fridge."

Genuinely touched by her efforts, I grinned and took the mug and sandwich. "You are an absolute life saver, thank you. And you're impressively innovative in the kitchen." I lifted the sandwich in a little salute to her talents.

She held her hands behind her back and beamed up at me.

"Oh, here's some cash." I balanced the sandwich on top of the coffee mug and dug in my hip pocket, finding a wad of folded bills and passing them to her. "Buy whatever you like. There's an extra key in the antique tea kettle on top of the fridge. I'm not sure what time I'll be home, but I'll text you."

"Okay, thanks." She wrapped her finger around the cash. "I'll get stuff for dinner. I know how to make spaghetti."

I started toward the door. I needed to get going so I wouldn't be late for morning briefing. "That sounds awesome," I said over my shoulder.

"Invite Damien to dinner," she called after me as I let myself out. "And Johnny!"

I laughed. "Will do. Have a good day with Loki."

Feeling oddly buoyant knowing Roxanne and Loki would be waiting when I arrived home, I took a bite of Cheerio-PB-and-J. The cereal added a surprisingly satisfying crunch to the sandwich. I wolfed it and downed the entire mug of coffee, scalding my mouth in the process, on the short drive to the station. Normally I preferred to walk to work, especially during the summer, but I was running late, plus I needed my truck because I planned to take off for Gregori Industries right after my shift ended. And I wanted to give my cut up soles as much a break as possible before subjecting them to a long day on my feet.

I parked and went inside, hobbling to the break room to quickly refill my mug with gross but potent station coffee, and then found Damien in the briefing room and slid into the chair next to him. When my bruised spine touched the seat back, I winced and leaned forward.

"Morning," I mumbled. I gulped more coffee and glanced over at him. He was staring at me as if I'd grown a second nose overnight.

"What the hell happened to you? You look like you got into a fight. And lost," he said.

I slumped, closed my eyes, and pinched my temples between my middle finger and my thumb. "I, uh, did some really clumsy sleepwalking last night." I glanced away.

He leaned closer to me, his clear eyes intent and his J Crew catalog model face tense. "Bullshit," he said in a low voice.

He peered at me as if he could see straight into my brain. My pulse gave a little bump and I fought the urge to squirm under his gaze. Was he reading or sensing something, or was I just that bad a liar? Maybe his magical aptitude made him a human lie detector, or slightly psychic, or perhaps he could sense the residue of my insane midnight escapade still clinging to me like invisible cobwebs.

I squinted at him from the corners of my eyes. "What, you think I have some kind of secret night life?" I twisted fully to face him and deadpanned, "You know the first rule of Fight Club."

I forced a laugh and sipped some more coffee, hoping he'd drop it.

"Ella, what's going on? Is someone after you? Harassing you?"

I almost laughed. No, someone wasn't after me. It had already found me, and it seemed to want to boot me out of my own body and take over.

"Nah, it's nothing like that, I swear. I'm just an extremely klutzy sleepwalker."

I flicked a furtive look at him again. His jaw muscles pulsed, his eyes clouded with worry, and it was obvious he wasn't buying my story. But Sergeant Devereux had arrived and everyone quieted as he took the podium. All through briefing, I could feel Damien's attention, his awareness flicking my way.

Devereux's eyes paused on me a few times while he spoke, and I wasn't sure if it was due to my scraped chin and bloodshot eyes or because I was on his radar after running over to Crystal Ball Lane in the middle of shift yesterday. Oh, and the stolen demon can. *Cans*, actually. Yeah, it was probably my multiple transgressions rather than my appearance. I was pretty sure he didn't give a damn about the fact that I looked like I'd spent the night falling down stairs. He just wanted to avoid more paperwork. I shrank down in my seat, trying to look rule-abiding and blend in with my fellow officers.

When Devereux dismissed us, I managed to push myself up without moaning in pain, and turned to Damien. "I wanna hear more about the research you're doing. What kinds of things can affect magical power?" I asked. I was a little curious, but I was mostly aiming to steer him away from his earlier line of questioning.

His eyes ticked around at the officers near us. "Let's wait until we get outside." He slung his backpack around and slipped his arms through the straps.

As we exited the station and headed toward our central downtown beat, I realized my feet didn't hurt nearly as badly as I'd expected, though they did feel uncomfortably warm in my boots. Maybe I'd hit on the perfect combo of caffeine and Advil. I experimentally touched the back of my head, where it had smacked the ground after I fell from the chain-link fence. The lump was completely gone, and there was only a hot bruised sensation where the goose egg had been. I should have been glad, but instead suspicion curled through me. I hadn't even iced the bump, and I'd expected it to take at least a couple of days to go down.

"When I was in school, I did some exploratory research," Damien said. Still distracted by my internal inventory of my injuries, it took me a split second to remember that I'd asked him to tell me more about his secret notebook studies. "Some of it was for my degree, but some I did on my own. I was particularly interested in whether a person's magical aptitude setpoint could, well, change. I had a theory that the setpoint wasn't as fixed as we'd always been taught, and I thought that with the right knowledge and—"

He cut off, and his boots scuffed to a halt so abruptly I carried on another step or two before my own feet registered that he'd stopped. I wheeled around and looked up at him, and conflicting emotions flashed across his face.

"Ella, what I'm about to tell you is . . . secret. Kind of like what you told me and Johnny last night."

"Okay," I said slowly.

His eyes were locked unblinking on mine, and he remained

silent for a beat or two, maybe waiting for some signal that I wouldn't keep my word.

"I know how to keep a secret, Damien."

He nodded, just barely. "I've discovered some ways to increase a person's magical aptitude."

My chin dropped, and I gaped open-mouthed at him.

I wanted to laugh at him outright or punch him in the arm. You couldn't *change* someone's magical aptitude.

I snapped my mouth closed with a click of my teeth. "That's quite a claim," I said, doubt drawing out my words.

He shrugged one shoulder. "Yeah, I know."

"I assume none of this is public knowledge," I said. "It would be huge news."

He shook his head. "I haven't published any of my findings. I still have a lot of experiments to run."

"Does your family know?"

"*No.*" He said the word with such emphasis my eyes widened just a little.

"Don't you think they'd be proud that you'd discovered such a thing? It's monumental. It's like discovering that you can change your height, or . . . or your IQ."

He looked away. "I doubt it. I'm still not a mage. They'd probably just see it as a feeble attempt to be like them."

Sadness for Damien flooded through me in an unexpected rush that stilled my breath for a moment. I'd never particularly cared that I was so weak magically, but for Damien . . . his aptitude—or lack of it—had been his torment. My mind constructed a story of his past, one that might not be exactly accurate but was probably close enough to the truth. It was painfully obvious that with his research he'd been chasing an impossible dream, one that had formed in his young adolescent mind as soon as he discovered he wasn't like the rest of his family: he wanted to become a mage. If he was telling the truth, maybe his dream wasn't so impossible.

About a dozen questions crowded into my mind, but just then a voice came through our walkies. It informed us of a bunch of minor demons loose in the basement of one of the government buildings near the capitol—a metaphorical bubble that had traveled from the demonic dimension to ours, releasing a flock of Rip spawn. A bubble-up wasn't an uncommon occurrence this close to a major Rip, but their timing and locations were pretty random.

Damien hitched his backpack higher on his shoulders while I checked in with dispatch to report us as responding. We jogged toward the address dispatch read off, and I noted with another flash of wonder that my feet barely hurt at all. In fact, all of my injuries were healing remarkably quickly. Inhumanly quickly. Was this an unexpected gift from the *other*? I wasn't sure how to confirm that, but I couldn't think of any other explanation.

We reached the building, a brick and cement structure with lots of tall narrow windows. The architectural style was probably the bees' knees when it was built, but to me it just looked antiquated and institutional. Employees were streaming out and gathering on the sidewalk and lawn across the street.

"Is it really necessary to evacuate everyone?" Damien asked.

I was about to respond that they were probably just following policy when a black Supernatural Strike Team Hummer raced in, its red bubble lights twirling, and screeched to a dramatic, abrupt halt at the curb. The driver door popped open, and Brady Chancellor jumped out. I groaned loudly.

"What?" Damien looked at me, alarmed.

"Oh, it's nothing, I just would have preferred any other Strike Team but that one." I felt my mouth twist into a grimace. Chancellor was a mistake I'd made back in training, and I didn't enjoy being reminded about it. He was a good-looking guy stuffed with enough ego for three people. Though admittedly, if he and I didn't have a history, I probably wouldn't find him quite so annoying.

"Strike is here because of the number of minor demons reported, right?"

"Yeah," I said, angling toward Chancellor and his crew. Like it or not, his arrival at the scene meant I was under his command for this call. I tried to stifle my withering sigh. "Dispatch will send Strike if there are six or more minor demons—suspected or confirmed. Now that they're here, they're in charge."

Chancellor was talking to his guys, holding his enormous combo gun in one muscled arm. The weapon looked like something out of a Mad Max movie, and it was completely unnecessary for this job, like bringing a wrecking ball when a sledgehammer would do. Strike weapons were like Demon Patrol stun guns on a truckload of steroids. The larger guns used magically enhanced supersonic blasts to temporarily confuse and slow arch-demons. Chancellor was one of those crew-cut types who seemed to think he was playing real-life G.I. Joe, and he loved to wave his oversized weapon around. Which probably was more than enough insight into what our brief fling had been like.

He caught sight of me and Damien. "Demon Patrol, wait out here on my order. Strike will enter first," he barked. His guys turned to gawk and smirk at us.

I ground my teeth and then forced my jaw muscles to loosen so I could respond. Chancellor was showing off. There was nothing in protocol that allowed him to try to keep me and Damien out of the action. "If there are only minor demons, and according to dispatch that's the case, we enter the building with your team. Why are we still standing around, anyway? If it were up to me, we'd have already gotten in there and fried at least three or four of them."

His face reddened—he knew I was right—but he ignored me, and for show he spouted some unnecessarily-military-sounding tactical instructions to the rest of the Strike Team. I folded my arms, waiting for him to finish, and then beckoned Damien to come along when Chancellor finally decided it was time to get to work. Once inside, I purposely hung back a little, waiting to see which route he was taking to the basement, and pulled up when Chancellor and his team made a right turn off the main corridor from the entrance.

I touched Damien's arm to get his attention and jerked my thumb over my shoulder. "This way," I mouthed.

We wheeled around, and I sped up. Past jobs in this building had given me some knowledge of the layout, and based on the information dispatch had passed along, I knew exactly where the demons were and how Damien and I could beat Chancellor there.

"Grab a couple of brimstone burners off your belt and have them ready," I said. I pulled two of my own burners, holding them both in one hand so I could remove their lids and slip them back into my burner pouch.

We pounded down a couple of sets of stairs. I sensed the presence of the demons but not their exact location.

"You feel them?" I asked, hoping Damien could better pinpoint where they were.

"Yeah, there's one close, heading right—"

He cut off and I swore, dropped my burners, and reached for my stun gun as a bat-like creature swooped toward us. It abruptly halted mid-dive and let out its eerie demon screech. I shuffled forward a few steps, trying to provoke it into charging me so I could shoot it down when it got within range of my gun. But in a move that reminded me of what happened with the demon at Roxanne's place, the creature backpedaled. My brows raised in surprise.

My skin prickled as a current of magic flowed past. Behind me, Damien was gathering his power. Like before, he trapped the demon in a sphere of magic. I quickly holstered my gun, grabbed another burner off my belt, opened it, and set it on the floor. While Damien moved the trapped demon down to the burner, I retrieved the other traps I'd dropped when I'd reached for my gun.

I heard the sizzle of the trap as it captured and fried the demon and squinted in the sulphurous puff of smoke it emitted. The whole thing had taken less than a minute.

"It was afraid of you," Damien said.

I coughed. "What?"

"The demon. It didn't want to get close to you. I haven't seen many of them in real life, but in training they showed us dozens and dozens of videos of demon encounters. None of them ever behaved the way that one just did."

I considered brushing off his observation, denying it, but he was right. Maybe he could help me figure out why demons seemed to be afraid of me. I scooped up the warm trap, slapped the cap over the charred demon remains, and set off at a jog. There were more demons ahead.

"You seem to like theories," I said as he caught up and drew even with me. "Got one about what happened back there?"

He skidded to a stop and swore. "Incoming."

He hadn't fully released the magic that filled him, and I watched as he raised his hand and two thin glowing green lines shot from his palm like arcs of electricity. The lines angled away from us, into the gloom of the poorly-lit basement, and around a left turn up ahead. He was going to trap a couple of demons that were completely out of his line of vision. That was almost as cool as seeing through walls. I shot him an impressed look, but his focus was elsewhere.

"Stay right there," he said. "I'm going to bring them close to you before we fry them. I want to see what happens."

"Uhh . . ." I took an apprehensive step back.

"Don't worry, they're contained and won't be able to get at you."

Two greenish glowing orbs, each with a demon inside,

appeared from around the corner. I clutched a burner in each hand, noting with some irritation the nervous sweat dampening my palms. Before my accident, a couple of minor demons wouldn't have made me blink twice. Logically I knew they weren't capable of doing much more than scratching the hell out of me, but I'd just as soon see them fried as quickly as possible. I planted my feet and held my ground as Damien drew the spheres closer. When they were about ten feet out, the demons went berserk, squealing and ramming against the back walls of their magical containments. He moved them a couple of feet nearer and the demons' panic intensified.

"Whoa," he breathed.

I set the brimstone burners down and backed away, eager to see the creatures safely disposed. Not that I didn't trust Damien, but as he'd admitted himself, his experience with demons was limited at this point.

We caught one more, bringing our total catch to four, by the time Chancellor and his team figured out where we were.

He stalked toward me. "You should have stayed with us."

I gave my head an innocent little shake. "We're only Demon Patrol, so you know, we're not that bright. We got lost. Couldn't keep up with all you Strike Team badasses."

When we all emerged outside, the discovery of Devereux on site didn't even dampen my glee over Damien and me catching one more demon than Chancellor's team. Strike operations always required a sergeant on site as well as official statements and paperwork, so we ate up the rest of the morning at the scene.

Smaller incidents kept me and Damien busy in the afternoon, and the day passed in a blur.

After my shift, instead of heading home, I exchanged my Patrol shirt for a light blue fitted t-shirt emblazoned with the logo of a local brewery and got in my truck and went south away from the heart of the city. With Damien and Johnny following me in Johnny's black Mustang, I left Boise city limits. My stomach clenched as the heavy, almost impossibly high fence surrounding the Gregori Industries campus came into view. I eased up to the security gate and waited. A glance back showed that Johnny had pulled to the side of the road right next to the entrance. He gave me a little wave.

A metallic clang drew my attention forward again, and I watched the security gate pull to the left. My heart stuttered as I lifted my foot from the brake, and my truck rolled forward into the no-man's-land of Gregori Industries.

Three guards manned the security booth, and they looked more like ex-SEALS than mall cops. They were dressed in smart dark gray uniforms with the Gregori logo on the breast pocket, which made me wonder if Jacob's little pseudo-nation did indeed have its own military. One of the men actually gripped an intimidating automatic weapon, as if this were some war-torn country instead of the outskirts of a mid-sized Northwest U.S. town where most people considered it impolite to use a car horn.

"Welcome to Gregori Industries. Please shut off the engine, ma'am." A muscular, tawny-skinned guard—not the one with the assault gun—had approached my open window. I twisted the key in the ignition and the motor died. "Identification, please."

Digging into one of the pockets of my cargo pants, I pulled out a little foldover wallet that held some cash and my essential cards. I slipped my driver's license from the clear pocket.

"Here you go." I passed the card to the guard's waiting hand.

Without a word, he took it into the booth. One of the other guards picked up a chunky walkie-talkie and muttered a few words into it, while the guy who had my ID stood at a laptop typing. I watched him hold up my license to the computer's camera presumably to snap a picture of it. The third guy came out and went to the front of my truck, where he took a picture of the license plate with his phone.

The guard at the laptop finished his typing and stepped out of the booth, and I glanced at the Sig holstered at his side. He returned my license and then looked ahead and gestured with his hand outstretched, pointing in a sharp, precise motion with his thumb tucked against his palm and his fingers straight out. Yeah, he was definitely ex-military or SWAT or something.

"You'll proceed to the white building fifty yards ahead. There you'll relinquish your phone and any weapons and go through a scanner."

My brows lifted. "Like at the airport?"

"Yes, ma'am, the security scanner is similar to the devices you see in airport security."

Great, then Gregori Industries would have a nice semi-naked X-ray style shot of me on file. It seemed like a violation of privacy, but what could I do? The corporate campus was outside the city and outside the law. With an uncomfortable lurch in my chest, I suddenly wondered what happened if someone died on the property.

I gave the guy a little salute. "Okay, thank you."

I started the truck and rolled forward on the paved road. When I neared the squat cube-shaped white structure, I noticed a row of half a dozen white vans identical to the one that had hauled the gargoyle away. Another guard emerged to direct me into one of the handful of marked parking spots. He had the same build and mannerisms as the ones at the front gate. Orange-red crew cut, fair skin, serious weight lifter. He looked around my age, maybe a year or two older.

I parked and got out, not bothering to lock my truck. If they wanted to search it while I was with Jacob, I had no doubt they'd do so whether it was locked or not.

"Good evening, ma'am. Come on inside and we'll get you processed. Any weapons?" He let me go in ahead of him.

"Nope," I said. I'd left my service belt behind.

Inside, the climate-controlled air hit me like a cool splash. The building was mostly one big room, with only a little windowed office at the back where another guard watched us. In the middle stood the security scanner, along with a few folding tables. At the wall was a row of about twenty full-length lockers.

The ginger guard walked backward, beckoning me with his fingers toward the scanner as if he were lining up a hundred people to process instead of just me. I fought the urge to snort a laugh. He pointed with his index and middle finger at one of the tables. "Please place your phone, any jewelry, magically charged items, and all the contents of your pockets on the table."

I did as he asked, briefly wondering how he'd react if I said I had a nipple ring. I didn't, but it almost would have been worth it just to see whether Gregori Industries had a policy for them. Once I'd relieved myself of everything I carried—I wasn't wearing any jewelry and didn't have any magical charms or amulets on me—he directed me into the scanner. I stood in the requisite legs-spread, arms-raised position while the mechanism whirled around me, checking for any weapons as well as scanning for certain types of magical items. When I exited the device, he handed me a clear plastic bag from a stack on the table.

"Place your possessions in here and then lock them in one of the lockers." He nodded at the wall behind me. "Set the lock by pressing your thumb on the blue pad."

By the time I'd finished, the guard in the office had emerged. I must have passed the scan because he handed me a generic visitor badge on a lanyard.

"Keep this visible at all times," he said.

I settled the cord around my neck. "Will do."

"Mr. Gregori will meet you just outside the door," the ginger said. He flicked his eyes to the exit, indicating I could escort myself out.

"Alrighty, thank you, gentlemen."

I sauntered casually off, but a sheen of clammy sweat coated my skin. It felt like I'd entered a maximum security prison. Gregori Industries had such a legacy of secrecy and skirting the law I might as well be on another planet. Memories of Mom's and Grandma Barbara's anger toward Jacob rippled through my mind. They'd clearly believed he was dangerous and dishonest and hardly hid their suspicion that he'd had a hand in my father's death. I'd been thinking that surely I was safe, as his own flesh and blood. But maybe my confidence was misplaced.

I tried to shake off the dark fears curling around my heart and bring my focus to the task at hand. I had to get Nathan released. I needed to bring Roxanne's brother back to her. She and Nathan had become too entwined with my guilt and regrets about Evan, and I couldn't accept another failure.

Outside, the sun sat at a low angle above the western horizon. Days were long this time of year, and I really hoped I could finish my business before sunset. The idea of being on Gregori property after dark gave me the willies. The evening sun glinted off the lens of a camera mounted on the side of a building a few dozen feet away. It was pointed straight at me. A sweeping glance showed there were at least half a dozen cameras within view, and I guessed there more were hidden behind the tinted windows of nearby structures. I suspected drones were circling high overhead as well.

A soft electric whirring noise drew my attention, and I took a few steps away from the security building for a better view down the paved road leading into the heart of the campus. A golf cart with a man behind the wheel approached. Even from a distance, I recognized Jacob. His face appeared in the news every so often, but he was familiar for more personal reasons, too. I swallowed hard as he drew closer. My memories of my father were faint, but photos of him that I still had and remembered well reminded me that he and his brother bore a close resemblance.

Jacob stopped the cart a few feet away from me, pulled the hand brake, and stepped out.

"Ella." He greeted me with a broad smile. He was slim and stood over six feet—I'd gotten my height from the Gregori side—with slightly stooped shoulders that made him look studious, especially with his wire-rimmed glasses.

I nodded but didn't move toward him. "Jacob. Thank you for seeing me."

To my relief, he didn't attempt to hug me. He tipped his head at the cart, still smiling. "Come on, I'll give you the grand tour."

I stayed where I was. "I don't have a whole lot of time, actually. I'm here on behalf of Nathan and his sister, and I need to know when we can expect him to come home. I'd like to see the gargoyle and proof that he's okay."

His smile faltered but only by the tiniest fraction. He gave me a slow blink and a little bow of his head. "I understand. Forgive me, I was excited to hear from you and have the opportunity to spend a few minutes with my niece."

That made me feel like kind of an ass for being so abrupt, but I also saw through his welcoming veneer. I'd spent some time around him before my dad died, but I didn't really remember it and didn't know him well enough to understand what was lurking behind his apparent warmth. But perhaps indulging him just a little would give me an opportunity to figure him out.

I gave him a tight stretch of my lips that I hoped resembled a smile. "Why don't we compromise? We can take the long way to where Nathan is being held."

I faltered a little on the last couple of words, realizing too late that they sounded more accusatory than I'd intended. Jacob either didn't notice or hid his reaction well. I swung onto the golf cart's passenger seat.

"I like that plan." He took the wheel, and I peeked at him out of the corners of my eyes. His profile was distinguished—solid nose, full mouth, slightly slanted forehead with a hairline that hadn't begun to creep backward.

He steered off the main road and onto a narrower cement walkway.

Another golf cart approached, and the guard driving it nodded at Jacob. "Evening, Mr. Gregori."

The place was eerily empty, though maybe it was due to the hour—most employees would have gone home for the day.

Jacob pointed to a building with a cheerful fountain bubbling up in the middle of a round pool at the front. "The cafeteria is in there."

"How many people work here?" I asked.

He flicked a glance at me. "Several dozen."

Vague much? What, was he afraid I was going to make some kind of report to the IRS? The place was huge, and I was sure he was lying. There had to be hundreds of people employed here. Gregori Industries had a reputation, sure, but the job market had been weak in this area for a long time, and rumor was that Gregori jobs paid very well. People might not be eager to admit their association with the corporation, but Gregori needed workers just like any other company. I'd also heard that when corporate headquarters moved here from the East Coast, many employees had relocated to keep their jobs.

"Do you live on campus?"

He grinned as if I were eight years old and my question were adorable. "I do have quarters on site, and yes, I often stay overnight."

I listened with one ear while he pointed out other buildings. We seemed to be making a loose spiral around the grounds, heading toward the tallest structure that was roughly in the center. There was something foreboding about it, though for the most part it looked like any other generic corporate building. When we drew closer, I realized the windows didn't start until about thirty feet up. No windows on the first two floors? My gut tightened as Jacob slowed at the end of the walkway leading to the building's entrance. I tilted my head back as I followed him to the double doors, but I couldn't see anything through the heavily tinted glass above. Despite the heat, I shivered with the sudden creeping sense that someone was up there watching us.

He placed his hand on the scanner mounted next to the door. A green light illuminated, and there was a heavy metallic *chunk* sound from the doors. He grasped the door handle, twisted it, and threw his weight back to pull the door open and hold it for me. Passing through the doorway, I noticed the door was seriously thick, almost as formidable-looking as a vault. Inside, overhead lights cast their fluorescent illumination through the empty hallways that branched off from the entrance. The lock mechanism activated as soon as the door closed behind us.

"To put your mind at ease, we'll pay a visit on your friend," Jacob said.

He turned to the hallway branching off to the right, and I kept pace with him. The casual way he spoke about Nathan and the gargoyle sent ire prickling through me. With each windowless door we passed, I felt a little more closed in. I wasn't usually prone to claustrophobia, but the building was starting to feel like a thinly-disguised prison.

"What are you doing with the gargoyles, Jacob?"

He led us to an elevator, where he pressed his palm to another security scanner like the one outside.

His lips thinned as he angled his gaze downward, seeming to consider what to say.

"The work is confidential and still in the early stages, but I suppose there's no real harm in telling you. I assure you, it's legal. I want you to know that the boy getting caught up in the trap was a freak accident. The traps are only supposed to trap demons, and it was a very unfortunate fluke that a human got mixed up in the process." He cast me an apologetic look, the inner corners of his eyebrows drawn in and up.

I believed that he never intended a human to get trapped in the gargoyle, but his declaration that the work wasn't illegal sent off warning pings in my mind. Gregori Industries was infamous for finding loopholes in the law.

The elevator dinged, the sound overly sharp and loud in the quiet hallway, and the doors parted. We stepped on, and again he had to scan his hand before punching the button with the 6 on it.

"I'm trying to build a better mousetrap, in a manner of speaking," he said. "Demon trap, actually. Not for the harmless little ones, but for the arch-demons. In my opinion, those suckers are still responsible for way too much misery and death."

He shook his head, as if so deeply personally affronted by the tragedies caused by arch-demons he was temporarily at a loss for words. Something about his manner made me suspect he was putting on a bit of an act, but I couldn't argue with the heart of his cause. After all, I made my living trying to clean up the smaller Rip spawn that bubbled through, and my own brother had been abducted by an arch-demon. And if there was anyone in the world who carried the weight of responsibility for keeping humanity safe from arch-demons, it was the CEO of fricking Gregori Industries. But his methods, his cavalier attitude, rubbed me wrong.

I squinted at him as indignation began to bleed through me. "You're using live gargoyles to bait and trap arch-demons. Don't you think that's a pretty bad way to treat a rare, intelligent creature? Surely with all the resources you have, you could come up with something a lot more ethical," I challenged.

He gave me a look that was something between great patience and pity. "Ella. We're at war. We must do everything in our power to fight back against what the Rip has unleashed into our world, and war requires sacrifices. If there's a way to trap arch-demons that doesn't put any human lives at risk, isn't that a worthy sacrifice?" He tipped his head a little in question, and I realized he was honestly waiting for my response.

The elevator stopped and the doors opened, giving me a moment to collect myself.

"It certainly wouldn't be the first time other species have been used or sacrificed for the greater good," he said, seeming to take my hesitation as a prompt to further his argument. "Do you have any idea how many of the things you use every day were tested on animals?"

I took a slow count to three before I spoke. "There are plenty of people in the world who believe testing on animals is immoral, and subjecting gargoyles to demonic possession is *hardly* in the same league as testing eye shadow on rabbits. Gargoyles didn't cause the Rip. Humans did." It took everything I had to say "humans" instead of "Gregori Industries."

He placed a hand on his chest, and his eyes rounded behind the lenses of his glasses. "Everything you say is true, Ella. Believe me, I get no pleasure from it, and I wouldn't blame anyone for their moral outrage."

"How can you do it, then?"

We'd stopped just beyond the elevator alcove, facing off.

His face hardened, and his hand dropped to his side. "Because my life's work is to clean up the horrors that have come through the Rip to torment us, and ultimately to seal the Rip. I will use *any* means necessary to see it through." His words became ragged-edged with ferocity, and his cheeks took on a faint flush.

I stiffened as if he'd shouted at me, though in fact he'd not raised his voice at all. Looking into his eyes, I searched for any glint of madness. But even if he was entitled and ego-driven—characteristics that bled through in the media even when he assumed his public persona—he seemed of sound mind. In fact, his passionate declaration was probably the most honest thing he'd said since I'd arrived.

I nodded once and then cast my gaze down the hallway. I still didn't agree with his methods, but I had a mission to focus on. With relief I noticed windows spaced along the walls, and some open doorways, which made it feel more normal and less like a prison.

"Is Nathan here?" I asked.

The fire dissipated from his eyes, and he assumed his former fake-ish smile and even-tempered tone. "Yes, but before I take you to him I need to check with his—caretakers." His tiny stutter over "caretakers" made me wonder what other word he'd had in mind.

Jacob took me to a conference room with a big TV screen mounted at one end and a long table surrounded by high-backed chairs. It was the type of generic corporate set-up that was so bland I actually felt a faint sense of disappointment.

"I'll return for you in a moment," he said and left.

I sat down in one of the chairs and leaned back, testing its bounce, and then pushed off with my feet to spin it around.

When the doorway flashed through my visual field, I planted my shoes on the carpet to stop my twirling. A man stood there—not a man, a ghost. It couldn't be the man I thought because he was supposed to be dead.

He took a step into the room, his eyes growing beady. He moistened his lips with his tongue, pulling his bottom lip in as if he were gazing at a ribeye he couldn't wait to slice into.

I stood in one swift motion, every muscle in my body stringing tight and my pulse speeding as adrenaline flooded into my veins. The shadows around the edges of my vision were going berserk. The man wasn't imposing by any means—several inches shorter than me, a good four decades older, and completely devoid of brawn or any physically intimidating feature. But I'd instantly recognized him as one of the most notorious people in the world, and I couldn't help staring openly even as everything in me recoiled and wished to flee as far from him as possible.

Before me was Phillip Zarella—the man wanted for some of history's most heinous crimes and rumored to have done things that were almost beyond belief. He half-raised a hand, either reaching toward me or pointing, and the hungry gleam in his eyes deepened.

"Reaper," he breathed, with a rapt look on his face.

My pulse stuttered, and it took all of my resolve to stand less than a dozen feet from Phillip Zarella, the mad scientist himself. This was no ghost, somehow Zarella was alive and well and *here*. I'd seen pictures of him, probably even some short clips of footage. But live and in person I could actually feel something dark and dreadful emanating from him, as if his crimes surrounded him like an aura.

Hurried footfalls in the corridor broke the tension of our locked gazes. Zarella's expression turned to irritation as Jacob appeared. The Gregori CEO looked deeply displeased, as if he'd come home to find his dog had chewed up an arm of the sofa. I could only stare at the two of them, wondering how in the hell—and why—Jacob Gregori had brought Phillip Zarella to the campus. Then it hit me, and a violent shudder snaked up my spine. He was beyond the reach of the law here. Jacob *wanted* him here. For some reason my uncle wanted Phillip Zarella free in spite of the long list of atrocities that would have meant multiple death penalties had Zarella not escaped from a maximum security prison last year. Escaped, and supposedly been shot and killed in the ensuing attempt to recapture him.

"Excuse me a moment," Jacob said hastily to me, grabbing

Zarella's arm and pulling him away from the doorway and out of sight.

I stiffened my knees to keep them from buckling as I truly began to realize what I'd seen—what I was positive I wasn't supposed to see. Phillip Zarella was dead. After his escape, he'd been caught trying to cross the border into Canada. There'd been a shootout, and he'd gone down. At least that's what had been reported far and wide not six months back.

My pulse surged again, and my hands began to shake as I suddenly feared I might not leave the Gregori campus alive. I pushed to my feet and ran to the doorway, intending to find a way out. But I nearly crashed into Jacob's chest. My feet tangled, and when I stumbled, he caught my upper arm and kept me from falling. I looked into his face, unable to mask what was probably a look of pure terror.

"The feds know he's here, Ella," Jacob said. He let go of my arm and moved to the side.

I blinked several times. "They . . . do?"

He lowered his lids and nodded once. "They do. I regret that he startled you like that, he wasn't supposed to be in this wing, but please don't worry about any repercussions of witnessing his presence here."

I took a shaking breath and swallowed, still trying to wrap my mind around the fact that Zarella's death had been staged. "Why the hell would you give asylum to Phillip Zarella?" I made no effort to hide my repulsion.

His mouth twisted in genuine disgust. "I know how it must

look, but I have him here only for his knowledge. There are things he understands about demons and the dimension on the other side of the Rip that no one else does. As abhorrent a human being as he is, I need him to achieve my goals."

"And the feds are okay with it?"

"We have an agreement."

I gave my head a shake as I felt my adrenaline fading and my temples beginning to pound.

Jacob bent a little to peer into my face. "Do you want to sit down for a moment? Do you need some water?"

"No." I gestured down the hallway with a flip of my hand. "I want to see Nathan."

I did my best to pull my shit together as we passed more conference rooms and offices, and then I took a left turn into an area that appeared to be part-zoo and part-laboratory.

"On this floor we keep minor demons for study," Jacob explained when we paused a windowed room where several of the bat-like creatures were perched like a flock of crows on what looked like a jungle-gym type structure you might see in a park. It was set up at the back wall, and the juxtaposition between the Rip spawn and the brightly-colored plastic toy was almost absurd. "We need to know everything we can about our enemy."

Remembering how demons had been reacting to me lately, I stayed as far from the windows as possible without being too obvious about it. The last thing I needed was to cause a scene that piqued Jacob's interest, or I might end up in one of these cages. In all seriousness, my fear probably wasn't all that far-fetched.

He stopped in front of a window and tipped his head at it. "And here we are."

Inside stood the familiar stone form of the crouched creature with the narrow feline face.

"How do I know Nathan is okay?" I asked.

Jacob stepped over to a panel on the wall. He entered a code and then beckoned to me. The image on the panel showed three separate shapes—gargoyle, demon, and human—and next to each there were vital sign readouts.

"See?" Jacob pointed to the human. "Vital signs normal. He seems to be in a deep sleep, actually."

Or maybe a brain-dead coma.

I faced him and waited until his gaze met mine. "When will you release him?"

He blinked and his tongue darted to the corner of his mouth, immediately raising my suspicions that whatever he was about to say might not be the whole truth. "We have to wake up the gargoyle first and then separate the human from the gargoyle."

"*Nathan*," I said. "The human's name is Nathan."

"Yes, of course. Anyway, once Nathan is free from the gargoyle we expect he'll still be in a state of demonic possession. So then we'll have to remedy that."

"You still haven't answered my question. When will he come home?"

Jacob's demeanor shifted so abruptly it felt like someone had snuck up and flipped a switch between his shoulder blades.

His face closed off. "We'd planned to keep the creatures in this state for several weeks so we could observe the symbiosis. In the original study we'd intended to conduct several experiments," he said with all the concern of someone talking about tomorrow's forecast.

My mouth dropped open, but before I could voice my outrage he raised a finger and continued.

"But because there is a human involved—yes, Nathan—we will attempt the separation after an abbreviated period of observation."

I felt my nostrils flaring, and my breath came rapidly through my still-open mouth. "How long?"

"Another three weeks. But I'll shorten it to two weeks if you'll do something for me in return," he said.

"What?"

"Allow me to help you find your brother."

I pulled my head back in confusion. "I don't understand."

"I want to do something for you to—well, to help alleviate my guilt, I suppose." He looked away, scratched the side of his head, and then resettled his glasses and met my eyes with his. "If your father hadn't died on that trip, he'd be here today. He would've been there when your mother passed, and he would've taken care of you and Evan. And maybe if he'd been there, Evan would have stayed out of trouble and he'd be okay. I was the one who pushed your father to go with me into a region we knew was dangerous, and I've regretted it every day since."

"If you want to find Evan, you can do that on your own. You don't need me to agree to anything."

"No, that's true. But I want you to agree. I want it to be

something we pursue together."

The thought of doing anything with Jacob sent a wave of distaste through me.

I shook my head, suddenly hyper aware of the tightness in my chest and a deep, desperate need to escape this place. "Fine, okay. We'll hunt for Evan together. But two weeks is too long. We need Nathan released as soon as possible. His sister needs him to come home."

"It's the best I can do." The words fell like bricks.

He folded his arms, and his face became an expressionless wall, except for the glint in his eye, the same one I'd seen when he'd spoken of defeating the Rip at all costs. I knew Jacob wasn't going to negotiate, and I also suspected he was lying. I would bet my paycheck that Jacob Gregori had no intention of releasing Nathan. He would continue to come up with vague excuses about why he couldn't. And knowing he was working with Phillip Zarella only reaffirmed and deepened my fears in the worst way. Zarella was brilliant, but he was the most notorious psychopath in history, completely devoid of any moral center. He'd think nothing of allowing Nathan to die, if only for the sake of his twisted curiosity.

I ground my teeth. I wasn't waiting two weeks, and I didn't need his help finding Evan. The *other* had already given me a clue about his whereabouts, and I would find a way to get it to show me more.

"It's been grand, but I need to get home," I said, not even attempting a pleasant tone.

Jacob took me back to the elevator and tried to make small talk on the way down and out of the facility, to which I gave minimal responses. Outside, one of the buzz-cut guys was waiting in a golf cart to take me back to my truck. Apparently Jacob was done with me.

I retrieved my things from the locker, got into my truck, and retraced my route back to the main entrance. The sun had set, but it wasn't full dark yet. Outside the gate, Johnny's car was still waiting. I pulled up next to it and rolled down the window. Johnny lowered his, too, and the guys peered at me anxiously.

"Are you okay?" Damien asked.

"What did he say?" Johnny said at the same time.

I let out a breath and realized my fingers were curled in a death grip on the wheel. I loosened my hands.

"I'm fine. He's keeping Nathan another couple of weeks," I said. "But I don't want to wait that long. I'll fill you in on the details, but I want to get back home. Roxanne is waiting."

I kept my foot on the brake while I sent Roxanne a quick text to let her know I was on my way. With a heavy heart, I told her that Nathan wasn't free yet, but he was safe and he'd be out soon.

Then I rolled forward and saw Johnny flip a U-turn in my rearview mirror. His headlights were an unexpectedly reassuring presence all the way back to the North End and my apartment.

When I finally parked and shut off the engine, I slumped for a moment, drained. But there was no time for rest. We had work to do.

The warm, savory aroma of spaghetti sauce filled my apartment, and for a moment my anxiety eased. Loki bounded forward to greet me, and Roxanne poked her head through the kitchen doorway, a sauce-smeared wooden spoon in her hand.

"Oh good, you're home. The spaghetti is in the pot keeping warm, and the salad is made." She was all business about dinner, but I could tell she was trying to mask her disappointment about Nathan. I was pretty sure she'd hoped I would be coming home with him, even though I'd told her there was no guarantee that would be the result of my meeting with Jacob, and even when Nathan was released he'd need medical attention. "Can you help me with the garlic bread?"

"Of course." I followed the sounds of preparations in the kitchen and inhaled deeply. "It smells amazing. Johnny and Damien are coming, too."

She was standing at the stove, stirring. "You should invite your friend Deb."

"It's a long drive for her and she has to get up early, but I'll tell her you wanted her to come. She'll be bummed she missed it."

I took up a bowl of melted butter and began drizzling it onto the loaf of French bread that was halved on a cookie sheet. She'd already minced garlic, which was waiting on the cutting board.

"This is really impressive," I said, watching her. "Do you cook dinner a lot at home?"

She flipped a glance at me and lifted one shoulder nonchalantly. "Eh, it's just spaghetti. But yeah, I'm in charge of meals a lot." She set the spoon down on a little plate and turned to me, leaning back against the counter. Her posture might have appeared casual, but her eyes were wide and tense. "So what exactly did they say about Nathan?"

I set down the butter bowl so I could face her fully. "Gregori Industries says they will let him go, but not soon enough for my liking. So I'm going to find a way to get him home faster."

"And he's still stuck in the statue?"

"Yes, but he's okay."

Her gaze tilted to the floor and she nodded, taking a deep breath. I could tell she was trying to be brave, but I caught the welling of tears in her eyes. My throat thickened in sympathy. She was obviously capable of caring for herself when she had to and was accustomed to doing so, but at the same time there was something so small and vulnerable about her.

The sound of the front door swishing open caused both of us to straighten and blink away our emotion. Damien appeared in the kitchen doorway with a white baker's box.

"I brought dessert, hope you like cupcakes," he said. I could tell he was trying to cheer up Roxanne, and I shot him a grateful smile.

"Yum!" Roxanne rewarded him with a grin.

I heard the door open again. "Sounds like Johnny's here. I'm going to talk to the guys for just a minute, and then I'll come back to finish the bread."

I beckoned Damien to follow. I grabbed Johnny's arm and towed him back out to the front porch, where I turned to the two of them.

"I don't want her to hear, and I'm gonna talk fast. Jacob has Phillip Zarella on campus." Shock registered on both their faces, but I didn't have time to acknowledge it. Words spilled from my lips. "Although Jacob said he'd release Nathan unharmed in a couple of weeks, I don't trust him. Especially not with that psychopath roaming the facilities. I want to break Nathan out. Damien and I saw that three men were able to get the statue onto a hand truck. I say we hijack a Gregori van, get onto campus, and take the statue."

Johnny gave me a sidelong look out of the corners of his eyes. "I'm not arguing with the urgency of the situation, but that sounds awfully risky. Not to mention potentially, oh, I don't know, impossible?"

I made a face at him. "Those vans are all over the place. I saw half a dozen when I was there, and they're close to the main gate. Three guys moved the statue with a hand truck, and we have the advantage of Damien's magic to help us with the heavy part."

"And you think you could get us into wherever Nathan is being held?" Damien asked, his voice pitched high with doubt.

"I know which building it is, what floor, and what room." I looked at Johnny. "I'd, uh, need you to hack the security system, though. There's a hand scanner, and then I think the cell requires a code to open it."

Johnny planted his hands on his hips and shook his head, his lids lowered partway over his dark eyes. "I appreciate your confidence, but I think those things are beyond my skillset."

I shot him a withering look. "Whatever, dude. You could do that stuff in your sleep, and we both know it."

His expression grew grave. "I'm all for saving Roxanne's brother, but once we're on the Gregori campus, it's like the frickin' Wild West. If we get caught, they can basically do whatever they want with us. *To* us."

In the silence that followed, I knew all three of us were thinking of Phillip Zarella. I swallowed as an uncomfortable tightening sensation gripped my chest.

"Dinner's about ready, Ella just needs to toast the bread."

We all jumped and turned to see Roxanne peering at us through the cracked door. I pasted on a big smile. "On it!"

I cast a glance back at the guys, widening my eyes. How much had Roxanne overheard? Probably not the part about Zarella hiding out on Gregori Industries property. She was plenty old enough to know about Zarella's notorious crimes. If she'd heard me talking about Zarella at Gregori, I doubted she could have hidden her reaction. I watched the back of her pale blond head, concerned about what she knew. How did parents do it? All the worrying, the managing of expectations, and the soothing of fears. I felt the sudden weight of my responsibility for Roxanne settle in my chest, and for a moment it was monumentally overwhelming.

In the kitchen, I narrowed my focus to the present and helping Roxanne finish dinner preparations. As I carried my plate loaded

with spaghetti, spinach salad with sliced cherry tomatoes, and a
hunk of garlic bread, I marveled that for the second night in a row
I seemed to have ended up hosting a dinner party. We gathered
around the coffee table again—my little kitchen nook table only
had two chairs and wasn't big enough for all four of us anyway—
with Roxanne in between Johnny and me on the sofa and Damien
on the leather ottoman. As soon as we were settled, Johnny lifted
his water glass.

"To Roxanne and her culinary bad-assery," he said, and
Damien and I raised our glasses too.

She giggled and her cheeks pinked as we all clinked our glasses
in a toast, and when she flicked her eyes up at Johnny, her blush
deepened. We all dug in, and I had to give her props—she put
together a great meal. I had a forkful of pasta halfway to my mouth
when Roxanne's hand stilled at either side of her plate, and she
looked up at us.

"So you're going to jailbreak my brother out of Gregori
Industries?" Her expression was equal parts fearful and hopeful,
and the raw vulnerability on her face made my heart ache.

I set down my fork. "That's what I want to do. What do you
think of the idea?"

"I just want him home as soon as possible." Her voice was high
and small, like a child's, and her lips trembled just barely before
she clamped them together and looked down at the plate in her
lap, but I knew Damien and Johnny saw it, too. She'd been so stoic,
and a good sport about staying with me, but I could see her hope
wavering.

"Then we'll figure out how to break him free," Johnny said quietly.

She raised her head and gave him a watery smile, swiping at the single tear that had begun to slip down one cheek.

I caught Johnny's eye over Roxanne's head and silently mouthed "thank you." He responded with a smile, and his dark eyes glowed with warmth. I meant to look away, but for some reason my gaze snagged on his, and I couldn't break the connection. An unexpected spark lit in the center of my stomach, and I inhaled sharply through my nose. Snapping out of the odd little moment, I dropped my eyes to my plate, but I could still feel Johnny's attention lingering on me like the heat of the low-angled sun in the evening. A bit rattled and curiously off-balance, I lifted my fork and took a bite, forcing myself to chew.

It had only been a second or two, maybe not even that long, but my face and chest felt as if they glowed a bit too warm, and I had the urge to splash cold water over my face. What the hell was that? Johnny just wasn't that kind of guy, not for me. For other women he was, for a *lot* of women, according to his reputation and extrapolating from the times I'd seen him in action. I wasn't an idiot—he was movie-star handsome and had a twinkling, charming vibe about him, but he was too obvious, too out-there with the way he pursued women, calling all of us "sugar" and "gorgeous" and getting all croony with his smooth voice. I preferred more subtlety.

I gave myself a mental shake. This was so not the moment to be entertaining silly little flutters in my stomach that probably meant nothing. What I really needed was some time alone with

Johnny and Damien to figure out a game plan. Luckily, Damien and I had the next two days off, which was perfect timing. We could bust Nathan out tomorrow, I could catch up on some much-needed sleep the next day, and I'd be fresh and ready to return to work the following day. Easy-peasy, lemon-squeezy.

Johnny's phone bleeped, and he picked it up and flicked his thumb across the screen in a few quick motions. His eyebrows drew together, and he set his plate on the coffee table to focus more fully on whatever message had come through.

He grabbed his plate in one hand and sidestepped out from between the sofa and coffee table. "Damn, I'm sorry, but I'm going to have to run. I'm on call as a consultant for the local police, and they're paging me to come to a crime scene."

With an internal sag of disappointment—which I tried to tell myself was purely due to Johnny's departure ruining my plans for figuring out our next move against Gregori—I turned and watched him quickly load his plate and fork into the dishwasher. He retraced his steps to the living room and paused at the end of the coffee table, but I could tell his mind was already jumping ahead to the case that awaited him. Work and women seemed to be his two main points of focus in life, and he could get equally immersed in either.

"Call me when you can?" I asked.

"It'll be late," he said.

"No problem, I'll be up."

He flashed me a nod and half-grin, squeezed Roxanne's thin shoulder, and then he was off to the front door, leaving a little stir of air in his wake.

I turned back to find Damien aiming a smug little smile my way.

"What?" I asked.

"Nothing." He gave me an exaggerated wide-eyed look. He bent his head down to push a piece of spinach around on his plate with his fork, but I still saw the uplift of the corners of his mouth, as if he were enjoying a private joke.

I exchanged a glance with Roxanne, and we both shrugged. Exhaustion tugged at my limbs, but I forced myself up off the sofa.

"Let's get the kitchen cleaned up so we can crash out," I said. "We've got a big day tomorrow."

Roxanne hopped up and went ahead of me, and I let her go and stalled near Damien.

"What was that about?" I stage whispered.

He shook his head. "Nothing important. But I have something for you." He flicked a look at the kitchen doorway, signaling it was something he didn't want Roxanne to see.

That piqued my curiosity. We got the sauce-splattered kitchen wiped down and loaded the dishwasher. Once the machine was humming, I helped Roxanne fold out the hide-a-bed and found the remote for her. Within a minute she was zoned out, alternating her attention between the TV and her phone, and I beckoned Damien to follow me out to the back patio. Loki came too, bounding into the yard and then sticking his nose to the ground to sniff.

It was full dark, and the air had cooled enough that we wouldn't break a sweat sitting on the patio. I noticed Damien had brought his backpack.

"Should I turn on the outside light?" I asked.

He glanced up. "Let's let our eyes adjust. This will be cooler in the dark."

I didn't even have a wild guess at what he wanted to show me, and I craned to see what he was digging for in his pack. He withdrew his hand, and it appeared he held a coil of rope. But when he kept hold of one end and let it unfurl, it began to glow with a subtle green light of earth magic. The faint prickle of nearby magic raised the hairs on my forearms. I focused inward and then down, drawing up a weak thread of earth magic in an attempt to sense what he was doing, but couldn't feel much more than a low vibration that seemed to emanate from the rope.

"What is it?" I asked.

Instead of answering, he flicked his wrist. The rope blurred through the air and there was a satisfying, sharp snap that startled Loki. He looked at us from the corner of the little yard with the glow of hellfire in his eyes and then went back to snuffling along the fence line.

"A whip that you've . . . charmed?" I ventured.

"Yes," he said, his tone warm and pleased. "I minored in charmed weapons in college."

"I, uh, actually don't know how a charmed weapon works." I rarely felt self-conscious about my lack of magical knowledge, but it struck me that between Damien's ability, his exposure to mage-level craft through his family, and formal education, he was probably an expert on a lot of things. I couldn't help feeling again that his talents were wasted on Demon Patrol.

"You use magic to connect yourself with the weapon. Let the energy become a live current that flows from your body to the object and vice-versa. It allows you to direct the weapon in more precise ways, as if the two of you are working in concert rather than you just wielding it."

He flicked his wrist again, and instead of biting the empty air, the whip snaked out to one of my lawn chairs. The end of it wrapped around one leg. With another rapid movement of his hand, Damien flipped the chair into the air. It turned a full somersault and clattered back down on the cement slab, landing neatly on its four feet. The whole demonstration took maybe a second.

Then he raised the handle of the whip overhead and circled his arm in a quick lasso motion. A flare of green magic sped from his hand, down the length of the twirling whip, and then stretched off the end, as if it were an extension of the whip itself. The strand of magic extended, reaching for a branch high above, and wrapped around the limb like a hand. When Damien tugged the whip, the bough dipped.

He released his magic, and the green light extinguished as the whip's tail fell to the ground.

"You can also use it to cast a large circle really fast," he said. "That could come in handy in a pinch."

I wrapped my arms around my middle, eyeing the length of the whip. "That's really nifty, but I doubt I have enough juice to make any sort of use of it."

He stretched out his arm, offering me the handle. "Even with your current level of ability, I think you can do something with this. I noticed you seem to have an affinity for earth magic over the other elements, so I charged the whip to easily channel that energy."

Reluctantly, I took the whip, my stomach tightening with the expectation that I would disappoint Damien. As soon as my palm contacted the handle, a zing of his residual magic warmed my palm. The whip itself was warm, almost as if it were a living thing.

"I use earth magic because it's the easiest," I said. Every kid with any level of magical ability was taught to use earth magic first. It was the most concrete and abundant of the elemental magics. "I don't really have an affinity for any of the elements."

"You're wrong," he said. "You're definitely an earth crafter, but you also have a strong affinity for fire. We'd need to do some training before you could do much with it. Try projecting your magic into the whip. Once you feel it, visualize what you want it to do and then flick your hand and send your intention outward through the whip. It's all in the wrist."

He moved several paces off to the side, well out of the way.

I knew my face betrayed my apprehension, and I was suddenly extremely glad it was so dark outside. In spite of my misgivings, I closed my eyes and stilled my mind, and imagined my feet growing roots into the soil, reaching for the magical energy stored there. When I felt the warm hum of it in my feet, I coaxed it up through my body, as much as I was capable of drawing.

As if the whip and magic were magnet and iron, the sensation swelled to a vibration, and the magic raced through me to the hand that held the handle, raising goosebumps in its wake. I sucked in a surprised breath. The whip glowed with strands of green earth magic, amplifying the supernatural power I fed it. The end of the whip twitched over the patio like a predator itching to strike out.

I eyed the dark shape of the folded umbrella in the middle of my glass-topped patio table. Visualizing the whip spiraling around it, my pulse accelerated, and I gripped the handle tighter. Holding my focus, I raised my hand and tried to imitate Damien's demonstration. Magic sparked down the whip and flew off the end, arcing to the umbrella. Instead of twining around it as I'd intended, the magic flew outward in one glob, missed the umbrella completely, and smacked into the wood fence with a bang, rattling the slats with the solid force of earth magic as if I'd walked up and kicked them. At the same time, the shadows in my periphery went wild, and my head thumped hard enough to make me wince. The *other* reacting to my magic? The strands of green spread out in a paint-splatter pattern before fading and leaving the faint scent of ozone hanging in the air.

I crowed a laugh in spite of the misfire and the smoky shapes swirling frantically in a frame around my vision. I'd never felt such an abundance of magic before, and certainly never wielded it that way. My ability was too meager to perform distal magic—magic at a distance of more than a couple of feet—and my heart galloped at the thrill of slinging magic for the first time in my life.

I grinned at Damien in the dark. "This thing kicks ass." His face was shadowed, but I had the sense that he was grinning back.

I drew more earth magic and shook my hand back and forth, and the whip skipped across the patio leaving green in its wake. I did it again just for the fun of it.

He chuckled at my playing. "I'm glad you like it. I can teach you to do some specific maneuvers if you want."

I released the earth magic and began coiling the whip, suddenly aware of the familiar drained sensation seeping into my body. There was always a price to wielding magic, and the lower the ability, the faster the crafter tired. A shiver passed through me as the faint chill left by the absence of magic set in. There was a little strap on the base of the handle, which was probably for keeping the coils in place. I wrapped the strap around the whip and snapped it.

The thumping in my head was still going strong, and something from my visit to the Gregori campus pinged in my memory. I shivered again as I remembered the look on Phillip Zarella's face when he'd appeared in the doorway of the conference room. He'd looked at me like he wanted to devour me and muttered the word "reaper."

I licked my dry lips. "Zarella said something to me. It was before Jacob showed up and shooed him away." My words came haltingly as a vague tightness clutched at my insides.

"What was it?" Damien's head tilted in curiosity.

"He said 'reaper.' And it wasn't just what he said but the look on his face. Like he wanted to whisk me back to his lab and take a saw to my skull so he could poke around in my head." I hunched forward and wrapped one arm around my waist.

Damien went still. "Are you sure that's what he said?"

"Positive. You're knowledgeable. Any idea what he meant by that?"

He let out a harsh scoffing breath, an expression of disgust. "No, and I have no desire to understand the inner workings of a psychopath's mind. He's a necromancer, so he has an affinity for anything related to death. But he's also clinically insane. I wouldn't put much stock in anything that comes out of his mouth."

"Yeah, you're probably right . . ." I trailed off.

But a chill passed through me. I'd forgotten that in addition to Zarella's atrocities against humans, vampires, and any other species he could get his hands on, he was one of only a few necromancers in the world. He'd raised zombies and then controlled them using telepathy. It was rumored that he could see through the eyes of any zombie, demon, or vamp—anything or anyone that had been touched by death or the Rip—and steer them around like a kid with a radio control car.

Anything that had been touched by death.

My mind flashed to the moment I'd awakened on a gurney under a sheet, queued for the autopsy lab along the side of a dark hallway in the basement of St. Luke's Hospital with two other stiffs. Talk about a real life nightmare that would haunt me for the rest of my days. The poor orderly would need therapy for the next decade after witnessing me bolt upright, screaming bloody murder as the sheet fell away.

I'd definitely been touched by death. More than touched. It had claimed me for eighteen minutes, and by some unknown miracle,

I'd escaped. My forehead thumped its rhythm, that foreign beat that didn't line up with my pulse, as if to remind me of the passenger I'd carried since returning to the living. Zarella had seen *something* when he looked at me, and I didn't think it was just a hallucination of an insane man.

Damien's voice jolted me from my thoughts. "If you did some focused training, you could do a lot more with the whip."

"I seriously doubt I could do all that much," I said.

"I disagree. I think you have more capacity."

"Why?" I asked.

He cocked his head. "It's hard to explain, and I admit I have nothing particularly concrete to base it on, just a sort of sixth-sense pinging. It's almost like you were supposed to have a higher level of aptitude and then . . . I don't know, something interfered at a critical moment and left you with only a bit of ability. Did you have any sort of traumatic event around puberty? A bad accident or serious illness?"

"Huh uh. Actually that was one of the few periods of my life that was fairly normal." I looked at him. "This is really cool and all, but we need to figure out this thing with Roxanne's brother. I was hoping Johnny would be able to stick around."

He gave a low laugh and moved to two of the chairs, pulling them closer together with a soft screech of the metal legs across concrete. He lowered himself into one of them, crossed one ankle over the other knee and rocked the chair back on two legs, clearly waiting for me to sit.

I remained where I was, folding my arms and keeping the

coiled whip clutched in one hand. "Why are you so smug and chuckly all of a sudden?"

"Come on, Ella. If we talk about it, we'll spoil the mystique."

"What the hell are you talking about?"

"You and Johnny. Duh," he said it in such a perfect imitation of Roxanne's tone of adolescent impatience I had to hold tight to my irritation to keep from cracking a smile. But Damien's mention of me and Johnny caused my stomach to do an unwelcome somersault.

"Um, there is *no* me and Johnny."

"Sure. Sure, there isn't." His annoyingly patronizing tone made me want to push his chair over backward.

I let out an exasperated breath, went to the vacant chair, and yanked it back a few inches out of spite before slouching onto it.

"We have more important things to discuss." I straightened and tried to tamp down the little flip-flop that was still echoing around in my stomach. "Here's what we should do. We'll wait near the Gregori campus for one of those vans to leave. We'll follow it 'til it's out of sight of the campus but not yet in the city. Then we'll borrow it and drive it back in through the security gate, go get the statue, and take it in the van."

A deep laugh floated toward us from over the fence, and I half-rose in alarm. The gate latch released with a *plink,* and the hinges squeaked as the gate swung open. A broad-shouldered form came through.

"Johnny?" I asked in surprise.

"You know you're insane, right?" Johnny took off his leather jacket, laid it on the table, and lifted a chair and carried it over to me and Damien. "I admire your intent, but that's an idiotic plan. And you might not want to be so loud about your criminal intentions. I could hear you from the sidewalk."

"Oh come on, that's a little harsh," I said indignantly. "Maybe my idea isn't very practical, but I haven't come up with anything better." I cleared my throat, trying to reclaim my composure. "I mean, how are we going to get in there? And what are you doing back here, anyway? I thought you had some emergency case."

"There were no supernatural forces at work in the crime scene," he said, his voice irritatingly level and soothing. "Newb cop called me in prematurely. Your plan is too rash, and it'll never work. But when I said you were insane, I meant it as a compliment."

Damien snickered while I opened my mouth and then snapped it closed, unable to come up with a good retort.

I sighed and leaned back. Getting prickly wasn't going to bring Nathan home any faster. "Okay, how do we do this?"

I knew Johnny was committed to the rescue mission because he'd promised Roxanne, and I realized I was genuinely curious about whether he had a plan of his own. He had a ton of connections I didn't, and I couldn't deny that he was probably better equipped to get us in and out of the Gregori campus.

"There's another Gregori gargoyle loose," Johnny said.

I perked up. "We have proof of what he's doing to gargoyles."

"Yup, that's what I was thinking. A friend of mine has eyes on it right now. He agreed to look the other way and pretend it was never there while we come and get it."

"We need to do it now," Damien said. "Tonight, before Gregori has a chance to track it down and claim it. Then we can go to the press in the morning."

"Yeah, I agree." I glanced through the kitchen's screen door. The dull flickers of light indicated Roxanne still had the TV on.

"You think that'll be enough to get Nathan released?" Damien asked.

"We won't know until we try. But Jacob seems to want to redeem Gregori Industries in the eyes of the public, if only to help his own reputation," I said, already standing and moving toward the door. "I'm pretty sure he doesn't want more bad press."

Johnny stood too and looked into the house. "What do we do about the kid?"

I bit the inside of my cheek for a moment and then shrugged. "Let's take her with us. Hey, Roxanne," I called into the living room. "How'd you like to go on a gargoyle mission with us?"

Her blond head popped up over the back of the sofa. "Can I pick a secret code name?"

I laughed. "Absolutely!"

Without a Gregori van to transport the wayward gargoyle, we needed something that could handle the weight of the stone creature. Fortunately, Johnny's father had a trailer we could hook up to my truck. The gargoyle would be exposed but shouldn't attract much notice in the middle of the night—or so we hoped.

Johnny and I got in my pickup to go get the trailer while Damien and Roxanne went to the apartment complex near the Boise River where Johnny's buddy had spotted the gargoyle. They were going to stand watch and make sure it didn't go anywhere. We figured if the gargoyle tried to take flight, or anything else of a supernatural nature occurred, Damien's magic was our best shot at keeping it contained.

So that left me alone with Johnny. I tried to keep my focus on the task at hand but caught myself becoming annoyingly aware of the aroma of his cologne, which was a distracting scent reminiscent of both sea and mountain forest. Between that, the swirling shadows around the edges of my vision, and the faint thump behind my forehead, I had my work cut out for me just keeping the truck on the right side of the yellow line.

"You see your dad much?" I asked. I didn't know anything about his family, though the way he'd mentioned his dad made it clear he lived alone. Johnny and I had crossed paths several times through work, and occasionally our social circles overlapped. Actually, it was probably more accurate to say his social circle pretty much engulfed mine. He was one of those people who seemed to know just about everyone, either directly or through one or two degrees of separation, especially when it came to people around our age in town. But I didn't know much of anything about his background.

"He spends a lot of time at his cabin in eastern Idaho in the summer. In the winter he goes south to Arizona." His tone was curiously flat.

My eyes ticked over to his face, trying to read his expression. Maybe he wasn't on the best of terms with his pops.

"Wow, three homes," I said. I wouldn't have guessed Johnny came from money. He worked hard and his services were in demand, and I knew he did quite well on his own. He was no trust fund silver-spoon kid. "Why does he hang onto the place here in Boise? Sounds like he doesn't use it much."

I looked over to see Johnny's non-committal shrug. "I don't know for sure. I think he does it out of loyalty to Mom's memory." His eyebrows were drawn low, as if trying to hide his eyes.

"I didn't know you lost mother. I'm sorry to hear that. That's sweet that he keeps the place in her honor."

"She's been gone a long time."

I wanted to say something comforting, but I got the sense the topic of his mother's death was one he tried to avoid.

"Who's the mysterious exorcist lady you know?" I asked, hoping a topic change would lighten his mood.

He shifted in his seat, straightening and unfolding his arms. "Her name's Lynnette LeBlanc. She's a witch who specializes in dark-edge magic."

The name sounded familiar, but I couldn't manage to pull any references from my memory. The unfamiliar term he used piqued my curiosity and sent off a little ping of warning at the back of my mind. "That's not the same as black crafting, is it?"

Not many were stupid enough to get mixed up in black magic. It was forbidden in the magic community, and it was dangerous—black magic was always accompanied by unpredictable and unintended results. A black love spell, for example, might achieve the goal of getting someone to fall in love with you, but then the love interest might get run over by a truck a month later. Or something equally terrible and random could happen to someone in proximity to the black magic practitioner—like a neighbor or family member.

"She doesn't practice any dark arts. She says her specialty is 'around' the black." Johnny lifted his hands to make air quotes with his fingers. "But I believe her. She's smart and really talented, but I don't think she's reckless."

I snorted as I swung the wheel around to take a left off Park Center Boulevard into an upscale subdivision. "I'm not sure how you can practice *around* the black without dipping into it."

"Yeah, I know it sounds weird. Her talent has to do with grave magic and things of that nature." His voice changed as his attention swung over to me. "She reminds me of you, actually."

My heart and my forehead thumped at the same time, as if

the *other* and I both took notice of his comment in the same way. I blinked a few times, and for a moment I had the wild urge to tell Johnny that I wasn't alone inside my own head, that something had come with me back from death and I needed to figure out how to communicate with it because it somehow knew where my brother was.

Instead, I sucked in a breath and then gave him a sly glance. "Well, she sounds like a badass, so I can see why you'd say that."

With a flip of his index finger, he indicated I should take the next right. "It's the third one on the left."

I pulled over to the curb and cut the engine.

He'd twisted to face me, and in doing so closed some of the space between us. "Ella, I'm glad I'm getting the chance to know you a little better. I have to admit you're part of the reason I'm getting swept up in this little rescue mission."

My pulse sped as my eyes stayed locked on his. They wanted to flick down to his lips, but I resisted. If I let my focus wander to his mouth, I'd probably kiss him and that would be stupid, just me giving into those silly flutters in my stomach and getting swept up in his gallant desire to help Roxanne. Despite his apparent sincerity and his admittedly charming declaration, I knew it was just a moment. I was well aware of his reputation. Tomorrow night or the next night he'd be saying something like that to another woman. That's how Johnny was—charm and yes, there was genuine sincerity there, but he had no interest in anything more than the passion of the moment.

So what did that say about me? That I actually wanted

something that lasted more than just a moment? I scoffed at myself and my entire irrelevant train of thought. We were there to save Roxanne's brother. Once that was done, I'd go back to trying to figure out how to get the thing in my head to show me where I could find Evan, and then I was going to bring my brother home.

I forced a grin. "Well, then let's get on with the mission," I said, trying to sound jaunty.

Hopping out of the truck and pulling in a deep breath of night air, I felt a little more like myself. I was used to moving and doing, not chit-chatting and exchanging silent glances. My fingers brushed the loops of the whip, attached to a clip on my Patrol belt that was positioned at the front of my left hip, and a tingle of residual magic raised the tiny hairs on my forearm. That was me— coiled and ready for action.

Johnny went to punch a code into the keypad mounted in the garage door frame, opening one side of the four-car garage. The noise of the door raising seemed to blast into the silence of the quiet residential street, but I was actually grateful for the racket because it filled the void left by the absence of conversation between us. We found the trailer inside and pulled away the bricks that were wedged in front of the tires, and then I jumped into my truck and backed it into the driveway so we could hitch up the trailer. Johnny also grabbed a rolling dolly and a mess of rope and bungee cords.

We pulled away with the trailer bumping along behind the truck and the dolly in the bed. It was just a five-minute drive to where Damien and Roxanne stood watch over the gargoyle, which we passed in silence that I tried to convince myself wasn't awkward at all. Due to the extra length of the trailer, I had to park on the street edging the apartment complex, rather than the nearly-full lot. I left the truck idling. Damien was supposed to give us the exact location of the gargoyle.

Johnny was fiddling with his phone. "They're at the northwest corner by the river. No parking nearby."

"Damn." I killed the engine and pulled out the key. "We'll have to take the dolly and hope no one looks out a window and thinks we're stealing something."

"Nah, people are moving stuff in and out of apartments all the time," Johnny said. "We should be okay."

We got out, and he reached into the back to hoist the dolly. I grabbed the bundle of cords. He pointed to a sidewalk that threaded between two of the complex's buildings.

"So Damien can't just lift the statue and float it to the trailer?" Johnny whispered as we passed an apartment balcony with TV sounds drifting through the screen door.

I gave a short laugh. "That's not how magic works."

He raised his free hand and shrugged. "I'm not a crafter, I don't know."

I narrowed my eyes at him. "You may not have magical aptitude, but you know plenty about magic."

"But seriously, why doesn't it work that way? He's walking around with a lotta juice."

I was pretty sure he knew the answer—if anything, he probably knew more about magic than I did—but sensed he was trying to keep the conversation light.

"Most magic makes use of the four main magical elements—earth, fire, water, air. In order to move an object, he'd have to use one or more elements." I paused, considering. "Maybe build up enough earth energy underneath the statue, in theory, since earth is the most solid of the elements. I'm not sure a mage could even do that, not with an object the size and weight of the gargoyle. I bet he could lift something smaller. Either way, the point is that magic still has rules."

"Rules? Booor-ring," Johnny sing-songed.

I grinned. "Once we have it the gargoyle on the dolly, he should be able to help us keep it balanced and maybe even give it a magical push to make it easier to move."

"I guess that's better than nothing."

We both slowed and then stopped. We were back in the shadows. Over the sound of crickets I could hear the soft watery flow of the Boise River, which was a few dozen feet ahead of us. The scents of decaying leaves, cool water, and moist soil mixed and filled my nose.

"Hey, it's over here." A low voice drifted to us in the dark, and I whipped around.

Damien's tall form with Roxanne's shorter one alongside approached from the Greenbelt that ran along the river.

"No Gregori henchmen yet, I take it?" I whispered when they joined us.

"Nope, we've got the statue to ourselves." Damien looked around, rubbing one arm up and down the other. "But I think there are some Rip spawn nearby, so we need to get our asses in gear."

He seemed a little jumpy, and the tempo of my pulse quickened.

"Lead the way, Agent Storm," Johnny said to Roxanne.

She was a Marvel comic book fan, so our secret agent names honored her favorite characters.

"Prepare yourself, Agent Iron Man," she said, half turning and flipping her fingers in a beckoning motion. "This is one ugly gargoyle."

We followed her, jogging with quiet footfalls along the paved bike and pedestrian path that followed the Boise River. I couldn't help casting a furtive glance behind me and darting looks into the deep shadows of the underbrush along the river bank. As long as I could remember, I'd been told to stay off the Greenbelt after dark. Parts of it were quite isolated from roads or houses. The coils of my whip, bouncing against my left thigh as I ran, and the more familiar weight of my service weapon at my right hip brought me some measure of comfort. I focused on the back of Roxanne's head, hidden in the hood of her sweatshirt, as if keeping my eyes on her would ensure her safety.

She veered off the Greenbelt onto a patch of lawn edging one side of an apartment building. Slowing, she led us around the corner and then stopped. We were on another of the pathways in between buildings, and all the nearby windows were dark. I passed the bundle of cords to Damien so I could reach for my small service flashlight. I released it from my belt but didn't switch it on. No light was required to spot the bulky mass of the gargoyle, planted in the grass just off the sidewalk.

My head thumped hard, and I reflexively winced and squeezed

my eyes closed for a second. When I opened them, my vision swam with so many swirling shadows it was like trying to see through thick smoke. Panic spiked my pulse and clenched my chest. I shook my head and blinked hard, and the dark shapes retreated back to the edges of my vision.

The faint aroma of Johnny's cologne wafted to my nose, and I heard the leathery rustle of his jacket beside me. "Are you all right?" he whispered.

I moistened my dry lips. "Yeah, fine."

With my heart still racing, I pressed my fingers over the end of the flashlight to partially shield it and switched it on as I approached the hulking form, aiming the beam at the statue's base. It stood at about five feet tall, shorter than me but somehow seeming much bigger because of its bulk. I had to walk partway around it to find the Gregori stamp.

A hissing screech sent my pulse racing again, and I sucked in a sharp breath through my nose. The sound had come from within the gargoyle, but it was also inside my head and I was sure no one else had heard it. Cold sweat sprang up on my palms, neck, and chest. As if drawn by an unseen force, my hand—the one muting the flashlight's illumination—reached out toward the statue's wing. When my fingertips made contact, the first thing I registered was that the surface was hot to the touch, like Roxanne's gargoyle. I hoped the heat only indicated the demonic energy of a trapped Rip spawn and not a human as well.

My eyes filled with a shadowy image, and the only thing I knew for sure was that it was cast in the strange blue and yellow hues of my previous dreams and visions. A terrible choking feeling of claustrophobia stole my breath. Only, it wasn't *my* lungs that felt compressed. I could feel my chest moving, nearly hyperventilating as my breaths came too fast. My mind reeled, trying to reconcile the sensations that belonged to me and the other things I felt, the foreign perceptions that somehow filtered through me.

I blinked blindly, trying to clear the images that came through the eyes of the *other*. The vision sharpened, and my eyes sprang wide in shock as I recognized my own face. I was somehow looking through the gargoyle's eyes, or—no, through the eyes of the demon locked inside.

"Ella? Can you hear me?"

"Is she breathing? Should I call an ambulance?"

Faces in front of me swam into focus. An arm was slung around my upper back to support my slack body, and hands held the useless weight of my head. In a reflexive spasm of my lungs, I sucked in a loud breath and then coughed and panted, drinking air in hungry lungfuls as if I'd just been dragged from the water and resuscitated. Nausea poured through me as unwanted recognition registered in my fogged brain. I knew this feeling. It was the same sickening, surfacing sensation that had filled me when I'd awakened on the gurney. When I'd narrowly escaped the grave.

Roxanne's face, slashed with shadows from the off-angle beam of light coming from the flashlight I'd dropped, crumpled in tearful relief.

"Ella, are you okay?"

My focus shifted to Johnny's face. I nodded and opened my mouth to respond but produced only a weak croaking sound. I cleared my throat and tried again.

"Yeah, I think so."

I sat up under my own power, let my head fall forward, and pushed the heels of my palms over my closed eyelids. When I dropped my hands to the cool grass to push myself up, the world tilted dizzily and I groaned. With Johnny grasping one arm and Damien holding the other, they carefully hoisted me to my feet.

"What happened?" Damien asked, still keeping hold of me.

I swallowed hard against the foul taste of bile, trying to work some moisture back into my dry throat. "I, uh, passed out I guess. But I'm fine," I insisted.

I bent down to pick up my flashlight, forcing Damien to let go of my arm. When I straightened, I realized Roxanne was staring at me, her eyes huge and round and her hands pulled inside the cuffs of her sweatshirt and pressed over her mouth.

"Hey, I'm okay, really," I said, softening. "What do you say we get this thing loaded and get out of here?"

I gestured to the gargoyle but didn't touch it. I wasn't a complete idiot.

No one moved. I cast my light around at the three people staring at me, aiming at their chests so I wouldn't blind them. They all wore similar expressions of apprehension and concern. Damien took half a step forward and started to lift his hand toward me. He stopped short of actually reaching for me. Smart guy.

"Ella," he said. "It's only been a matter of weeks since you experienced something really traumatic. Maybe you haven't given yourself enough time to—"

"Look, I'm just tired and a little out of condition," I interrupted. "I haven't slept much lately. After we get Nathan back, I'm going to rest. I'm planning to catch up on sleep and take it easy the next couple of days, I swear. Now can we please get on with it before someone shows up to snatch our bargaining chip out from under us?"

I tried to look bright and energetic, but I didn't think they bought it. Regardless, Johnny went to retrieve the dolly he'd dropped a few feet away, and Damien gathered the rope and bungee cords. I knew I'd have to touch the gargoyle again to help move it, but I hesitated, looking around for something to put between my hands and the stone. I couldn't afford a repeat of what had happened a few minutes ago. I quickly untied my boots and slipped out of them so I could pull off my socks. Both Johnny and Damien gave me long, wordless looks, and I knew I'd have to answer their questions at some point.

With my socks on my hands as makeshift gloves, the guys and I tipped the statue, and Roxanne shoved the dolly under the lifted edge of the base. When we pushed the gargoyle upright, the dolly creaked a warning at us, but it held. The weight caused the wheels to sink into the damp grass, however, and there was no way the three of us were going to muscle it to the nearby sidewalk unaided.

The tingle of magic brushed over me as Damien gathered his power. I recognized heavy rope-like strands of green earth energy with much smaller filaments of yellow air magic intertwined. Air energy was the hardest of the four elements to master, and integrating it with another element required a high degree of skill. The gargoyle shifted under our hands as Damien raised the wheels of the dolly just enough to allow us to push it over to the pavement.

By the time we got it to the nearest parking lot, all of us were grunting and sweating with the effort, even with the assist from

Damien's magic. I left them to go move the truck closer, noting as I ran around the back of the truck to the driver's side that the trailer had no ramp. I pulled as close as I could to the walkway where the others waited with the statue, and as I got out I dared a tiny smile of victory over the fact that no one had called security or come out to question what we were doing.

I should have saved it. We'd just tipped the gargoyle onto the trailer, with Damien's magic to keep us from dropping it, and were working on shoving it into the middle of the platform when a sickening icy shiver passed over me like a chilly wind. I froze, my eyes scanning the sky.

"Do you feel that?" I heard Damien ask.

Roxanne gasped. "Something's coming," she said with fear thickening her voice.

I spotted the dark form of a large demon briefly silhouetted against the moonlit sky before it dipped back down into the dark cover of the tree line. The creature was still near the river, but somehow I knew it was headed straight for us.

My heart plummeted into my stomach like a stone dropped into a pond. "Arch-demon. Get in the truck!"

I had a few brimstone burners on me, but they were for minor demons and wouldn't do a thing against a Rip spawn that size. Thanks to my prominent position on Devereux's shit list, I'd been unable to swipe a large demon can from the station.

We left the gargoyle where it was, still partially hanging off the back of the trailer. Damien and I exchanged a glance as he followed Johnny to the passenger side. I hurried Roxanne ahead of me to the driver's side, and my new partner and I seemed to silently arrive at the same thought. Magic didn't conduct through glass. A stun gun wouldn't work from inside the truck, either. He closed the door after Johnny was in, and I did the same once Roxanne's hand was clear of the doorjamb.

In a newer vehicle, we would have been safe inside, as cars built within the past twelve or thirteen years came standard with mage-charmed materials that couldn't be penetrated by demonic energy. But I couldn't afford the upgrade on my pickup, so it was unprotected.

Damien and I remained outside on either side of the truck. Magic buffeted me and sent electric pulses zipping over my skin as he rapidly drew a huge current of power. As I pulled my gun from my belt and hit the charge button, the demon rose like a specter above the rooftop of the nearest apartment building. Like a prehistoric winged hell-creature, in flight it was easily over a dozen feet from wingtip to wingtip.

"Call it in, Johnny!" I shouted without taking my eyes off the creature. I had no idea whether Damien's abilities could contain a demon of this size, but even if he could handle it, we'd need Strike Team to bring a trap sooner or later. I preferred sooner.

The creature circled above us, letting out an otherworldly hissing screech that seemed to resonate deep into my bones. The pulse of the *other* in my forehead intensified, almost as if answering the demon's call. I planted my feet wide and extended my arms with both hands gripped around my gun, trying to aim through the shadows gyrating in my vision.

As soon as the demon was within range, I pulled the trigger sending electric pulses zapping through the air. My shots hit with satisfying little pops of violet-blue sparks, but they weren't enough to paralyze or kill the demon. Mostly they just seemed to piss it off, but I only hoped to distract it long enough to allow Damien a chance to fully rev up his magic.

And rev it up he did. I'd never felt anything like it. It was as if he sucked in power from all directions, creating an energetic tornado around himself. Every inch of my exposed skin was alive in the current of magic he drew. Meanwhile the demon darted and dipped at us, but like the ones before it shied away from approaching close enough to possess me. Damien's magic also gave it pause, and it screamed in frustration. The horrible sound scraped my eardrums, and I winced and clenched my teeth.

"Stop firing," Damien ground out, clearly at his max.

I obediently lowered my gun, glancing at him just in time to see streams of magic that blended all four elements shoot from the fingers of his right hand. The glowing threads arched up and back, surrounding us and the truck in a sort of spherical lattice. He must have determined that forming a protective live ward around us was safer than attempting to contain the Rip spawn in a bubble of magic as he'd done before with the minor demons.

After the energy he'd already expended to help us move the gargoyle, I couldn't imagine how he was able to summon enough to hold the barrier. But I could hear the wail of a siren approaching fast. Strike Team would arrive within seconds. Damien just had to hang on for another minute or two.

I started to breathe a little easier when the demon reared up and screamed. Its eyes were two orbs of flame in its dark, ugly head, and they were trained on something behind us. I whirled and spotted a young woman in yoga capris with a blond ponytail, probably a student from nearby Boise State University, illuminated by a parking lot light and standing on a patch of grass between two walkways. She held a leash while her little cocker spaniel lifted his leg against the trunk of a tree. She was partially turned away, her eyes on something else, and I could see the cord coming from an earbud in her ear. I knew it was useless—if she hadn't heard the demon's call, she wouldn't hear my warning—but I screamed at her anyway.

She didn't even turn around. Just as Strike Team's trucks screamed into the parking lot, the demon dove at the woman. At the last minute it twisted in the air above her and darted straight at her face. In a shift that couldn't be explained by traditional science, the demon shrank and morphed into an elongated streak of darkness that bifurcated into two prongs, one entering each of the woman's eyes.

Her head jerked back as if she'd been punched. Her entire body grew rigid, and she released her hold on the leash. Her cocker wisely tucked tail and sprinted away. I called to him and clapped my hands, and he ran at me. Damien opened a space in the sphere for the little dog to slide through. I scooped him up in my arms and held him as he quivered.

The woman turned to face us, but she no longer looked like the perky college student of a few minutes ago. Her skin had paled to the dead gray color of ash, and her eyes were burning coals in her head. Strike Team would have an exorcist with them and should be able to save the woman before she made a kill. If they didn't and she managed to take a life while possessed, there would be no way to separate her from the demon possessing her.

Strike members streamed from two Hummers and formed a half-circle around the woman, firing bursts of blinding, pearly white—ethereal magic energy created with the aid of mages—until she collapsed. The shots weren't lethal. They were just meant to incapacitate until the possessed woman could be safely contained. Then an exorcist would perform the separation in a special enclosure so the demon couldn't escape. A handful of Strike men and women had hung back to make sure no one approached too close to their operation. One of them was positioned behind the trailer, and I glanced back just in time to seem him eyeing the gargoyle's base. He touched his earpiece, and his lips moved.

My skin tingled as Damien dropped the live ward he'd formed around us. I blinked, trying to clear the after-images left by the absent strands of magic and the bright bursts from Strike's weapons.

He groaned, and there was a dull *thunk* as he half-collapsed against the truck. I tucked the dog under my arm and ran around to Damien's side. His lids were pinched closed, and he panted like he'd just sprinted around the block. I reached out to take his arm and steady him, but Johnny jumped out and engulfed me and the dog in a bear hug.

"I've never been so pissed about not being a crafter," he said, his words muffled against my hair. He pulled back to look at me.

"You didn't get hurt, did you?"

"Uh, no, I'm fine," I assured him, still reeling from his embrace.

I looked into his eyes, and the depth of worry in them made my cheeks heat. I wanted to crack a joke but stood there tongue tied.

"Thanks for your concern, man," Damien said sarcastically, saving me. "Little help here? You know, for the guy who just saved your pretty ass?"

Johnny and I both shot surprised looks at Damien and then at each other. Apparently magical exhaustion brought out his sharper edges. I kind of liked it.

While Johnny slung an arm around Damien and helped him around the open door to the driver's seat so he could sit down, I went to Roxanne's side. She was still sitting in the truck, looking dazed.

"You okay?" I asked, awkwardly patting her forearm.

She nodded, but her eyes were still glassy. "Is that lady going to die?"

Knowing she was thinking of her brother, I followed her gaze to where Strike Team had bagged up the possessed girl in what looked like a mummy sleeping bag but with white mage-spelled magic woven through it. They had her on a gurney, and it did look a little like they were going to wheel her off to the morgue. My stomach did a slow flop at my memory of my almost-trip into a drawer in the basement of the hospital.

"No, they got here in time," I assured Roxanne. "She didn't hurt anyone else, so she'll be okay. They're going to take her to a safe place where someone will separate her from the demon. If Nathan needs this kind of help, we'll make sure he gets it too." I offered her the cocker. "Would you hold him? I think he could use a buddy."

She nodded, a faint smile touching her lips as she gathered the little dog into her lap.

One of the Strike guys broke away and sauntered toward us. I groaned internally. Of course it was Brady Chancellor.

His eyes flicked over the four of us. "Anybody here need medical attention?" he asked. Genuine concern clouded his face.

"We've got one case of mild magic exhaustion, but otherwise we're okay," I said.

He nodded and then turned to rejoin his team.

I was just beginning to wonder if we should make our getaway, when a regular police car pulled to a stop nose-to-nose with my truck. The lights were on, but there was no siren.

The doors winged out, and two officers emerged. They walked past us toward the back, quickly checked the base of the gargoyle with their flashlights, and then turned the beams on us.

"Who's the owner of this vehicle?" asked the one with beefy arms and dark brown skin.

I stepped away from Roxanne and squinted in the light trained on me. "I am," I said, suddenly feeling sure that I didn't want to be the owner of the vehicle.

Beefcake reached for his cuffs and came at me. "Ma'am, you're under arrest for possession of stolen property."

I dropped my head back and groaned up into the night sky. The guys were protesting, speaking over each other, but I knew it would do no good. Cool metal rings laced with anti-magic threads clicked around my wrists, and Beefcake packed me into the back of the patrol car as he read me my rights.

I searched the uniformed Strike members, looking for the guy who'd been staring at the gargoyle during his team's operation. Instead of calling Supernatural Crimes when he'd spotted the statue, he must have called the regular police. Or maybe he'd contacted someone at Gregori directly. Regardless, it appeared that Jacob had at least one friend on Strike, and probably at least a few in the police force. I fumed and silently cursed his name all the way to the station.

Gregori had dropped the charges by the time we'd reached the station, and I was back home an hour later, but Jacob's men had claimed the gargoyle in the meantime. Our bargaining chip was gone.

Deb had shown up at the house while I was gone, and we'd spoken for a few minutes in my bedroom. She was still pissed at Keith, apparently.

I let Deb take my room, and I lay next to Roxanne on the foldout bed with Loki snoozing at our feet, the TV flickering in the dark room. The arch-demon and the possession had really shaken her, and she didn't want to be alone. She'd fallen asleep an hour ago, but I was still awake, caught in that state of over-exhaustion where your body longs to slip into unconsciousness but your mind won't allow it.

The events of the evening spun through my head and kept snagging on the moment when I'd touched the gargoyle. I'd replayed it dozens of times, slowing at the point when I'd seemed to look through the gargoyle's eyes and saw myself. My insides twisted as I forced myself to return to the painfully obvious implication—I hadn't seen through the gargoyle's eyes, but through the eyes of the demon that had possessed the gargoyle. The statue had been warm with demonic energy. And from what little I'd learned about the skittish stone creatures, it surely would have flown away under its own power long before we arrived, if it had been able. Gargoyles commonly hid atop tall buildings in their stone forms during the day, but at night they flew and hunted. A Gregori gargoyle was somehow altered to attract a demon and then once possessed trap the demon by turning to stone.

So. I had looked through the eyes of a demon. The only people able to do such things were necromancers. The mere idea that I could possibly have anything in common with Philip Zarella made me want to pull my own skin off.

But I couldn't help wondering: did Zarella have necro-vision like mine? Did he see random images in dreams, like I did? And the million-dollar question . . . did Zarella know how to control the vision to seek out something specific, or *someone* specific? That's what I needed to do—discover how to control the necro-vision to find Evan.

I nearly snorted a wry laugh. *Necro-vision.* Like my brief death had turned me into some kind of superhero, a character from Roxanne's comic books.

I closed my eyes, wanting sleep and more images of my brother. I lay there for several minutes, still wide awake and thinking about Nathan and Roxanne. It didn't take a PhD in psychology to see that my desire to help them was driven at least partly by my own past and my need to save my brother.

Evan had begun slipping away from me early, at least it had felt that way. He'd always been a quirky little kid, often lost and playing in his own made-up games or coming up with off-the-wall observations about the world that made me and Mom laugh. But around the time he turned twelve, he started to withdraw. His magical aptitude developed—he was a high Level I—and that just seemed to make him even more reticent. By the time Grandma Barbara passed, when Evan was thirteen, he was already experimenting with drugs. I'd been trying to deal with our grandmother's rapidly failing health, money problems, and finishing high school. I knew Evan was sliding headlong down a dangerous path, but he seemed determined to self-destruct regardless of anything I tried to do to pull him back. It had all happened so quickly, and he'd seemed to slip through my grasp like smoke.

I needed to find him.

My breath was coming slower, and weariness was beginning to claim me. But before I drifted off, a thought bubbled up. My efforts to save Nathan had so far fallen short, and I realized I needed to enlist stronger forces. We'd intended to use the gargoyle to expose Gregori through the media, but I thought of something even better: Rafael St. James. No one could whip up outcry over injustice more effectively than he could. I wasn't sure how quickly he could act, but first thing in the morning I'd get in touch with him.

Sleep finally came, but it was dreamless.

I woke to Roxanne bending over me with her hand on my forearm.

"Ella," she said. "I'm leaving now. I have a babysitting job today. Will you text me and tell me what's going on with Nathan?"

"Of course." I pushed up onto one elbow, passing the back of my hand over my eyes as I tried to sharpen my mind through the haze of sleep-brain. "Do you need a ride?"

She shook her head. "No, that's okay. It's only a few blocks away, so I'll walk."

"Okay, text me so I know whether you'll be home for dinner."

We stared at each other for a moment and then both busted up.

"Will do, *Mom*," she said with that adolescent edge to her voice, but she shot me a grateful smile as she slipped out the front door.

I flopped back and stretched, tempted to try to get another thirty minutes of sleep but knowing it wouldn't happen. I had too much I needed to do, and first and foremost was to get hold of Raf.

I scooped up my phone and sent him a text, saying that I had an urgent humanitarian situation and needed his help.

The bedroom door swung open, and I turned my head and watched Deb emerge, looking fairly rested, all things considered. But her eyes narrowed as she came and stood over me, holding up the remnants of a candle in one hand and pinching a piece of paper between the thumb and forefinger of the other.

"What are these?" she demanded, and jiggled the paper. "I told you to see a hedge witch to get something medicinal for your insomnia, not buy a sleeping spell."

My eyes popped wide as I recognized the sheet for the spell I'd purchased on Crystal Ball Lane. For a moment my mind raced, searching for an excuse, a story I could feed her. I sat up and raked my fingers through my hair. No story. I needed to come clean.

"You'd better sit down," I said.

She did so, placing the spell items in her lap and looking at me expectantly.

Then I told her everything. I described the shadows that had appeared after my accident, the dreams, the visions, and what had happened the night I used the spell.

The color drained from her face. "The thing that's . . . *with* you now, it took you to the fenced-off house on Sixteenth? Six-thirty-seven North Sixteenth?"

"I don't remember the address, but yeah that's probably about right. Why?"

"It used to be a foster home, lots of kids went through that house." She clasped her hands together and pulled them into her chest where her fingers twitched in nervous little movements on the fluorite stone she wore on a chain, a subconscious gesture she often made when unwanted memories of her childhood surfaced. "I lived there for a little while. There was a fire. Kids died."

I swallowed hard. Silence thickened in the room for several seconds, and I heard the bathroom faucet drip with tiny, measured *plinks.*

"So those *were* ghosts I saw," I finally said. Necro-vision was seeming more and more apt.

"Sounds like it." She shook her head as if trying to jar loose some thoughts. "But that's not important right now. You need help, Ella."

The *other* had been drawn to ghosts, the wandering souls of the dead that hadn't been put to rest. It had its own desires, but

I didn't yet know the exact nature of them. Something told me I needed to learn what they were if I wanted it to cooperate with my search for Evan.

I scrubbed my hands down the sides of my face. "Yeah, I guess. At first I thought I wanted to get rid of the thing, the *other*, but after the visions of Evan I just want to figure out a way to use it so I can find him."

She grabbed my wrist, gripping it with surprising strength. "No. You need to have it extracted, exorcised, whatever. It's dangerous. I don't know how I missed it before." Her eyes roved the air around me. "I guess I was too preoccupied with my own crap, but now that I'm paying attention . . . this is bad, this thing clinging to you. I don't know what it is, but you've got to get rid of it ASAP."

I pulled my wrist out of her grasp. "I *can't*, Deb. It knows where Evan is. It somehow sees him. I'm not getting rid of it until I find my brother. I don't care if it kills me." I spoke with such ferocity, my voice cracked.

We stared at each other for a long moment, and she finally nodded. "You have to let me take you to someone who might be able to tell you what it is. Will you agree to that, at least?"

"Yes," I said. I pushed myself up from the sofa bed, eager to leave the topic behind. My phone chirped, giving me an excuse to pick it up.

It was a message from Raf saying he was going to Eats and Java soon, a coffee house a few blocks away from my apartment, and he could meet me there or talk after.

I quickly filled Deb in on my idea to involve Raf. "Up for some coffee and eggs?" I asked.

"Absolutely." She quirked a smile at me, but I could tell by the intent look in her eyes that she was worrying about my condition.

We got dressed and headed out. A pleasant sense of normalcy washed over me as we walked to Eats and Java. I filled her in on my communication with Raf. A glance around told me we'd beaten Raf, and by the time our food arrived he still hadn't shown. While we sat at one of the outside tables with our drinks and omelets, Keith tried to call Deb about ten times. She ignored all of them and finally shut off her phone, and I started to wonder if she might actually be serious about leaving him.

During a pause in our conversation, I looked up and spotted Raf heading our way, holding the hand of a willowy brunette with dewy skin and trendy side-swept short bangs. His usual entourage of do-gooders followed—guys wearing beanies even though it was almost eighty degrees out and fresh-faced girls who looked like they'd just hiked a mountain.

He caught my eye and flipped the fingers of his free hand in a little wave. He said something to his girl, and she and the rest of the group continued on toward the front entrance of Eats and Java. The girl half-turned and shot him a lazy lidded smile, and then slinked away with a loose-limbed model's stride. I was about her height and build, but I couldn't pull off that walk if my life depended on it. I'd look like a drunken giraffe if I tried.

I pushed my chair back and stood up. "I'll be right back," I said to Deb.

"What's up?" Raf asked.

I took a deep breath, and then gave him the Reader's Digest version of our situation with Roxanne's brother and Gregori. I left out the part about being Jacob Gregori's niece. Raf's face registered some surprise when I described the gargoyles. His arrow-straight brows lowered as I spoke, until he was practically scowling.

"As far as I can tell, Gregori is committing any number of atrocities," I said, trying to wrap it up. "What they're doing to gargoyles, using them as bait for demon possession, is tantamount to torture. And Roxanne's brother, Nathan, has been trapped inside a gargoyle, most likely demon-possessed himself, for days now. I wanted to talk to you to see whether you have any contacts who could help us free Nathan and shed light on what Gregori is doing with the gargoyles. At the very least, we need to get Nathan out of there fast."

His lips pressed into a grim line, bringing out his dimples. He pulled his phone from his hip pocket. "You're right, Gregori is violating the rights of the gargoyles as well as holding a human prisoner against his will. Atrocity is definitely the word," he said, giving me that intense gaze. "I'm going to need a day or so to coordinate some things. I'll be in touch soon, okay?"

I tried not to look too relieved. I hadn't really wanted Raf's contacts. I'd hoped he would want to jump in himself. As I watched him, I remembered how Damien had identified Raf as a shifter, but I still couldn't wrap my mind around it. Pack animal shifters, as most of them were, tended to keep to themselves and spend most of their time in tight communities on the outskirts of cities or deep in the wilderness. And they all had an indescribable but unmistakable wildness to their eyes. He just didn't fit the profile. But then, until recently I didn't know it was possible for a gargoyle, human, and demon to get into a three-way possession, so who was I to say what was impossible?

I grabbed his forearm in both of mine. "Thank you so much, Raf."

He nodded and pulled out his phone, already swiping the screen with short strokes of his finger.

"I'll be in touch," he whispered to me, with his mouth away from his phone. He gave me one last look and then put his phone to his ear and started walking toward the coffee house door.

This humanitarian, champion of the underdog stuff was what Raf was famous for, and getting him on board for our cause was huge. Monumental. I straightened, feeling a grin spread across my face. I probably looked like a moron, but I didn't care.

I returned to the table where Deb sat holding her mug—herbal tea, as she'd decided to give up coffee while she was pregnant—and I sank into my chair.

"You look elated," she said, laughing.

"I kinda am elated."

"Why? You meeting up with him tonight after he sends Twiggy home?" She brought her mug up to take a sip, but not before I caught her wicked little grin.

"*No.*" I shot her an irritated look. "That was eons ago. I'm just really glad he's agreed to help us."

"I want in, too," she said. "Promise you'll include me in whatever you're doing?"

"Of course!" I narrowed my eyes and tried not to chuckle. "You got a thing for Raf, Deb?"

She scoffed. "Who doesn't? But seriously, he's your type, not mine. And you're clearly more his type than I am."

"He's not my type," I protested. "That was just a brief little opportunistic nothing. It lasted, what, a week?"

"Um, yeah, exactly." She stared at me wide-eyed, as if I were missing something stupid-obvious. "Flashy, hot guy. Short term. It's the Ella Grey special."

"But, no, that's not . . . my . . ." I trailed off into a frown.

Brady Chancellor. Flashy, check. Hot, check. Less than two months, check. Raf was basically the same, though not an asshole like Brady, and there had been a couple of other short dalliances in between Brady and Raf. And recently those little flutters over Johnny . . .

I slouched low and groaned, and Deb threw back her head and laughed.

"Seriously? You really didn't know that was your thing?" she asked. Her eyes sparked with a bit of amusement, but I knew she actually cared about my answer.

The death glare I aimed at her didn't do a thing to curb her mirth. "Go ahead," I growled. "Get it out of your system."

She giggled another fifteen seconds. "Okay, I'm done."

I planted my elbows on the table and propped my chin on my knuckles. "I know how dumb it sounds, but it's actually not how I thought of myself. I don't know, in my mind I thought I was attracted to guys who were . . . more subtle and refined? More private? I don't know why I thought that. I'm clearly an idiot without a shred of self-awareness."

Deb chewed her bottom lip, and her face turned serious as she tilted her gaze down at the table top. She scratched at an old coffee stain with her thumbnail. "You're not an idiot . . . I'd say most of us think of ourselves as making better decisions, or maybe just different ones, than we actually do." Her hand snuck down to briefly rest over her belly.

We both went quiet for a few seconds.

"Are you going to stay at my place tonight?" I asked.

"Is that okay?"

"Absolutely, stay as long as you need to. Hell, let's go get all your shit and move you in."

She snorted.

"Seriously, if you're ready I'll go with you to pick up your stuff."

"No." She gave a tiny sigh. "Not yet."

I knew better than to push her right now. She became so fragile in sadness, I had to allow her to work through some of it, wait until her sadness became infused with a little anger before I tried to press her about leaving Keith.

"Hey, you promised me something, don't think I've forgotten." She pulled out her phone and powered it on. "I'm gonna find someone who can examine you ASAP."

I grumbled deep in my throat. "Ugh. Fine. Let's get it over with."

Despite my sullen response, I curled the fingers of one hand into a loose fist and tapped my knuckles nervously against my lips as I watched Deb sitting across from me with her hair falling forward in a curtain as she bent over her phone.

"Okay." Deb looked up and set her phone on the table. "My friend Jennifer is a witch who has an affinity for death-related stuff."

"Wait," I interrupted her. "Let me guess. She practices dark-edge magic?"

She blinked a few times, and then nodded. "I'm surprised you know that term."

"I heard it recently for the first time."

I peered at her from under hooded lids, suddenly wondering if she knew a lot of dark-edge witches. I never would have pegged Deb for the type to be interested in that sort of thing. She'd hadn't ever mentioned it to me, at least. But then, I didn't pay a whole lot of attention to the witch and coven stuff.

She looked down at her phone. "She says we can come over to her place now."

We booth stood and stacked our silverware, mugs, and crumpled paper napkins on our plates and shuttled them to the cart stacked with tubs for dirty dishes.

"What are her rates?" I asked, already dreading how much cash I'd need to pull from an ATM. I wasn't terribly eager to shell out more of my hard-earned money for help of the magical variety, seeing as how well the sleeping beauty spell had gone.

"She won't charge us," Deb said.

We started off at a brisk clip back toward my place.

"Really?" I eyed her again. "She must be a pretty good friend.

Either that or she owes you."

Deb slid a look at me and then shifted her gaze ahead. "She's part of a group I'm in. A few of us are making a bid for the same coven, and we decided banding together and presenting ourselves as a cohesive package of skills and women who work well together might help our odds. We've gotten to know each other fairly well."

I let a couple of seconds of silence pass. I trusted Deb not to dabble in anything dangerous, but a tiny warning was pinging at the back of my mind. "Are there other dark-edge witches in your group?"

She shrugged with nonchalance that I saw right through. "A couple."

"Deb." I waited until she was looking at me. "Are you sure they're all safe? Good witches, no black magic?"

"They're good people, I swear. You'll see when you meet Jennifer, I think you'll like her."

I loved Deb, but I wasn't going to take her word for it about Jennifer or any other dark-edge witch. Sometimes Deb seemed to miss giant red flags in other people's behavior. Or maybe she was just too willing to overlook them, like with her husband. She wanted to think the best about people, and it was an endearing quality, but more than once it had led her to trust the wrong person.

Her phone jangled, and she glanced down at it. From the expression on her face, I figured it had to be Keith.

"You're gonna have to talk to him at some point," I said quietly. "Even if he's an ass, he's still your husband."

She made a face. "Yeah, yeah." It looked like she was deleting a string of texts from Keith.

"Maybe you should at least text him so he knows you're okay."
I could hardly believe I was saying anything that made me sound
like Keith's advocate—believe me, I'd never been a fan—but part of
me wanted Deb to face the situation and either find a way to work
it out or make the decision to leave.

She hummed a noise of assent, quickly tapped out a message,
and then shoved her phone in the back pocket of her cutoff shorts.

My place felt strangely quiet when we went in my apartment.
Loki hopped off the foldout bed to greet us, and I let him out into
the back yard while Deb used the restroom. I was tempted to
check in with Roxanne via text, but didn't want to *seem* like I was
checking in. Instead, I snapped a picture of Loki in the yard and
sent it to her.

*He misses his buddy! I think he's been sleeping on your pillow
all day.*

Roxanne sent back a smiley face, and then a message: *These
kids are turds. I think I need a raise.*

I replied: *LOL*

Deb came out looking green. "Do you have any gum?"

"Yeah, in the junk drawer, I'll get you some. Morning sickness?"

She blew out a long breath. "I guess so. I don't puke that much.
I just spend like half the day feeling on the verge of it, which is
almost worse. Minty things seem to settle my stomach a little."

I let Loki in and then locked the back door while I was in the
kitchen getting Deb's gum. When I returned to the living room
she was slumped on the blue leather ottoman. I scrunched up my

mouth in sympathy and passed her an unopened dollar store pack of spearmint.

"Do you need to rest before we go to Jennifer's?"

She shook her head. "If I rest every time I feel nauseous, I'll spend the whole day lying around."

Deb drove us in her old blue Honda Civic with her phone plugged into the stereo and playing indie rock from the 90s at high volume. She often went through phases of listening to a certain era of music for months at a time. The AC didn't work, so we rode with the windows down and our hair whipping around us, giving me flashbacks of when we were in high school and Deb had just bought the used Honda, which she'd named Deep Blue.

I hadn't thought to ask where Jennifer lived, but when Deb headed west on Hill Road, a thought struck me.

"Is Jennifer a vampire?" I asked.

She glanced at me. "Yeah. She lives in Sunshine Valley."

There was a large neighborhood nestled against the foothills where a vampire community had grown. I'd only been there once before and remembered that the immediate surrounding area was desert, which gave it a sense of isolation even though it was only minutes from a couple of main thoroughfares.

I squinted up at the hills to my right, trying to wrap my mind around the idea of a vampire witch.

"I've never heard of a vampire joining a witches' coven," I finally said, my voice raised to carry over the music. "I don't think I've ever heard of a vampire with magical aptitude, actually."

"I don't think there are many of them, and I suspect the few crafting vampires out there just keep their ability to themselves." She let out a little exhalation and reached over to the stereo console to turn down the volume. "I don't blame them at all."

"Yeah, me either. Just one more thing for the anti-vamp groups to latch onto. Your friend is brave."

"Well, she's not exactly taking out an ad in the Statesman to announce her magical ability or coven bid. It's not secret, but it's not something she really wants spread around."

"Gotcha." Maybe Deb was right about Jennifer. I had to at least give her credit for being a pioneer. If she got into a coven, I assumed she'd be the first of her kind to do so.

I gave Deb a sidelong look, considering both her and her bid for a coven in a new light. My friend had aligned herself with a vampire witch. That took some guts.

"Now I get why she has an affinity for death-related stuff," I said.

Deb flipped me a wry nod.

Vampires were considered a species of undead, like zombies. The VAMP2 virus killed the human body, and then it reanimated in its vampire form. Unlike zombies, which didn't retain any of their former memories, skills, or personalities, vampire minds were preserved and they brought with them everything their minds had held and experienced in their human lives. The classification of "undead" basically required two things: reanimation after physical death, and subsequent physiology that was markedly different than human physiology.

My heart seemed to stop for a moment.

I met the first criterion.

As my stomach began a slow twisting tumble, I rubbed my palms up and down the tops of my thighs a few times. "This should be interesting," I whispered to myself.

By the time we passed under the arch that welcomed us to
Sunshine Valley, the sun was high in the sky, and I guessed the
temperature was over 80 degrees. I wasn't just sweating from
the late summer heat and the twenty-minute drive without AC,
though. Anticipation churned rhythmically around in my gut like
the agitator of a washing machine.

At first glance, the sprawling subdivision looked like many
of the others in the area. There were SUVs parked in driveways,
teenagers on bikes, and a pickup game of basketball was in
progress at neighborhood's park. But a closer look revealed that
everyone here possessed the ethereal glow of vampirism. In an
odd sort of irony, the VAMP2 virus that killed them gave them
smooth, flawless skin that was ageless. Literally ageless. Whatever
age the human was when infected with VAMP2 was the age he or
she remained forever, in appearance at least. In what was perhaps
a merciful turn of nature and magic, children under the age of
fifteen or so never survived the virus to come back as vampires.
Occasionally VAMP2 killed older teenagers and adults as well, but
it was unusual.

The ones who did survive the virus were essentially immortal,
invulnerable to human diseases and the breakdown of old age.

The ugly and violent period following the Rip had, unfortunately, shown exactly what methods were required to end a vampire's existence permanently. Docile vampires could be killed only by silver poisoning, a stab through the heart with any type of wood or wood-laced object, or beheading. Wild vampires—those without implants—could be killed by those methods in addition to sunlight.

Deb steered through the residential streets and then pulled over to the curb in front of a one-story starter home with a neat yard and upgraded finishes. She killed the engine, and I saw the curtains stir in one of the windows.

When we were partway up the front walk, the door opened and a vampire with shining brown eyes greeted us. Jennifer was barely over five feet, with slim legs, a generous chest, and some extra weight around her torso—no, not all vampires were model thin and perfect looking, contrary to what certain movies and TV shows portrayed. But she did have that incredible skin and the magnetism that was a weak, implant-dulled manifestation of vampire glamor. She smiled at Deb and pulled her into a quick hug and then turned her attention to me.

"You must be Ella." Jennifer held out her hand.

I grasped it, the coolness of her skin almost stone-like against mine. The shadows edging my vision stirred as if a sudden wind had disturbed them.

"Thank you for making time to see us," I said. As soon as I let go of her hand, the swirling in my periphery settled.

"Are you kidding? I'm thrilled to help Deb. And what little she told me has me curious as shit about you." She gave a throaty little cackle. Her face lit up when she spoke, and she moved her hands in little animated gestures. There was faint evidence of an upper East Coast accent, which piqued my curiosity. Could she be one of the early generations of post-Rip vampires?

I grinned, already warming up to the vampire witch.

"Do you live alone?" I asked, taking a quick look around.

The living room was cozy, with a handmade afghan thrown across the back of an overstuffed sofa, a cheerful variety of plants lining the narrow table under the front window, and a basket heaped with yarn and a couple of half-finished knitting projects next to a worn leather La-Z-Boy that faced the TV. A side table held a messy stack of trashy gossip magazines.

"Yup, bachelorette bitch, that's me." Jennifer moved farther into the room. "Can I offer you some iced tea? I still drink it all the time, out of habit."

"Sure, that sounds great," Deb said, and I nodded in agreement.

"Have a seat, make yourselves comfortable." Our host disappeared into the kitchen, and a moment later I heard the sounds of ice cubes clinking into glasses.

As I sank down onto the sofa, I started to relax. This wasn't at all how I'd pictured the abode of a dark-edge vampire-witch. Jennifer seemed like any young single woman in her first home. I didn't even see any evidence of her devotion to witchcraft.

Jennifer brought in a little tray with three tall, slim glasses of iced tea and some packets of sweetener. I passed on the artificial stuff and drank mine straight.

We chitchatted for a couple of minutes about how we knew each other. Deb and Jennifer had met through a mutual witch friend about a year back. The vampire witch had indeed come from the East Coast, though she didn't specify when. It could have been a couple of years ago or a couple of decades ago. That was the thing with vampires, you couldn't tell how long ago they'd turned. There was speculation that very old vampires would eventually develop distinguishing characteristics, and there were a few whack jobs out there who claimed to have seen VAMP1 vampires—the secretive vamps of legends that had originated in the Old World, who would have been hundreds of years old by now if any still survived—but the VAMP2 population that was reborn after the Rip was too young to have any aged vamps.

During a little pause in the conversation, Jennifer gave one of her thighs a slap. "Well! Shall we see what we can discover about Ella's predicament?"

"Sure," Deb said. She smiled, but I read apprehension in her eyes.

My mouth had gone a little dry, so I just nodded.

The vampire witch stood, and Deb and I followed suit.

"I've got a witchy area set up in the spare bedroom," Jennifer said. We followed her past the TV to a short hallway, and into a dark room.

My eyes began to adjust, and I saw there was a pagan altar set up on a trunk along the north wall. Blackout curtains were drawn over the single window. There was the scrape of a struck match and then a little flame, and I watched as Jennifer lit the two candles on the altar and then struck a second match for the three pillar jars that stood on a corner table. The light reflected off a couple of smoked glass mirrors that were propped against the walls at a right angle to each other.

She turned to us, shaking the match to extinguish it. "I'm going to cast a circle with Ella sitting in the middle facing me. Deb, you can sit in the circle behind her if you like, just take care not to disturb anything I weave. And fair warning to both of you, grave magic is chilly business, so get ready to cut glass with your—well, you know how the saying goes."

I snorted a laugh, but the term "grave magic" was ringing around in my head like a bell's toll echoing off the hills. Jennifer opened a narrow door and pulled three cushions out of the closet. She set them up in a north-south line on the floor. I settled cross-legged on the middle one with the altar in front of me and watched as she gathered a few items, including one of the mirrors.

"Ella, grave magic is different than regular magic," Jennifer said. "You have to pass through a gateway to access it. I don't know what form that will take for you—it's a fairly personal thing. For me, it's usually jumping off a cliff. Imaginary, of course. It'll probably be something you'll want to resist. Just be prepared to take some sort of leap, so to speak."

"Just go for it, got it," I said.

I heard Deb sit down behind me and took some comfort in her presence. I was confident Jennifer wouldn't harm me. My apprehension stemmed from a certainty that the next few minutes would reveal answers to my questions, and you know what they say about being careful what you ask for? I smoothed my damp palms along my cargo shorts and took a slow breath.

Stillness seemed to settle over the room like a morning mist, and I watched Jennifer's back as she stood facing her altar. She was whispering to herself, but I couldn't quite make out the words. Then, she turned and began moving clockwise from the altar. In her right hand she held a crystal wand—a white stone, selenite, perhaps. She pointed it at the ground, tracing a magical circle as she recited a casting spell. I suddenly realized I hadn't sensed her level of magical aptitude. I still couldn't, and I wondered if she had some sort of powerful obfuscation spell that masked her abilities, or if being a vamp made them invisible. She was casting a circle that glowed as a faint magenta trace, a color of magic I'd never witnessed.

When she made her way back around to the altar and completed the circle, the air seemed to pressurize slightly, pushing against my eardrums. She turned, and I sucked in a sharp breath as I took in the two glowing points of her irises. Her eyes illuminated with the same purple-pink light of her circle.

My pulse ratcheted up as she lowered herself to the cushion in front of me. She mirrored my posture, crossing her legs, and our knees were only inches from each other. Her breathing slowed as her casting trance deepened, and her gaze seemed to go right through me.

Goosebumps raised along my skin, rippling over me in a wave, and I realized the air in the room was growing chillier by the second. Not only was it cold, it felt heavy, as if we were deep underground. I clamped my arms to my sides to keep from shivering too obviously. The sensations in the room intensified, and I fought to keep still, focusing on the lights in the vampire witch's eyes and realizing too late that I probably should have asked her what she intended and what she expected to happen.

I began to sink into my own trance, my eyes unfocused, and my body settled into the cold until it felt oddly comfortable. Almost without trying, I felt my own magic begin to rise from the earth. For a split second I tensed, thinking to push it away, but then decided to let it flow. Jennifer was probably powerful enough to block it if she needed to.

She took a breath, and I expectantly returned my focus to her face.

"Elements of nature, I invite your presence and power," she intoned. "Lift the veil to reveal the truest, deepest essence of your child, Ella Grey."

I expected more—some of Deb's spells and incantations were fairly long—but instead of continuing, Jennifer reached for the smoked glass mirror and lifted it, positioning it between our faces.

The candles in the room flared, and my entire body went rigid as I gazed into the mirror. Panic set off a spike of adrenaline as I realized I couldn't move, not even to blink. I expected the *other* to take over, but it didn't, and after a moment my alarm began to subside. I could see the lights of Jennifer's eyes through the mirror—it was a glass, actually—in addition to my own reflection.

The image in the mirror was shifting, my features morphing and moving as if reflected on a watery surface. As I watched, I realized with relief that I could move under my own power again. My face dissolved as the glass went dark.

A small blue flame appeared in the center of the glass, just one dancing point, but then it began to bleed outward in all directions. As it spread beyond the edges of the glass, a burning cold hit my skin. It hurt like the searing press of ice and the sensation grew as the flames seemed to wrap around and engulf me. My pulse quickened. This must be the gateway. The pain intensified, and my eyes darted around, looking for a way through. I knew I was still sitting on a cushion on Jennifer's floor, but I was also somehow standing in the middle of an ice-cold inferno.

The flames were pressing inward, and the air was growing thin as they consumed the oxygen. I glanced up, but the flames covered me. I let my eyes close, pulled in a breath, and propelled myself forward. The icy-hot pain flared and then snuffed out.

I looked around, and I was back in the center of Jennifer's circle, with the glass between me and the vampire witch. I stared into it, and something new began to clarify. I recognized my own eyes, but the rest . . . that face was not mine, I knew it even though it was partially obscured by a hood. It was like looking at a hologram. The face in the glass was hollow and skull-like one moment and then resolved to my own features the next. It shimmered back and forth a few times and then settled on the skull with my own eyes overlaid. My mouth dropped open as I gazed, and my breath puffed white in the cold. I tilted my head slightly, and the skull moved with me.

In that second, my own body, my *self* seemed to evaporate,

leaving only the empty skull reflected in the glass. I gasped, jerking back, as a sudden, horrifying sense of loss and confusion rushed through me, torrential and dark. It wasn't so much what I saw but what I felt, and it terrified me. Ella was gone, and only a yawning, endless chasm of timeless space between worlds remained. I squeezed my eyes closed and pushed my fists to my temples, but felt only the dry scratch of bone on bone and the realization that I *couldn't* close my eyes because there were no lids to cover them. I shook my head violently, and the room swung around in my vision and then blurred.

"Ella."

A gentle hand touched my arm. I opened my eyes, blinking a few times, and felt a rush of gratitude that indeed I had working eyelids again. Thankful for eyelids. That was a new one.

Jennifer was leaning toward me, her pupils normal again and reflecting the warm candlelight.

"Ella, focus on the floor beneath you," she said. "Ground yourself."

I flattened my palms on the carpet and visualized my anxiety and the memory of what I'd seen flowing down, into the earth where it was safely absorbed. After a few seconds, I could breathe normally.

Jennifer stood. "I'm going to open the circle. Just focus on your breath."

She said a few quick words to close the spell and moved counterclockwise to dissolve the circle she'd cast. The air around me began to lose its chill. I brushed my hands up and down my bare arms and filled my lungs slowly.

She went to the wall and turned on the overhead light, keeping it dimmed low, and then went around the room extinguishing the candles with a little metal bell-shaped flame tamper. She pulled her cushion around to form a triangle between the three of us and sat down on it.

I swallowed hard and looked at her expectantly.

"I saw the same thing you saw in the glass," she said. "It looks like you've got a spare soul tethered to you."

I blinked several times and flicked a quick glance at Deb, but she looked as mystified as I felt.

"Like a ghost?" I asked. "Am I permanently haunted?"

I didn't bother trying to hide my look of horror, and Jennifer cracked a smile.

"No, it's not a ghost, it's a *soul*." She watched me patiently, allowing it to sink in.

I scrubbed one hand down the side of my face. "Okay, I don't know what that means."

"Every person has a soul. Every living being, actually, though animal souls are a bit different than human ones, and plant souls are different still. I believe that in the course of your accident, another soul somehow got snagged onto you."

I squinted at her. "How does that explain all the weird things that have happened? And my two-toned necro-vision?"

Her face tightened, and for the first time I sensed some apprehension. "I'm fairly certain it's not a human soul."

My brows shot up, but I just stared at her without a clue how to respond. Then a dreadful thought occurred to me. "Please tell me it's not a demon soul," I rasped, my throat suddenly dry.

She shook her head firmly. "No, it's not a demon."

I slumped in relief and let out a breath. "Okay, so what are the other possibilities?"

"Vampire or zombie, in theory. But I know what those look like, and that's not what I saw. There's another possibility I'm aware of. Another creature of death, but an extraordinarily powerful one, and one that didn't begin life as a human like vampires and zombies do." She hesitated and moistened her lips, and then her words came slowly, almost reluctantly. "It . . . could be an angel of death. I've never seen the soul of one, so I don't know for sure."

My lips parted and for a moment I couldn't speak. "A reaper?" I whispered.

A faint smile ghosted across her lips, and she nodded. "That's another term for angel of death."

"I think that's what it is." I found I felt no real surprise at her confirmation. After all, she wasn't the first to tell me.

"It looks like you now have some new talents as a result of this extra soul. Necromancer-related, which aligns with some of the things you've experienced. Very rare, as I'm sure you know." Jennifer bit her lower lip, and then took a heavy breath. "You need to have it exorcised or cut loose. Reaped from your being. I'm not sure what the right term is. But a reaper won't be content to just ride along as a passenger in your life."

"Yeah, no shit." I gave a short, humorless laugh. "It's taken the wheel a few times already."

Instead of mirroring my amusement, her face grew deadly serious. My chest clenched as if bracing against what was coming.

"There's something else I saw," she said. "Ella, it's already started consuming your soul. If you don't get rid of it, you'll, well, *disappear*. In the most profound and permanent sense of the word."

Deb let out a little sound of dismay, and I glanced over at her. She had her fingertips pressed to her lips, and her blue eyes were starting to well up. She gave a little sigh and dropped her hands to her lap.

"You'll keep this confidential?" I asked Jennifer. "What you saw and what we're talking about?"

"Of course," she said. "But this is incredibly serious, and you need to do something as soon as possible. Deb and I can put you in touch with someone who—"

"I appreciate the gravity of what you're saying," I cut in, my voice low. "Believe me, I do. But I can't cut this spare soul loose. Not yet, anyway. I—I need it."

I gave her some brief background on my brother and then told her about how I'd seen him through the necro-vision.

"You have a talent for magic in this area, and you're obviously powerful," I said. "Is there anything you can do, a spell or charm or something, that might slow down what the reaper is doing to me? I'll pay you, I'd be glad to. Whatever it takes."

"I'm not sure if I can do it, but I'll try. It'll take me some time. I need to consult with more experienced crafters and do some research. Do I have your permission to talk about what we've learned? I won't use your name."

I gave the vampire witch a nod.

She turned a hard look on me. "But in the meantime, I want you to promise you'll reconsider. There's no way to tell how fast the reaper's soul might consume yours. For all we know, it may reach a tipping point where it gains the upper hand, and then suddenly you're done for. It could happen tomorrow or next week or a year from now. There's no way to predict it, and no guarantee of time enough to find your brother or to come up with protective magic if there is any. There are people in your life who care about you and don't want anything bad to happen to you. And Ella, if the reaper claims your soul there will be nothing for your brother to come back to."

My defenses prickled at what she was implying, that keeping the reaper around and using the necro-vision to try to find Evan wasn't worth the danger. But Jennifer was clearly a woman who called things as she saw them, and it was a quality I appreciated. She was trying to help, and she didn't have to do it.

I nodded. "I understand, and I promise I'll think about it." I swallowed hard, not daring to look at Deb for fear of what I'd see on her face, and more so how I'd feel when I saw it. "Thank you so much for everything. Deb is lucky to have a friend like you, and I'm glad we got the chance to meet."

I slowly unfolded my legs and began to rise. I didn't want to seem rude, but I needed to escape, to be alone to try to process what I'd learned.

Deb and Jennifer followed my lead.

I dug into a pocket of my cargo shorts and pulled out a slim foldover wallet that held my I.D., bank card, credit card, and some cash. "I want to give you a down payment on the work you're doing for me."

Jennifer held up her hand and shook her head. "I'm not taking your money. Not today. If I can come up with something that'll help, I'll clean you out, though."

I stared at her for a beat before I realized she was joking, and I managed to crack a shaky grin. "Fair enough." I shoved my wallet back into my pocket.

Deb didn't smile, and in my periphery she was too still. I ticked a glance her way. She looked stricken, staring past us at nothing. The tightness in my chest began to transform into a dull ache of guilt. Deb didn't need this burden, not right now when she was in the midst of her own crisis. I silently cursed myself for being the cause of more stress in her life.

Jennifer saw us to the door, and Deb and I trudged out to her Honda. Once we were in the car and buckled in, she just sat there with the keys in her hand.

"Do you want me to drive?" I asked gently.

She shook her head, but didn't move to start the car. She just stared straight ahead through the windshield.

"I know what you're thinking. I know you're feeling guilty that all of this . . . this angel of death stuff is putting more stress on me," she said. "But it's okay. Really, it is, because the alternative is that you'd be dead. You wouldn't have come back after your accident, and I'd be visiting your grave. I'd be pregnant and struggling with my marriage and unsure about what to do next, and I'd have to do it all without you. I'd rather have you here with a ticking time bomb leeching your soul than dead. Because you're not going to die again, Ella, we're simply not going to allow that to happen. This reaper thing *is not going to kill you.*"

She spoke with such intensity, her voice broke just about the time a tear welled over the lower lid of my right eye and slid down my cheek. The emotion snagging in my throat wasn't about me or my strange predicament. It was more about the reversal of our roles—Deb trying to reassure me instead of the other way around—and the unexpected strength and determination she was radiating.

She turned to me with a piercing look, but all I could do was nod.

Then to my great relief, she started the car. I rolled down the passenger window and closed my eyes as the hot early evening breeze blasted my face and swept away the last remnants of the chill left by Jennifer's grave magic.

Back at home, I let Loki out into the yard and then got in my truck, leaving Deb to wait for Roxanne to return from babysitting. Without exchanging a word, Deb understood that I needed a few minutes to myself. In spite of her brave words in the car, I could feel her worried attention like a spotlight trained on me.

When I stuck the key in the truck's ignition, there was a thump behind me. I twisted around to see Loki through the rear window.

"Aw, don't tell me you can jump over the fence." I narrowed my eyes, trying to look disapproving, but I couldn't help grinning back at him. I sent Deb a quick text to let her know he was coming with me.

I headed past my precinct, where the lot was full of cars belonging to the Demon Patrol officers on shift. East of downtown, I took a street that angled past the military reserve and up into some older Foothills neighborhoods. It was still a few hours before sunset, but the shadows were beginning to stretch eastward away from the lowering sun, highlighting and deepening the muted grays, taupes, and sages of the summer-baked hills. On a winding road that sloped gently upward, I made my way toward Tablerock, a mesa that overlooked the city.

The paved road ended, and I crunched onto a steeper dirt road.

Tablerock was a notorious hangout spot for teenagers, but this early in the evening I had the road to myself and there were only two other cars at the top. I parked and got out, and perspiration prickled my body. Up here with no cover, the sun was relentless.

Loki hopped out and trotted alongside as I angled away from the other people enjoying the view. I walked to the edge of the rocky plateau and took in the trees, streets, and buildings that filled the valley below. Here and there, the river revealed itself as a twinkling ribbon stretching westward. A faint brownish haze hung in a stripe that layered low across the blue sky parallel to the horizon, evidence of smoke from summer forest fires.

As always happened when I came up here, some of my tension began to melt away. I took a slow breath, wondering where Evan was and why he'd never tried to contact me. I'd always assumed it was because he was dead or lost in the haze of addiction, but . . . We hadn't been on the best terms when he'd disappeared. I'd been trying to get him into a rehab program, and he'd stubbornly refused all help. Maybe he didn't want to speak to me, just didn't want me to be part of his life. I pushed the thought away before the familiar ache could take hold of my heart.

Whether Evan was dead or alive, whether he ever wanted to see me again or not, I was risking my life to find him, and I'd never stop until I had answers. Or the angel of death claimed me, whichever came first.

I reached for Loki and scratched between his ears. "You scared the reaper away that night when I was spellbound. I don't suppose you know how to keep it at bay until I find Evan?" I looked down at him and he panted up at me, his pupils glinting maroon.

It was a chance I had to take. Evan was my brother, and it was my choice to leave the reaper soul right where it was. I pressed the fingers of one hand against my chest, as if I might feel it in there. I needed to learn more, to figure out how to control it before it consumed me.

But right at this moment there was a different fight to lead. I needed to focus on Roxanne's brother. I went back to my truck, got in, and pulled out my phone as Loki thunked onto the bed. Suddenly antsy to check in with Raf, I felt compelled to urge things along. Not just for Nathan's sake. I was now in a race against the reaper, and I wanted to see things through with Roxanne and her brother.

He answered on the first ring.

"Hi, it's Ella," I said. My gaze went out the front windshield to the view, but I had already pulled my focus inward to the future.

"Ella, good news," Raf said. "I've got the Global Supernatural Humanitarian Organization on board, as well as the World Human Protection Federation."

I nearly let out a whoop. "Advocates for both the gargoyle and the human involved—that's *perfect*. My only concern is how fast we can move on it."

"GSHO is sending in a representative, and she'll arrive on an early flight tomorrow morning. They're accustomed to swift interventions. I've worked with Human Protection in the past, and they're willing to let us appoint a local proxy. I want to move in on Gregori tomorrow."

"You're a miracle worker, Raf. You've gotta let me take the lead on something. What can I do to smooth things along?"

"Could we meet up in a half hour?"

I turned the key to start the truck. "Absolutely. Do you remember where I live?"

"Sure do." I could hear his faint smile as his voice warmed a notch.

"Come by whenever you're ready."

I arrived home to an empty house. Roxanne was still babysitting, and Deb had gone off somewhere, maybe home. I quickly made my way around the living room, straightening pillows and clearing away a couple of glasses. I stood in the middle of the room, giving it one last assessing glance, and glanced through the front bay window as a small foreign car pulled to the curb. I wasn't sure what make the car was, but would have bet my paycheck it was one of those new ultra-environmental European vehicles that ran solely on a magic-enhanced battery. It probably cost more than I made in a year.

I went to let Raf in, realizing too late that I probably should have folded up Roxanne's bed. He greeted me, and I could tell by the intensity in his pale green eyes that his mind was already jumping ahead to what we needed to accomplish. The hide-a-bed caught his eye, though.

"Houseguest," I said by way of explanation. "Let's go in the kitchen, we can use the table in there."

Remembering that he drank coffee at all hours of the day, I went to the electric brewer to start a new pot.

When I slid into the chair across from his, he'd already spread three tablets over the table. For the next hour or so, he sipped coffee and schooled me on the ins and outs of working with the two organizations he'd enlisted for our cause.

"So we'll have the GSHO agent," he said, pronouncing the acronym "gee-show." He sat back in the chair and gave me a penetrating look. "She's allowed two assistants, so we need people to do that, as well as two local proxies for Human Protection. Ideally, I'd like someone experienced with supernatural species as one of the assistants. And, one or two higher-level crafters would be good. Any ideas who to send in?"

I thought for a moment, my mind spinning. "Yeah. Actually, I think I can fill all four of those positions."

"How soon can you get them here?"

"Within two hours," I said automatically. I'd find a way.

He nodded with satisfaction and then glanced at his tablet to check the time. "Okay, I'm going to let my people know. Everyone will meet here at seven, if that's all right?"

"Let's do it." Purpose and anticipation charged through me.

I walked Raf to the door, my phone already in my hand. I sent a quick text to Damien and then dialed Johnny.

"Hey," I said when he answered. "You know that exorcist you called the night we went to Roxanne's?"

"Yeah, Lynnette."

"We're gonna need her to get Nathan out of Gregori's clutches. Any way you could sweet talk her into coming to my place at seven? We really, really need someone with her skills."

He chuckled. "Johnny's got your back, sugar."

I rolled my eyes but couldn't help a grin. "I need you to come too. I've got a job for you, if you're up for it."

"You know I am. Especially if it'll help Roxanne."

I let out a little breath of relief. Two down, now I just had to get Damien on board. "Awesome, thank you Johnny. See you soon."

By the time I ended the call, I had a response from Damien. I was surprised to see him hedging at my request that he act as one of the Human Protection proxies, but he agreed to come to the meeting. I'd have to wait until we were face-to-face to find out more about his reservations.

The next hour and a half passed in a blur as Roxanne arrived home from babysitting and Deb showed up too. We ate a hurried dinner and then cleaned up the place more thoroughly than I'd managed for Raf.

We had about twenty minutes before everyone would start arriving.

I watched Roxanne for a moment out of the corners of my eyes. She was curled up on the leather chair a few feet away from where Deb and I sat on the sofa. Deb had been checking her phone every few minutes, keeping tabs on social media, and found that Raf's press people were already making noise—posting articles and updates to draw eyes to our cause.

Roxanne's attention was glued to the TV, and her face had that slack look kids get when they're really absorbed in something. She was focused on some teenage reality show she'd found that I'd never heard of. She would see the online shit storm soon enough, it wasn't like I could hide that stuff from someone her age, but for some reason I wanted to give her just a few more minutes of peace. I'd considered sending her somewhere else while everyone gathered at my house but decided she deserved to know what was happening. And I wanted everyone involved to meet the girl who would be devastated if things went to hell, so there would be no abstraction in the events that followed.

I took one last look around, drawing a slow breath as I imagined my living room crowded with bodies. Things were about to get interesting.

Damien arrived first, followed by Johnny. I took both of them aside while Deb assumed my post at the door to greet people.

I led the guys back to the kitchen and gave them the very short version of what Raf had explained to me earlier.

"Because of the skills you each bring to the table, and your personal investment in Roxanne up to this point, I was hoping the two of you would act as the proxies for the Human Protection Federation," I said.

Johnny gave me a crisp nod. "I'm in."

I shot him a quick, grateful smile. We both turned to look at Damien.

"I truly want to help," he said slowly. "I just prefer to avoid anything that's going to put my name in lights." He shifted his weight, clearly uncomfortable.

I wasn't exactly sure why he was holding back, but suspected it had something to do with his family back East.

I chewed my lower lip for a second. "What if you went in as one of GSHO's agent assistants instead? It doesn't require the same paperwork as the other position. Oh, and maybe a low-level obfuscation spell to disguise your appearance a little?"

I really wanted Damien to be part of the party that would enter the Gregori grounds. He was the most powerful crafter I knew, and his presence would be extra insurance.

"Okay," Damien said, but I could tell he was still not completely at ease with the idea.

"Thank you, both of you," I said. "We're gonna get some more info from Raf soon. I should get back out there."

I caught Johnny's arm, holding him back as Damien turned to the living room.

"Did you bring your toys?" I asked Johnny.

"Yeah."

"Could you scan something for me later?"

Curiosity lit in his dark eyes. "Of course."

I nodded my thanks.

A steady stream of people trickled in, with Raf arriving somewhere in the middle. I recognized some of his regular crew, but there was no sign of the willowy girl who'd been with him at the coffee shop. Maybe she was just arm candy.

As more people came through, I did my best to keep track of names. At ten after seven, I went to the door to find a young woman around my age with black hair and glinting blue eyes. In spite of the temperature, she was dressed in imitation leather pants. The edge of one ear was lined with three little hoop earrings, and there was a tiny diamond stud on one side of her nose. She wore shiny black Doc Martens that laced partway up her shins. When she lifted her hand in greeting, her finger flashed with a silver sculpted ring that featured a tiny skull with pink crystals in the eye sockets. She gave me a smile that I could only describe as smoldering.

"Lynnette Leblanc. Are you Ella?" Magic hung around her like a sensuous perfume, and the strength of it indicated she was probably a mid-Level III, second only to Damien among the people gathered. I stood several inches taller than her, but the power she exuded gave her the presence of a much larger stature.

"Yeah, Ella Grey." I swung the door wider. "Please, come on in."

Her eyes flicked down once, passing over me as she walked in, and somehow that one split-second look seemed to take in everything. She was the exorcist Johnny had mentioned that first night at Roxanne's apartment. The shadows swirled a little in my periphery, as if interested in Lynette's arrival.

She waited for me to close the door. When her black-lined eyes met mine she still seemed to be evaluating me, but I thought I saw a flash of approval. "Johnny has mentioned you several times. It's good to finally meet you."

"You, too," I said, still a little dazed by her appearance. Her alt-goth getup might have looked overdone on someone else, but she gave it a surprising and unmistakable elegance. "Thank you for coming. I know this is really short notice and probably an odd request from someone you just met, but would you be willing to go onto the Gregori campus to perform an exorcism?" I shot a glance over my shoulder and then lowered my voice. "They're going to make this sound like a humanitarian inspection, but I intend to make it a rescue mission."

I hadn't actually told anyone that I wasn't planning to leave

Gregori without Nathan. Raf's setup was for humanitarian purposes, and he was hoping that with the media exposure and public pressure Gregori would release Nathan and the gargoyle. I wanted to take it a step further.

Her eyes lit with interest. "Johnny told me about the boy stuck in the gargoyle. A three species tangle, interesting case." She paused and gave me a long considering look. "All right. I'll do the exorcism on site. I usually charge for this sort of thing, but we can work out some sort of trade instead."

"Yeah, absolutely," I said, relief tingling through me. I had no idea what I could offer her, but I'd figure it out later. "That's really generous of you."

My phone was buzzing and chirping furiously in my pocket, and she glanced down at it, lifting one brow.

I pulled it out. "Uh, excuse me, I'd better check that."

There were a bunch of messages from Deb.

YOU DIDN'T TELL ME YOU KNEW LYNNETTE LEBLANC!!!

The next text was a row of surprised-looking emojis.

How could you not tell me?

More emojis, including an angry face.

You have to put in a good word! PLEASE.

Another smattering of emojis.

I looked up and caught Deb's eyes on me. Her brows were halfway up her forehead, and she was giving me a look that seemed to alternate between excitement and agitation. I made my way through the little knots of people, the largest crowd my apartment had ever seen, to where she stood. She grabbed one of my upper arms and squeezed it, making a little squeaking noise in the back of her throat.

"I don't know her," I said, keeping my voice low. "We've never met before. I swear."

"It's *her* coven," Deb said.

I gave her a sidelong, confused look.

She rolled her eyes and huffed with impatience. "Lynnette owns the charter for the coven I'm trying to get into. She's the one of the most powerful witches in the Northwest, and the youngest ever to be granted a charter."

"Well, now's your chance," I said. I gave her a little push toward where Lynnette and Johnny stood. "Go talk her up!"

"You're right," she said, her eyes narrowing with determination. She squared her shoulders and beelined for Lynnette.

I trailed after, catching Johnny's eye when Deb began to monopolize Lynnette's attention.

He broke away from Deb and the exorcist witch and joined me near the wall.

"Hey, thank you for being here," I said.

His teeth flashed in a smile, and I felt his fingertips brush the small of my back, which sent a ripple through me. "Of course, I wouldn't miss it," he said. "What is it you want me to check out?"

Out of the corner of my eye, I saw Raf had separated himself from the group, and the room was starting to quiet down.

"After," I whispered. I went to join him.

Everyone found a place to sit—several on the floor—except Johnny who remained standing against the wall.

Raf grinned and looked around the room, seeming to give every person a brief moment of eye contact. He rubbed his hands together briskly.

"Let's get down to business," he said. "First, I want to acknowledge Ella Grey, our host for the evening, and the woman who contacted me and alerted me to a gargoyle and a young man who desperately need our help."

He nodded at me, and heads swiveled my way. A few people clapped, and one of Raf's beanie-wearing guys whooped. I lifted my hand in acknowledgment.

"Next, Roxanne Harrington, the sister of the young man Gregori is holding."

Wedged between Deb and Damien on the floor, Roxanne sat cross-legged, twirling a strand of her pale blond hair around her finger. She smiled shyly up at Raf.

"Okay." Raf's face turned serious, his pale green eyes intent. "I'm in touch with the Global Supernatural Humanitarian Organization. As most of you probably know, their inspectors typically get involved in humanitarian missions involving vampires to help shed light on violations of their rights. But their activities extend to other species as well, you just don't hear about those as often. If the organization's governing body decides there's a threat against or possibility of mistreatment of any intelligent, supernatural being or group, by international law GSHO inspectors must be allowed entry to investigate. That means Jacob Gregori will be required to let our inspector in to see the gargoyle."

An excited murmur swept through the room, and I felt myself

getting caught up in the anticipation. For once, Gregori would have to submit to an outside authority.

"The other half of the equation is Nathan Harrington, who is presumably demon possessed and trapped inside the gargoyle. For Nathan we're also bringing in the World Human Protection Federation. GSHO protects supernaturals from abuse by humans, and WHP Fed gets involved when a human gets unduly caught up with a supernatural." He pronounced the abbreviated form of the organization's name as "whip-fed," with an ease that indicated it was probably commonly known as such. "So, we've got it covered both ways. Human Protection doesn't have the sway that GSHO has, but GSHO has agreed to take on WHP Fed's proxies as part of their party that will enter Gregori Industries. And we'll make sure there's plenty of media coverage."

A devious grin spread over Raf's face, and a few people gave low appreciative laughs.

"The inspector will arrive early tomorrow morning, and we're going to move in on Gregori immediately after," Raf continued. "We'll have the GSHO agent plus four others appointed by Ella who will enter the Gregori campus."

I took half a step forward, my eyes flicking to Lynnette. I hadn't had a chance to fully explain everything to her. She'd already agreed to do the exorcism, but now that she had more details, I hoped she was still on board. Her impassive, sultry expression didn't give me much to go on.

"Damien Stein, Johnny Beemer, and Lynnette Leblanc have generously agreed to do this," I said, pointing out each of them.

"And I'll round out the group myself. Among us we'll have a variety of special skills that I think perfectly meet the needs of the mission."

I avoided looking at Raf, not wanting him to read anything in my face that might indicate I had my own plan for the expedition to Gregori Industries. To my relief, when I flicked him a glance, he gave me a look of approval and then returned his attention to the group.

"Can they film it?" one of the women sitting on the floor asked.

"That'll be up to Gregori's discretion, and as such I'm guessing the answer will be no," Raf said. "There's nothing in the international accords that gives the GSHO the right to take live video during inspections."

I had no doubt he knew the international supernatural protection and humanitarian law backward and forward. He cast another look around the room, and I got the sense he was about to wrap things up.

"Those of you who've worked with me before know what to do," he said. "Social media, news stations, your journalist contacts, just do what you do best. If you have questions, Anthony is the primary contact on this and should be able to help you." Raf pointed at the beanie guy sitting closest to the door. "We're one step closer to exposing Gregori's mistreatment of gargoyles and bringing Nathan Harrington home."

He nodded firmly, winked at Roxanne, and then moved off to the side. Everyone took his cue and stood, and the din of conversation soon filled the room. Raising his chin to see over heads, Raf caught my eye and pointed at the back of the room, indicating he wanted me to meet him in the kitchen.

"I'll wait, find me later," Johnny said as I passed by him. He touched my hip with a light brush of his fingertips and then melted into the crowd.

"Thanks," I said.

Even though there was an open doorway between the kitchen and living room, it was substantially quieter away from where everyone was gathered. Raf entered and then turned and beckoned me off to the side near the stove where we were out of sight.

"This is incredible," I said. The way he'd mobilized the whole thing with such rapid efficiency left a deep impression. "Thank you again for taking on the cause."

"It's what we do," he said, with a brief smile that crinkled the outer corners of his eyes. He flipped a glance toward the open doorway. "How well do you know Lynnette Leblanc?"

"I don't. She's a friend of a friend, and tonight is the first time we've met. Why?"

"She's extremely powerful. She can also be quite persuasive. Be careful what you agree to, she has a way of using phrasing and subtle magic to bind people in conversation. Her magical talent is partly centered in spoken words, more so than the usual witch." He lifted a hand to push a lock of dark hair off his forehead. "Not that I think you really have cause to worry. She'll be focused on the task at hand, and she's a valuable ally to have."

"Thanks for the tip," I said, recalling that she'd asked for a trade instead of payment and I'd agreed without a second of thought. I'd felt an odd tingle at the time. She must have used a power word or two, and I just hadn't recognized them in the moment. I had no idea what she'd ask of me later, but I couldn't waste time worrying about it now.

The sound of Deb's laughter carried over the conversation in the living room, and suddenly I felt a ping of apprehension at her obsession with joining Lynnette's coven. I wished I'd paid more attention and asked some questions when Deb had talked about the exorcist witch. I needed to understand what Deb was seeking and why it was so important to her to be associated with Lynnette.

"You'll get a text from me later tonight with tomorrow's timeline," Raf said, back to his focused intensity and the mission at hand. "It may change by morning, so keep an eye out for updates."

"Will do, and thank you again," I said.

Raf headed toward the front door. His gang had mostly dispersed, probably to go make noise on social media and rouse their journalist contacts. Damien still sat next to Roxanne, and it looked like they were playing some sort of game on her phone. Johnny and Deb were straightening the room and putting things back in place. I watched for a moment, feeling an odd mix of affection, protectiveness, and the urge to sneak into my bedroom, lock the door, and sit in solitude until someone forced me to come out. But this was *my* crew, and I couldn't disappear just because having so many people around gave me a permanent case of the willies. They wanted to help Roxanne, but ultimately they were here because I'd persuaded them to get involved. Or they'd unwittingly gotten sucked in, like Damien.

Damien glanced up and noticed me lurking. "Hey, I want to show you how to do something. A new skill you can take with you tomorrow."

He tried for a smile, but his face was too tight. A nervous little bolt of adrenaline sharpened my senses and amped up my pulse. Right, tomorrow. When I'd be walking into the lion's den to take away the lion's favorite new toy.

I swallowed. "Sure, what do you have in mind?"

"We'll need your whip," he said.

Roxanne perked up, her phone momentarily forgotten as she glanced back and forth between me and Damien.

I went into my bedroom to retrieve the whip, letting the coils unfurl when I returned to the living room. A satisfying zing of magical energy hummed from the handle, into my palm, and up my arm. It made my insides tingle with the desire to reach into the earth and pull more magic, a sensation that was both foreign and delicious. I tended to use my magic as little as possible—my low aptitude meant I couldn't really rely on it for anything useful, and I'd put almost no effort into honing what little ability I had. Plus, there was always a vague sense of inadequacy whenever I wielded it. When most of the crafters around me could do the equivalent of magical backflips, or at least a really nice cartwheel or two, and I could barely manage to hop on one foot, well . . . my experiences with my personal magic were disappointing at best. The only time I'd ever been truly grateful for my paltry ability was when I decided to sign up for Demon Patrol, because magical aptitude was a requirement to join.

Damien beckoned me over to the area near the front bay window, where there was no furniture.

"I want you to know how to cast a circle with the whip. Casting that way will give you more power than you'd have normally," he said, taking on a professorial tone. "And eventually when you get good with the whip you'll be able to do it in the blink of an eye. The faster you can close a circle, the faster you're protected."

A circle was actually a type of protective ward. It was the first type of ward crafters were taught. My mother had shown me how to cast a circle, and I could manage it if I had to, but it had been a long time since I'd done it.

Johnny and Deb had stopped what they were doing, and they both stood near the kitchen doorway watching us. Great, an audience. Deb crossed her arms and cocked her head as she looked at the whip in my hand, and then a Cheshire grin spread over her face. I hadn't mentioned Damien's gift to her, and I could tell she was dying to grill me about it. She'd be stoked that I had a magical object. She used to encourage me to take more interest in developing my ability, but had just about given up in the past year or so.

"Ohh, it's charmed," Roxanne said in a cooing voice. Her eyes grew glassy and unfocused. "And it's charged, too. And Damien's signature is on it."

"You can *see* that it's charmed and charged? And you can tell who did it?" Deb asked, leaning forward at the waist and peering at Roxanne.

The girl nodded, her eyes flicking around at our faces as if she were suddenly afraid she'd done something wrong. Deb and Damien traded a look, and I got the sense that whatever Deb had discovered about Roxanne's abilities was of great interest to serious magic users. I wasn't sure what it meant. In fact, I couldn't even define the difference between charming an object and charging it. My mother had probably explained it to me at some point—she was my mentor when my magical aptitude came forth—but most of her teachings had faded in my memory. It was like calculus. I'd known it at some point, but damned if I could remember many of the details now. The dull weight of regret over my failure to take my mom's lessons to heart settled on my upper chest. I took a breath and tried to shake off my musings.

"Center yourself and call up your magic," Damien instructed.

I moistened my lips and tried to block out all the sets of eyes trained on me. I rarely summoned magic in front of someone else, let alone a group. I couldn't even remember the last time I'd cast a circle. But the magic-infused object in my hand made me feel more powerful, more attuned to magic than I ever had before.

I let my eyelids fall closed and extended my awareness downward, imagining myself as a tree with roots extending deep into the earth. Every cell in my body seemed to wake up as magic flowed through me like a conduit. As if aware of the object I held, the magic streamed up to my right shoulder and down my arm.

"Now use the whip to mark a circle around yourself," Damien said.

I opened my eyes just as he was moving clear of the whip's reach. Raising my hand, I whirled it like a lasso, with only enough momentum to carry it in a cone around me. Apparently it was too much—instead of tracing a stationary ring, magic flung off the end in little green sparks, like water flying from a wild hose. The sparks ticked loudly against whatever they hit but didn't cause any harm. At the end of the arc, the whip grabbed the curtain that was pushed over to the right of the bay window.

I grumbled and went to pull the fabric free. "How do I get the circle to stay put?" I asked.

"Instead of letting the magic fly free, keep control of it all the way down. Guide it, indicate where you want it to go. It's yours to wield, and it'll do what you tell it to do." Damien said it as if it were all quite obvious. Maybe it was to someone who had more than a spoonful of aptitude or training.

I tried again, with basically the same result.

He stepped forward. "Here, let's go outside where the dark will show the traces better."

I ticked a look at Johnny, and he winked at me and then hurdled over the back of the sofa to sit down next to Roxanne. Apparently he was willing to wait until my lesson with Damien was finished.

Deb remained inside, too, and I welcomed the cover of darkness with relief.

Damien reached for the whip, his face cut in planes by the weak light coming through the kitchen window. His brows were drawn low in concentration.

"Watch," he said.

His hand began to glow as if a pale green flame engulfed it, and the magic coiled down the length of the whip. With an easy swing of his arm, he twirled the whip around his head like I'd done inside, except instead of flying out in all directions,. his magic seemed to fall off the end of the whip and hover in a waist-high ring around him.

"You can set the circle on the ground or in mid-air," he said. "One isn't really easier than the other, but since you're more familiar with earth magic, try the ground one. Oh, and picture where you want the magic to land first. See the circle around you in your mind as a ring magnetized to magic, or a wire that will absorb and conduct magical energy."

"Ah," I said. The visual helped a lot. He passed the whip back to me.

I did as he instructed, visualizing the line of a circle formed of dry, flammable tinder that could only be lit by magical energy. Then I centered and called up earth magic. Without opening my eyes, I raised my right arm and circled my hand. When I heard the crack of the whip, I winced—too fast. My eyes popped open, and I expected to see magic splattered like paint around the yard. But instead, I stood in the center of a glowing ring. It was already fading, though. I thought I'd failed, so I hadn't bothered trying to keep the circle in place.

"Nice!" Damien said with approval brightening his voice. He strode toward me, his phone in his hand, and stood next to me. "You've already got the hang of it. Take a look."

He tapped his phone's screen. He'd videoed my attempt, and I was glad he did because what I saw wasn't what I would have expected. He put the video on a loop—it was only a few seconds long—and we watched it in silence a few times. Instead of swinging out straight, the whip seemed to coil in the space around me, tracing a much tighter circle than if it had flown free.

"See? It's like you're pulling it through water," Damien said, his voice charged with enthusiasm. "It stays close to your body because you're controlling it with magic instead of allowing the natural physics of momentum to make it flare wide."

I nodded and felt a slow grin break across my face. "It helps if I don't look while I'm doing it," I said.

"That's a good thing to know about your ability," he said, clearly excited about this development. "Most crafters can't work much beyond the context of their physical surroundings. If you're able to wield more effectively with your eyes closed, it means there's a strong visualization element to your ability." He turned to look me in the face. He his eyes were wide, but I wasn't sure what he was getting at.

I gave a little shrug. "Uh, okay?"

"That's awesome, Ella," he said. "It means you're not reliant on the reality that surrounds you. You can use your imagination to aid your craft. Believe me, it's a prized skill, and not one that's easily taught."

I snorted a laugh. "I don't see how you could know that after just one little demonstration."

"Trust me, I'm right. The way you wielded completely changed on that last one. It was the first time I've seen you do it with any kind of ease. You need to trust yourself more. And you need to practice. A *lot*. Push yourself and do it every day, and you'll be surprised how adept you can become."

"I don't have time to practice before we have to go to Gregori," I said. My stomach knotted as the next day's plans rushed back to the forefront of my mind.

"No, but now you know what it feels like. Do it a dozen more times before you go to bed tonight, and you might be able to make use of it if you have to tomorrow," Damien said. "And after, start a daily practice."

"Okay," I said, surprised to find myself agreeing to any sort of magical practice. Deb would pee herself with delight. "Thank you for showing me, and for this." I lifted the handle of the whip. "You're a really good teacher."

He shoved both hands in the front pockets of his jeans. "It's no problem at all." He tilted his head and looked at the ground, seeming embarrassed by my gratitude.

"I think I'll head home," he said after a beat of silence. "Big day tomorrow."

"You sure you're okay with being involved?" I asked.

"Yeah, I'm sure it'll all work out."

Inside, Roxanne had changed for bed and folded out the sofa, and she was lying on her side with her book spread beside her, with Loki taking up half the bed next to her. His tail thumped a couple of times when he saw me. The sound of Deb in the shower came from behind the closed bathroom door.

Johnny was sitting on the blue leather chair, his cheek propped against his fist as he flipped through messages on his phone. His arm was partially flexed, emphasizing the solid roundness of his bicep. His hair was just long enough to show some natural curl, and a dark C-shaped strand hooked over his ear. I blinked hard, mentally smacking myself. I really needed to get a grip. Just then he looked up and flashed me a smile, and I willed my cheeks not to flush.

Pushing to his feet, he grabbed the handle of the black case next to him. He must have run out to his car for his instruments while I was in the back yard with Damien. He glanced at Roxanne, who was thoroughly absorbed in her book, and then tipped his head toward the kitchen. I nodded, and we went through the doorway and over to the table, where he laid the case. But instead of opening it, he turned to me.

"So what is it you need examined?" He arched a brow, and a smile tugged at the corner of his mouth.

"Nothing that requires the removal of any clothing, so don't get excited." I shot him a withering look, feeling some relief at knowing we could still keep up our usual banter. "But I was wondering if you could use your supernatural X-ray thingy to, um, see what registers when you turn it on me."

His lips parted as his usual come-hither expression seemed to slide of his face, replaced by something I couldn't quite identify. He blinked a couple of times. "Are you in some kind of trouble, Ella?"

With a mirthless little laugh, I propped my hands on my hips and tilted my gaze downward. "A bit, yeah."

I looked up at him, and our eyes locked for a long moment. Then he turned and flipped the latches on the case and pulled out the tablet he'd used on the gargoyle that first night at Roxanne's.

When it powered on, it illuminated Johnny's face with the pale blue light of its screen. He tapped it a few times, glanced at me, and then trained his attention on the instrument. His eyebrows drew together, and a vertical crease formed between them.

My heart pattered nervously, and my chest felt tight. "What? What do you see?"

I tried to come around next to him to get a look, but he turned slightly, keeping it out of my view.

"Johnny, what is it?" I asked, expecting him to say that he detected two entities—me and the Reaper—similar to what he'd seen with the gargoyle.

He squinted at the screen, staring at it as if expecting it to say something else. "You . . . you're not entirely human, Ella."

When Johnny finally raised his eyes to mine and I saw the stricken look on his face, my heart stuttered in my chest.

Swallowing back the sour sensation of my stomach dropping straight through the floor, I grabbed one of the handles of Johnny's tablet and yanked it over so I could get a look at it. But of course I had no idea how to interpret what I saw. There was a grid with a bunch of numbers, plus one of those heat-map-type pictures.

"Where does it say I'm not human?" I demanded.

"You're human, but you're something else, too." He pointed to an area of the colored image, which looked like a blurry, misshapen, multi-colored hologram of me from the waist up. Then his finger moved over to the grid of numbers. "It's—I want to say it's something of an angelic nature, but it's not quite that. It's much too dark. It's almost like a cross between an angel and a zombie, with something else thrown in."

I took a deep breath, trying to settle the churning bile in my stomach. "Angel of death, maybe?"

He lowered the tablet and looked at me, still except for his eyes roving my face.

"Maybe," he said quietly. Pulling back a couple of steps, he held up the tablet. "Let me get a full-length image. It might help the numbers fall out a little more clearly."

I stood still while he snapped another picture. He absently reached for the nearest chair with one hand, pulled it out, and sat down. I dragged the other one next to him. Shoulder-to-shoulder, we stared at the screen. The numbers in the chart flickered and changed, and then after a moment they seemed to settle into their final values.

"I'm not really sure how to interpret this partial human aspect of the data." He swiped the screen to scroll down the chart.

"I need to know how much." I licked my dry lips. "What percentage of me is still human?"

"Sixty-seven percent." He set the tablet down and angled his body toward me, with one arm resting on the back of his chair and the other on the table. We were sitting so close together, his knee pressed against mine. His gaze was searching my face again. "You wanted me to confirm something you already know. Something that has you scared."

I pressed my lips together, trying to steel myself but feeling dazed and off-kilter. "A reaper's soul latched onto me when I died. Now it's trying to consume me. Apparently it could eat up my soul at any moment, and then *poof*! No more Ella Grey. Like, at all. My soul would cease to exist."

I made a sound that was something partway between a squeak and a sigh. I pushed one hand into my hair, surprised to find my fingers were trembling. I couldn't seem to catch my breath. For some reason Johnny's readings drove home my predicament in a new way. He was right, he was essentially confirming something

I already knew, but something about seeing it on the screen and hearing him say it brought it into a whole new level of reality.

Johnny grasped both my wrists, pulling my hands together in between his. "Hey. Look at me."

His voice sounded like it was coming down a long tube, like the cardboard ones in the middle of a roll of Christmas wrapping paper. Evan used to beg me to have sword fights with them when we were kids. We'd whack at each other, with me holding back to make the match more even, until one of our tubes buckled.

"Ella."

The firm pressure of Johnny's hands around mine finally brought me back. I focused on his face.

"You *died* and *came back*. You've survived this long with that thing riding around on your soul," he said. "You're going to make it long enough to figure out how to cut it loose. I'm sure there's a way, there's got to be."

I closed my eyes and slowly shook my head. "I can't get rid of it. I need it."

I gave him the short version of what happened to Evan, and why I wanted to keep the reaper around.

Johnny was silent, his jaw muscles working and his mouth pinched into a tense pucker.

"No," he said, his voice stony.

I pulled my hands away from his and stood. "What do you mean, 'no'? It's not your choice."

He rose too, his eyes fiery. "There's no choice to make, here. You don't need to risk your soul. There are other ways to find your brother."

"Yeah, there are other ways, but you know what? It's been five goddamn years and none of those have panned out," I hissed, trying not to raise my voice and attract Roxanne's attention.

His hand whipped out to grasp my wrist, and he stomped toward the back door, pulling me along. I tried to twist out of his hold, but he squeezed harder. Once he had me outside, he pushed the door closed and let go of me and planted his hands on his hips.

"You feel guilty about your brother, and you think making this sacrifice will somehow ease your guilt."

My hands clenched into fists against my thighs, my pulse high on a surge of anger. "What the hell do *you* know about how I feel? You haven't been living with this every day!" I knew he didn't deserve to be yelled at, but I couldn't seem to hold back the tension that had been building up in my chest all day.

He stepped closer, getting in my face. "You're being stupid, and it's not worth it."

"I know I am, but I'm going to do it anyway. I have to," I said. I let out a long breath, not in the mood to try to further defend my choice.

"No, you don't."

"Yes, I do." I shoved my fingers into my hair, pushing it back off my forehead.

"I'll help you try to find him," he said. "I'm a private eye, Ella."

"Look, I really appreciate everything you've done, everything you're doing. Really, thank you. But I have to do this."

We were silent for a couple of breaths. He lowered his chin and looked at the ground and gave a slight, reluctant nod. I knew he wasn't going to let the argument go, though.

"Don't thank me yet. Your IOU list is getting pretty damn long." He cocked his head and lowered his eyelids partway.

I snorted. "Yeah, well, you better collect soon. I may not be around long enough to pay up."

He moved closer, and for one insane second I thought he was going to try to kiss me, but instead he leaned in and with his cheek close to mine and his lips at my ear, whispered, "Fair warning, I just might do that. Prepare yourself, sugar."

My breath caught for a split second. I couldn't help it. But I managed to recover, remove myself from his personal space, and punch him lightly on the upper arm. "Don't assume it'll be that easy, *sweet cheeks*."

Too late, I realized my mistake as a new fire lit in his eyes. I'd inadvertently issued a challenge. Oops. I exhaled a soft laugh and turned to go back inside. He followed a few feet behind me.

Inside, the lamp beside the sofa was out, and Roxanne was a still, curled-up lump under the covers. I'd thought she might have trouble sleeping, considering what we were planning the next day, but it looked as if she was already sound asleep.

"See you tomorrow," Johnny whispered.

"'Night," I said.

I waited for him to leave and then locked the front deadbolt.

A vertical line of light shone from my room through the cracked door. I pushed it open and found Deb sitting on the bed in girl-style plaid boxer shorts and a pink tank top, with her book of shadows—a notebook bound in cream-colored faux leather that was a sort of journal of the witchy part of her life—spread open on her lap.

She looked up, closed her notebook, and raised a brow at me. "Was Johnny showing you his toys?" she asked in a purr.

I tossed her a withering look as I unbuttoned my shorts and let them slide to the floor, grabbed some cutoff sweats from a drawer and put them on, and hopped up on the bed. "Actually, yeah he was." I grabbed the edge of the quilt folded on the end of the bed and pulled it over my legs.

Shifting over on her hip so she was facing me, Deb waited for me to say more.

"Apparently I'm no longer a hundred percent human. He picked up the *other*, the reaper, on his scanner thingy, though he wasn't sure what it was."

"How much did you tell him?" she asked quietly.

"Pretty much everything. He tried to talk me out of keeping it."

"You like him, don't you." She said it in a wry tone with a hint of accusation, and there was no upturn of a question at the end.

I sagged back against the pillow and pushed the heels of my palms over my closed eyes. "Not really. I mean, I appreciate all he's done, but he can be a bit of an asswipe."

"He probably finds you really frustrating," she said. "You haven't succumbed to his charms, and it offends his inner Don Juan."

"All the more reason to keep resisting," I said.

She laughed. "That's just going to make you more and more

attractive."

I groaned, and she closed her book of shadows.

"We can't really help who we're drawn to," she said, and reached to turn out the bedside lamp.

I thought of Keith and wanted to ask her whether she'd talked to him—in particular if she'd told him yet she was pregnant—but sleep claimed me before I could form the words.

The alarm on my phone burst through my slumber way too soon. I moaned in protest as I reached down to the floor for my shorts, pulled the device out of a pocket, and snoozed it for ten minutes. Despite the lack of adequate sleep, I was wide awake. Deb turned over to her back and stretched beside me.

I had a text from Raf.

Someone will be there to pick you up between 6:15 and 6:30.

"Morning," I said. Another groan for good measure, and then I swung my feet to the floor and went over to the closet and opened it.

"It's so early," she grumbled.

Neither of us were morning people. My workout was the only thing that really got me going—well, that and a big cup of coffee— and I was determined to get in a quick run before the day kicked into gear. I wasn't okayed yet for strenuous exercise, but I figured *screw it.* I had an angel of death eating my soul. An aneurism brought on by jogging was the least of my worries.

I flipped through some of the clothes hanging in the closet. "What does one wear to a gargoyle rescue mission, anyway?"

Deb gave a short laugh, and I turned to the dresser and pulled out a pair of light running tights, a workout top, and an old Demon Patrol Trainee sweatshirt. I got dressed and tiptoed through the living room in my running shoes, pulling my hair up into a ponytail as I went. I grabbed Loki's leash, and he dropped from the pullout bed to the floor and joined me near the door.

Outside, it was still dark. The sun wouldn't be up for another couple of hours, but I enjoyed the cool air as it whisked away any remaining grogginess left by sleep. Getting into a rhythm of breath and footfalls with Loki doing the same beside me, I headed toward Harrison Boulevard, a street of mostly large, upscale, historic homes. I zoned out and my mind stilled, but I had to cut the run short. The GSHO inspector would be landing at the airport soon, and after that Raf would mobilize us to Gregori Industries.

Back home, Deb and Roxanne were up, and the smell of bacon and coffee filled the apartment. I quickly showered and then got dressed, settling on gray pants that looked respectable enough but were an outdoorsy brand so they had some stretch to them, plus a long-sleeved navy henley. There was no need to look dressed up, I'd decided, when it was likely I'd be trying to hold off an arch-demon. I strapped on my service belt, and snapped the tightly-coiled whip next to my left hip.

Shit. I'd meant to practice with the whip last night. My stomach knotted.

"Hey Ella," Roxanne called. "Damien is here to give us a ride to Gregori."

Oh well, it was too late now.

I filled a mug with coffee but didn't take any food. I was too keyed-up and preoccupied with kicking myself for forgetting to practice circle casting.

I slid into the plush front passenger seat of Damien's Lexus, and Deb and Roxanne got into the back.

"Hello, ladies," he greeted us. "Big day, huh?"

"I can't wait to see Nathan," Roxanne said, her excitement evident.

Damien and I exchanged a glance.

"This is just an inspection, remember?" I said gently, twisting around to look at her. I intended to walk out of Gregori with Nathan, but she didn't know that, and I definitely couldn't make any guarantees. "But we hope it will prompt his release."

She nodded, her expression turning solemn. I felt bad for dampening her enthusiasm, but I wanted her to be prepared. The sobering truth was that I didn't even know for sure that Nathan would make it out of the ordeal alive. Exorcisms were tricky business, and though it sounded like I had the best in Lynnette Leblanc, I didn't know what condition Nathan was in. He'd been alive during my last trip to Gregori, but even the best exorcist couldn't do much if the victim was too weak to handle the separation.

My insides laced tighter and tighter the closer we got to the Gregori campus. Half a mile away from the main gate, I could already tell it would be a mob scene. Vehicles lined the usually quiet two-lane highway beyond the edge of town, and I could see police cars blocking one lane farther down. Damien pulled over to the side of the road.

"Raf wants us to wait here." He turned to me. "He's sending a car so the five of us going in will arrive together."

I pressed my lips together, nodding and taking a slow breath in through my nose.

A car pulled up behind ours, and I turned to see it was Johnny's Mustang. He got out and ambled up to Damien's side, and leaned down to rest his forearms on the window. "Fancy running into you folks out here. How's everyone feeling?" His eyes rested on me for an extra beat before he looked around at everyone else.

"Hopeful," Roxanne said.

I reached back to pat her knee. "Same here."

Johnny stuck his hand into the pocket of his leather jacket and pulled out an object. He held it up, and his gaze locked on mine. "I thought you might want this."

A grin spread across my face.

"What is it?" Roxanne asked.

"It's a demon trap," I said. Johnny had somehow procured a Strike-level canister. I'd brought a couple of brimstone burners on my belt, even though they'd be useless against a Rip spawn large enough for possession.

I reached across Damien to take Johnny's can. "I don't know how you got that thing, but you're a lifesaver." I noticed he also had a flat black foam case, the type that usually held a laptop or a tablet.

His fingers brushed mine, and his smile widened. "Not a problem."

He straightened, looked back, and then smacked his hand lightly on the top of the car. "Looks like our ride is here."

I turned around to peer down the road just as a long black sedan eased over to a stop behind the Mustang.

I wasn't expecting a limo. I gave a wry laugh. "I feel a little underdressed for prom."

Deb leaned forward to squeeze my shoulder. "See you soon."

Damien handed her the keys so she and Roxanne could drive to the front gate.

I swung the door open and stepped out, and just as I turned to head to the limo, a blond-headed blur ran around the back of the Lexus and crashed into me. Roxanne's thin arms squeezed my waist as she pressed the side of her face into my sternum.

"Thank you, Ella."

I hugged her for a long moment. "You're welcome."

She stood next to the Lexus, watching as Johnny, Damien, and I got into the sedan. I waved, and she waved back. I pulled the door closed, and the driver turned around to give me a little salute. I recognized him as one of Raf's beanie guys.

"Morning," I said, nodding to him and Lynnette Leblanc, who sat in the front passenger seat.

The woman next to me, dressed in an orange and gold sari, offered her hand. "I'm Mishti Gupta, representative of the Global Supernatural Humanitarian Organization," she said in a lilting Indian accent.

I clasped her hand. "Ella Grey. Welcome to Boise, Ms. Gupta. Thank you for coming."

She had no magical aptitude, which didn't surprise me. I vaguely recalled that GSHO inspectors were non-crafters, though the organization did have many magic users on staff and their governing body included vampires, mages, and sub-mage crafters.

We were already approaching the main entrance of the Gregori campus. A few police officers manned the crowd barricades set up to keep people off the road. Another officer beckoned us forward and indicated Raf's guy should turn onto the patch of asphalt in front of the gate.

On her lap, Mishti held a thick binder with a couple of file folders stacked on top of it. She lifted them and tucked them against her chest with one arm.

"Stay in the car while I issue the GSHO order," she said.

An officer appeared to open her door, and she stepped out. Media people were lined up behind barricades on both sides of us, and Mishti's appearance set off the cameras. A member of the Gregori security team, an authoritative ex-military type I didn't recognize from my previous visit, exited the guard house and came to stand on the other side of the fence, his expression stony. She went up to the gate and pulled a document from one of her folders. Our driver cracked the windows down a few inches so we could hear.

"By international treaty, the Global Supernatural Humanitarian Organization requests immediate entry onto the premises," she said in a voice strong enough for the nearby cameras to pick up. "By law, our request must be granted. Here is our order and my identification as an official of the organization."

The guard didn't make a move to let her in, so Mishti had to bend down and slide the documents under the inch or so of space beneath the gate. I flipped a glance over my shoulder. There were a *lot* of people crowded around.

The guard carried the documents back to the guard house, and I could see him talking on a phone. Mishti was steadfast, standing at the gate alone with her binder and folders in one arm, waiting. She'd likely been in much sketchier places around the world than Boise, Idaho on behalf of GSHO, but Gregori Industries was like its own dimension.

The military guy, trailed by three armed guards, emerged from the little house. He said something to Mishti. Our driver rolled down the passenger window the rest of the way as she came back to the car.

"They won't allow us to drive in," she said. "But they're opening the gate for the five of us."

I took a deep breath as Damien swung the door open, and I followed by his side. I quickly secured Johnny's demon trap to my belt. The four of us split, Damien and I standing to Mishti's left and Lynnette and Johnny on her right, facing the gate as it began to roll to one side. I caught Damien's nervous scan of the gathered crowd and how he tried to angle his face away from the cameras. The petite Indian woman glanced up at each of us and nodded and then stepped forward. I squared my shoulders and tried to think calming thoughts, but my pulse was thin and fast with anticipation.

Together, the five of us entered Gregori territory.

The gate closed behind us with a soft rattle, but in my mind somehow the noise was much larger.

A large golf cart appeared—one of the big ones that was more like a little open bus than a cart—and we were instructed to sit in the second and third rows. The guards with their big guns got on too, one in the front and two standing in the cargo area at the back. As during my previous visit, we were ushered into the squat building with the scanner and lockers.

"Leave your belt and its contents here, ma'am," one of the square-jaws, a guy with quads that strained his fatigues, said to me.

I shook my head. "Sorry, this stuff comes with me. The young man trapped in the gargoyle is possessed. We need protection in case the Rip spawn decides one of us looks more attractive."

Lynnette and I both knew the real plan was to free Nathan from the gargoyle and exorcise the demon possessing him, but that sort of thing was definitely outside GSHO's humanitarian inspections. The organization likely wouldn't have sent a representative if they knew my true intention was to use them to get us onto the Gregori campus.

"We have protective measures in place." The end of Square Jaw's automatic weapon had been pointed at the ground next to his feet. It raised a few inches, and I wasn't sure if he was trying to remind me that armed guards surrounded me and I didn't need additional protection or give me a not-so-subtle nudge to follow his orders. Maybe both.

I pointed at his gun. "Regular ammunition is no use against arch-demons. We have the right to protect ourselves. The only thing I'm carrying that could be used to harm a human, though not lethally, is my stun gun. I'm willing to leave it here." I unstrapped it and held it up with my fingers splayed wide, well away from the trigger. I turned it and presented it handle-out to him, hoping the offering would be enough.

He took it from me and gestured to my belt. "Leave the whip, too, and we have a deal."

My insides knotted as I handed over my whip. Maybe this was my karmic punishment for not practicing like Damien had told me to. At least I still had Johnny's demon can.

Johnny had to open his black case for their inspection, revealing that it held the souped-up tablet with the handles. His supernatural scanner, as I'd come to think of it. Square-jaw allowed Johnny to keep it on condition that he keep a little device plugged into it that would prevent Johnny from sending any data, and after our inspection Johnny had to allow them to make sure he didn't capture any video.

Once we'd all relinquished our phones and my weapons and passed through the scanner, we were escorted back out to the cart. Instead of the circuitous route Jacob had taken me, we went straight to the tall central building where the gargoyle was held.

The guards surrounded us and marched us inside, into the elevator, and up to the second floor—one of the windowless ones. Instead of the cell-like viewing room where Jacob had shown me the gargoyle, we were taken to the door of a much larger room positioned in the center of the floor. It reminded me of a surgery theater, as it was two stories high and there were windows up above as well as on our level.

A hard-faced woman with a tight gray-streaked bun waited for us with her hands clasped in front of her. She wore a white lab coat and an ID badge on a lanyard around her neck identifying her as Dr. Bonnie Smith. Jacob stood a bit behind her. He was flanked by two men in suits who had to be lawyers.

Jacob's eyes were so hard as they fell on me I could almost feel his gaze drilling against my skin. The clenching and releasing of his jaw muscles were the only outward signs of his agitation.

Mishti pulled some paperwork from one of her folders.

"We require access to all health information for this specimen. In addition, we require access to the specimen itself," she said. She handed the papers to Dr. Smith, who only gave them a cursory shuffle and glance before passing them to Jacob. Dr. Smith waited for him to scan through them, and then when he nodded at her, she turned to an oversized tablet mounted on the wall. With the touch of her index finger, she activated the tablet.

"Here you'll see the live readouts for vital signs and supernatural activity."

Mishti stepped up to the tablet, adjusting her glasses, and examined it. She pulled a notebook from under her folders and produced a pen from a pocket, and began writing.

Lynnette sidled closer to me and leaned in so she could whisper. "They're trying to shield it in that room, but I can feel the Rip spawn even out here. Large arch-demon. I hope you're quick with your trap. When I exorcise it from the boy, it's going to be looking for another victim, and it's going to be angry." Her deep blue eyes, emphasized by her pale skin and dark hair, took on an intensity that reminded me of Raf.

My heart lurched, but I raised my chin and gave her a steady look. "You do your job, and I'll do mine."

She grinned like a cat about to pounce on a mouse, and I realized she was actually enjoying this.

"Ever performed a separation on a gargoyle before?" I asked.

"No, but it shouldn't be a problem. Species separation is all about the same when you boil it down."

"Gotcha." Actually, I didn't really know exactly what she meant, but as long as she had the exorcism part of our mission under control, that was all I cared about. "Any sense about how Nathan's doing in there?"

"Alive, that's about all I can tell." She peered at me with her intense, kohl-lined eyes. "Have you ever considered joining a coven?"

I pulled my head back in surprise. "Me? Seriously?" I almost forgot to whisper.

She opened her mouth to respond, but Mishti seemed to have gotten all she needed form the panel readouts.

"Please let us in to inspect the specimen," she said to Dr. Smith.

The lady in the lab coat went to another panel next to the doorframe and palmed it. It flashed green and the door mechanism made a metallic thwacking noise.

"By international agreement, you have up to thirty minutes to perform your inspection." She reached for the door handle and gave us a slight smirk. "I'm assuming that you won't be taking the additional thirty minutes allowed for interviewing the human subject, seeing as how that would be impossible in his current state."

She opened the door and Mishti went in. For a split second, my urge to grab the doctor's bun and try to twist it off her head was almost uncontrollable. The sudden frantic movement of the shadows in my periphery helped distract me from any tempting violence. I clamped my teeth and drew in a breath through flared nostrils, forcing my focus to the task at hand. Lynnette, Johnny, Damien, and I followed Mishti, and the door closed behind us.

I grabbed Damien's arm and pulled him close. "Lynnette's going to do an exorcism," I whispered rapidly. "Sorry to spring this on you, but we need your magic."

I didn't have a chance to say more as Lynnette's magic flared through the air, rushing around me like a sudden gale. The smoky shapes framing my vision were stirring in response, flapping like windsocks in a storm.

"Door's locked and warded. They won't get in until I release the ward. I'm going to begin the separation in a few seconds," Lynnette said to me in a low voice. "Get her to back up." She flicked a glance ahead at Mishti.

Lynnette gave me one final look, and I nodded once, trying not to get distracted by the shadows and the pulse of the *other* in my forehead. Lynnette closed her eyes, focusing within.

Mishti hadn't noticed that Lynnette had stopped, and of course hadn't felt the magic Lynnette had used to ward the door. The small Indian woman had continued on to the gargoyle and was looking it up and down. The room seemed to fill with a million buzzing hot points of magic that bounced off my skin like gnats. I couldn't see them, but the air felt alive with energy.

"Ella?" Johnny took a couple of steps toward me, his brows drawn in confusion.

Damien intercepted him and spoke to him in a low voice.

I went up to the GSHO inspector and grasped her arm gently but firmly. "I'm sorry, Ms. Gupta, but I need you to get away from the gargoyle."

She turned to me, her mouth half-open in surprise, and then her gaze went past me to Lynnette, who was swaying slightly, already deep in trance.

"What . . ." Mishti's eyes whipped up to mine. "What exactly is going on? What is she doing?"

"There's been a little change in our plans," I said, more forcibly tugging her away from the statue. "For your own safety, you need to get out of the way."

She planted her feet, refusing.

Movement caught my eye, and I looked past Mishti at the gargoyle, which seemed to shift as if surrounded by the heat shimmer of a hot flame. I caught a glimpse of demon eyes within the gargoyle's face, and my heart jumped into my throat. I bent at the knees and picked up Mishti, grunting as I slung her over my shoulder.

She protested more loudly as I carried her to the corner of the room, set her on her feet, and simultaneously whipped the demon can off my belt and whirled around. I mentally reached downward for earth magic.

"Stay back!" I yelled at the inspector.

Damn, I wished I had my whip.

I watched in fascinated horror as the gargoyle animated, a living, breathing stone creature. It was surrounded in writhing strands of multicolored magic and glowed as if it were on fire. It thrashed, spreading its wings, and then arched and screamed, and the sound was like a cat's screech combined with claws across a chalkboard. Cracks illuminated along its surface and angry red hellfire shone through. I wasn't sure how Nathan could be surviving this, but Lynnette had seemed confident she could separate Nathan from the two creatures without killing him.

Blue smoke began to seep from the glowing cracks in the gargoyle. The smoke was thick, almost opaque.

"Johnny?" I glanced behind me. He already had his tablet powered up. "You'll have to be our eyes if the smoke gets bad."

Damien had moved next to me, and my skin prickled as he pulled magic. "The demon will go for the most vulnerable of us," I said, talking fast. "Lynnette will be spent after the exorcism, and Nathan will be defenseless."

"They'll be too far apart," he said through gritted teeth. "I can't make a ward that encloses both of them."

"Focus on Lynnette, Mishti, and Johnny, then," I said. "I'll take care of Nathan."

If past experience held, the demon wouldn't try to possess me. I hoped that meant I'd be able to protect Nathan until the arch-demon was contained in the trap I'd brought.

Lynnette had managed to wake up both the gargoyle and the demon, but I couldn't see any sign of Nathan yet. As far as I could tell, all three species were still merged and at least two of them were pissed. Mishti was yelling behind me, but I was trying to ignore her and focus on keeping hold of what little magic I had to wield.

My pulse pounded in my head as adrenaline and earth magic bled into every cell. I glanced back at Lynnette, and I licked my dry lips. Her eyes had turned solid black. With a hard swallow, I moved a couple of steps ahead of Damien.

A low boom shook the floor, accompanied by a blinding flash, and I threw up an arm to shield my face. When I opened my eyes, a plume of heavy smoke completely obscured the gargoyle, and the smell of sulfur and burnt hair filled the air in an eye-watering stench. I happened to glance up over the smoke and caught sight of a face in one of the theater windows. At first I assumed it was Jacob, but it wasn't. It was Phillip Zarella. The look on the necromancer's face was a disturbing mix of insanity and glee, and his attention wasn't on the gargoyle. It was on me. A chill spiraled up my spine, but I didn't have time to consider what the maniac might be thinking.

"The gargoyle's free," Johnny called from behind me. "Nathan is still possessed."

Coughing, I held my sleeve over my mouth and nose. The smoke lifted a little to reveal two beings where a moment ago there'd been only the gargoyle.

The stone creature had stopped writhing. It shook its head in a feline movement, blinked its huge eyes, and then began licking a stony-skinned paw with its pale pink tongue. It seemed completely unconcerned about the demon-possessed human standing next to it.

I recognized Nathan by his pale blond hair that was the exact same color as Roxanne's. But his skin was dead gray, and his eyes burned red like two windows into hell. His clothing had survived the ordeal, but it was plastered to his skin, and he looked as if he'd been dusted all over with ashes. His chest was heaving, but other than that he stood stock still.

Angry red cracks began to peek out across his skin, indicating the separation of demon and human was imminent. At least Mishti had gone quiet. I risked a glance at Lynnette. Her eyes were still black as night, made even more otherworldly by her dark lashes and kohl-lined lids, and her lips moved as if she were silently chanting.

Damien lifted his arms and multi-element magic snaked from the ends of his fingers, ready but not yet curling around himself, Lynnette, Johnny, and Mishti.

I pulled the top off the demon can and shoved the lid into my pocket. The temperature in the room had risen several degrees, and sweat dripped down my temples. With my eyes glued on

Nathan, I moved forward a few steps and set the can on the floor.

The hellfire crevices in Nathan's skin were pulsing, widening. He threw his head back in silent agony as white flame flared around him. I squinted, watching as black vapor crept from the cracks in his skin—the start of the demon's exit from his body. The brightness intensified, and I squeezed my eyes closed against the sharp pain. Before I could blink through the after images, the demon was already screaming and tearing around the room. The human and the demon were separated. I felt the magical whoosh of Damien's power as he created a ward around himself, Lynnette, Johnny, and Mishti behind me.

Nathan had collapsed and appeared unconscious. I needed to protect him before the demon tried to possess him again. Without time to recover, the young man likely wouldn't survive another exorcism.

"Nathan!" I yelled, hoping to rouse him. He didn't move.

The demon screeched and circled overhead, its wingspan a dozen feet across and stirring up the air.

I snatched the can up and ran a few steps toward Nathan, waving the trap at the creature to get its attention. With an ear-splitting scream it darted toward me, but then like other demons had, it reared back, unwilling to get too close. It flapped, lifting higher, and then looked over at Nathan.

"No," I gritted out. Too many people had worked too hard for this. There was no way I was going out there and telling Roxanne we'd lost her brother.

I closed my eyes, summoned every shred of magic I was able

to pull, and then held my right arm up and imagined I grasped the charmed whip. I let my magic fly out, and a tight green orb hit the demon on the side of its head, momentarily distracting it from Nathan.

I ran toward him and threw myself over his crumpled form.

Turning my head, I could see the others. Mishti was wide-eyed and clearly terrified. She'd moved behind Lynnette to the door, alternately pounding on it with her fists and turning to look at the demon. Armed guards were outside beating on the door and jerking the handle, but they couldn't get through Lynnette's ward. I had no idea how long her ward would hold. The gargoyle had moved to a corner and reassumed its statue form, probably to protect itself from another possession.

I still grasped the trap, but the demon wouldn't come close enough to me to activate it. Damien couldn't hold his ward forever. I had to do something.

With my eyes on the demon, I moved off of Nathan and slipped my arm under one of his and across his chest. If I could just get him across the room and inside Damien's ward, he'd be safe. Heaving backward, I moved him a few feet.

The center of my forehead pounded so hard it felt like my skull was going to split wide open. It was like the *other* was trying to claw its way out. I stumbled, and Nathan fell from my grasp. Spots danced in my eyes, but they weren't due to the shadows. I was on the verge of passing out. I fell across Nathan's chest. The sensation grew so intense it overwhelmed everything. I jammed my hands against my temples, groaning through clenched teeth.

Behind my closed eyelids, random scenes flashed across the screen of my mind. Some of them were in the yellow-and-blue tint of my necro vision. And then the image settled and the pain subsided to an uncomfortable thump.

I opened my eyes, but the vision remained. Gasping, I scrambled backward on all fours. I was somewhere else . . . no, I was seeing from the *viewpoint* of somewhere else.

From above. Where Phillip Zarella stood.

Just as the realization slammed home, every muscle in my body went rigid. I fell back, my head smacking the floor. Everything went momentarily black and then cleared. I was staring up at the ceiling, from my own perspective again, but I couldn't move.

Then, as before when the *other* had taken command of me, my limbs began to shift. With my head throbbing at the back from my fall, I stood with wooden movements and turned to face the center of the room.

And that was when I felt it—his presence in my head.

Phillip Zarella was driving me.

I felt the same dark energy I'd sensed when I'd first met him, but this time it was inside my brain. The psychopathic necromancer was controlling me like I was a vampire or a demon. And he wanted to play.

I could feel his intention as clearly as if it were my own. He wanted the demon to come at me. The thought of it gave him a feeling of pleasure and anticipation that made my stomach roll sickeningly. He knew about the reaper, maybe not exactly how its soul was attached to me, but he'd sensed it when we'd first met, and

I could feel how it had captured his imagination. He wanted to dig around inside my mind and soul to examine it. He wanted to see what would happen if its host—me—became possessed.

He was driving the arch-demon, too. I wasn't sure how I knew it, but I could sense the creature's apprehension, its unwillingness to come too close to me despite Zarella's telepathic order, and I almost felt a fleeting wisp of pity for it. But I had my own problems.

Zarella forced me forward, stopped me when I got to the dropped demon trap, and drew my foot back. My movements were becoming more natural, as if he were getting the hang of manipulating me, and the realization brought bile up my throat. If I managed to survive this, I was positive I'd never feel completely clean again. He drew my foot back and sent it flying forward. The toe of my boot hit the can and sent it tumbling to the far side of the room.

The demon was darting nervously but hadn't tried to dive in for possession. Clearly Zarella didn't quite have full control of it because its fear of me was still winning. At least it wasn't going for Nathan.

My breath became ragged as I mentally probed around Zarella's presence in my mind. There had to be a way to push him out, to reclaim myself. Loki had knocked loose the reaper's control the night I was under the influence of the sleeping beauty spell, but I had no idea how he'd done it.

But if a hellhound could help me, maybe now the angel of death could, too.

I shifted my focus to the shadows swirling furiously in my

periphery. Cold sweat popped out on my forehead, chest, and neck as I tried to invite them in, to welcome them. I had no idea if embracing the reaper's soul would allow it to consume mine, but I had no choice. If it ate my soul and I died right here in the Gregori facility, at least I would die knowing I did everything I could to try to save Nathan and my friends.

My pulse slowed as the smoky shapes crowded in, drifting across my eyes and partially obscuring my vision. I felt the presence of the reaper and pushed past my dread, turning to it instead of cringing from it. I probed around inside myself, looking for where the *other* was centered, and my attention sank to a point just below my breastbone. And then I pulled my own will aside, making room for the reaper.

The deep cold I'd felt during my session with Jennifer, when I'd seen the face of the angel of death in the glass, bloomed in my core as if I'd swallowed a chunk of dry ice. Through the reaper, I felt the jagged darkness of chaos the arch-demon emanated. And I sensed the black fascination—no, more like kinship—with death within Phillip Zarella. I turned my attention to the *other* and tried to convey that I needed help pushing Zarella out of my mind, that together the reaper and I had to overpower him.

I could sense Zarella's confusion, but his hold on me wasn't changing, wasn't weakening. Through our telepathic connection, I realized Zarella knew what I was doing—and it excited him.

Shit. A fresh wave of dread flooded through me as Zarella's grasp on my mind seemed to tighten. I'd miscalculated. Instead of the reaper and me standing against Zarella, letting the reaper emerge within me had only made it easier for Zarella to control me—us.

If Zarella got his wish and the demon possessed me, I'd go after one of the humans in the room. I'd kill, and then there would be no saving me, exorcism would no longer be possible. The demon and I would be permanently fused, and I'd be euthanized.

Or maybe the angel of death would devour my soul first. I decided I preferred that to subjecting myself to Zarella's sick entertainment.

I mentally bore down, trying to shove Zarella aside. The shadows closed in, and for a moment it seemed as if the reaper and I were finally pushing in tandem against the madman. I was so focused on my internal battle I became almost completely unaware of anything happening around me.

But then there was a screech, a loud crash, and the tinkle of falling glass. I jerked in surprise. I glanced up just in time to see the gargoyle circling overhead and a large pane smashed out. It must have flown into the window at Zarella.

The distraction was enough to break his hold on my mind. The shadows receded to the edges of my vision and my head cleared. I sped across the room, snatched the demon trap, and wheeled around. But the demon was faster. It was already diving for Nathan.

"No!" I yelled. I pumped my arms, racing toward him.

He was still in an unmoving heap where I'd left him. I stopped and sucked up some earth magic and hurled a malformed wad of it at the demon. It burst weakly against one leathery wing, and the demon twisted its head to look at me but then turned back to its prey. It reared back, and I recognized the beginning of a possession dive. I reached for my magic again, but I was too drained to pull any more.

Beyond Nathan's crumpled form, Damien was still holding his ward around the others.

Stumbling forward, I stretched out the can, irrationally hoping I could somehow intercept the demon as it plunged. I flung myself forward like a shortstop diving for a hard hit in the gap, knowing even as I did it that I wasn't going to get there in time.

The next few seconds stretched out, happening in exquisitely painful slow motion. With a flash of multicolored magic, Damien shifted his ward to Nathan. Lynnette stirred just as I hit the floor with a grunt. She blinked and then looked up at the demon. She raised her hand and sent a small burst of fire magic from her palm. It hit the demon in the face and stopped its dive but didn't do any real damage. She clenched her fists, trying to recharge, but I could see she was still too weak from the exorcism. But it was enough.

I scrambled forward on all fours under the demon, turned, and rose to one knee. The creature began its dive, opening it beaky mouth wide in a hellish scream. I pulled my arm back and threw the trap at its yawning maw.

Throwing the can was a last-ditch tactic, and maybe not the brightest thing to do, but the can hit its target. The demon let out a surprised squeal, and then it seemed to turn in on itself, morphing and shrinking as it appeared to get sucked into the vortex of its own mouth. There was a pop and a flash, and then the can fell to the floor with a solid *thunk*.

I pushed to my feet and pulled the lid from my pocket as I went to retrieve the smoking trap. I snapped the cap on. I gripped the can in my fist, coughing on the trap vapors. When I looked up through watering eyes searching for Zarella, he was no longer there.

My attention swung over to the gargoyle, which once again sat serenely in the corner. Then I swiveled around, giving the other a glance as I bent to check Nathan, who was right where I'd left him and still breathing. I lifted one of his limp hands and felt the weak tap of his pulse in his wrist.

Damien had released his magic and fallen to one knee, taking some deep breaths. Lynnette was trying to stand on shaky legs, and Johnny sprang to her side to help her up. Behind them near the wall, Mishti sat huddled in a ball with her face tucked against her knees. I started to turn back to Nathan when I caught sight of Jacob. He stood watching through the window in the door.

On a wave of anger and new adrenaline, I strode to the door, staring straight into my uncle's eyes. Dr. Smith was behind him in the hallway, pressed up against the opposite wall. A breeze of magic whirled through the room as Lynnette removed her ward. I tried the handle, but someone had locked it from the outside.

"Let us out of here now, or I'm gonna get the gargoyle to bust us out!" I hollered, banging on the door with my fist. I didn't know if Jacob or his researcher could hear me, but I was sure they got the gist of my demand.

He opened the door. I strode out and got in Jacob's face, stretching to my full height. The armed guys surrounded me but didn't approach.

"There's an ambulance outside the front gate," I said. "Let the medics up here immediately." I held up the demon trap, and just then the creature knocked around against the inner walls. "You have to the count of three, or I'll shove you in that room, uncork this can, and toss it in there with you."

It wasn't possible to free a demon from a trap, not with my bare hands anyway, but my threat worked. He flipped his fingers at Dr. Smith, giving her a silent signal, and she reached into her lab coat pocket and produced a phone. With wide, dazed eyes, she made a quick call.

"Were you just going to stand there while we were trapped with an arch-demon? Or were you waiting for Zarella to carry out his little cage match fantasy?" I hissed at Jacob.

Red splotches bloomed on his cheeks and anger shone in his eyes. "You created that danger for *yourself*, Ella. You had no right to do what you did. This was to be an inspection, not an exorcism."

His breath was coming fast, and the truth hit me like a punch. All he cared about was his live demon trap. He was furious that I'd screwed up his experiment. I stared at him for a moment as it sank in.

"You're a monster," I spat and wheeled away to go to Nathan.

He was a mess—he looked like he'd been sweating nonstop the entire time he'd been trapped, and he smelled like it too. But he was breathing. He was alive. I gently rolled him over to his back. He let out a soft groan, but didn't open his eyes.

A moment later a stretcher arrived, and the medics quickly

loaded him up.

A contingent of half a dozen armed guards escorted all of us to the elevator, down, and out of the building. The ambulance was waiting right outside. Johnny and I had each taken one of Lynnette's arms to help her walk. Damien trailed behind us with still-stricken Mishti. His face was drawn and pale, and at first I thought it was due to magical exhaustion. But I sensed it was something more than that—he seemed agitated, maybe even a little angry. But there was no opportunity to ask him about it. We all got back on the golf cart, and a few minutes later we'd retrieved our belongings from the lockers and found ourselves deposited at the front gate.

We walked through, back out to freedom.

That night as dusk fell, I pulled the front door open to find Johnny standing on my porch.

He had his arms pulled behind his back, and he wore a faint grin.

"I'm surprised to see you," I said.

He brought his hands out, and he held a bottle of wine in one and a bouquet of wildflowers in the other.

"You deserve a celebration," he said. "I'm here to help you celebrate."

I narrowed my eyes, hesitating and remembering what Deb had said about him. About how my refusal to play into his little advances was a challenge to his inner Don Juan.

Ah, what the hell. I *did* deserve a celebration.

I nudged my head to one side by way of invitation, and as he slipped by me, I inhaled a nose-full of leather, aftershave, and something else that was deliciously male.

"Quiet," he remarked, looking around. He handed me the flowers, and Loki came up to nudge his free hand. Johnny scratched the hellhound-doodle behind the ear.

I closed the door and took the flowers into the kitchen.

"Yeah," I said over my shoulder. "Roxanne is spending the

night with Nathan in the hospital."

"What about Deb?"

I hadn't realized Johnny had caught on to the fact that Deb had stayed with me for a couple of nights. "She's back home."

She'd realized she shouldn't avoid Keith any longer, and regardless of what she decided to do long-term, she was going to have to talk to him at some point.

I found a wine bottle opener in a drawer and pulled two of my three wine glasses from a cupboard. I had no idea why I only owned three, but I couldn't even remember the last time I'd used them. And the last time a man brought me flowers—the *only* time that I could recall—was back in Demon Patrol training. Brady had done or said something stupid and brought flowers to apologize. Apology flowers kind of sucked. Regardless of Johnny's underlying intentions, the flowers were a nice gesture.

I rummaged around in the cabinets but couldn't come up with a proper vase, so I filled a water glass halfway and stuck the bouquet into the glass. With the bottle opener shoved in my pocket, the wine glasses clutched between the fingers of one hand, and the makeshift vase in the other, I returned to the living room.

Johnny had taken off his jacket, and he sat forward on the edge of the sofa. I caught his face in profile for a moment before he saw me. There was a faint smile on his lips that widened when I came into his view. I set the glasses down and handed him the opener. He uncorked the bottle while I centered the flowers on the coffee table.

"This was awfully nice of you," I said, sitting down on the sofa and curling my legs under me.

Johnny filled the two glasses with generous pours of white wine and handed me one of them. He held his up. "To a big win for the good guys."

We clinked, and I took a long sip. I wasn't usually a wine drinker, but I could tell it wasn't a bargain bottle—a pinot grigio, according to the label—smooth, with the perfect balance of sweet and dry.

"How's Nathan doing?" Johnny asked.

All of us—Damien, Johnny, Deb, Raf, Lynnette, and I—had stayed at the hospital for several hours with Roxanne until her brother regained consciousness and the doctors declared he was out of danger. They were keeping him overnight for observation and treatment for mild dehydration. I couldn't fathom how he was trapped in that gargoyle for days without suffering much worse effects, but then I didn't completely understand how a giant demon could fit into a trap the size of a soup can, either. Supernatural phenomena had their own set of rules.

"Roxanne texted an hour ago and said he ate some toast, which the doctors seemed pleased about. He should be able to go home tomorrow."

"That's great to hear. What about Raf?"

I grimaced. Raf hadn't known that I'd basically planned to use our humanitarian entry into Gregori as a cover to free Nathan. He had pulled me aside while we were at the hospital, and our discussion had become heated.

"He's got some explaining to do with GSHO, because we used

their authority to get into the Gregori campus," I said. I was being loose with the word "we"—I was the one who'd broken the rules. "But the Human Protection organization was actually thrilled that we came out with Nathan. So . . ."

I held out my hands and lifted each palm in turn, in a weigh-this-against-that motion.

"Is he pissed at you?" Johnny asked.

"Yeah, but it looks like the whole thing is going to generate so much more attention than he'd expected, I'm pretty sure he'll get over it."

I went silent for a moment, feeling my brows draw together as I recalled how withdrawn Damien had been at the hospital. I'd tried to ask him what was wrong, but he'd just muttered something about how he should have kept a low profile, and he brushed off my further attempts at getting him to explain his mood.

Johnny looked down for a moment and gave his head a slight shake. "Kind of hard to believe all that's happened in the past few days."

I thought back to when I'd entered Roxanne's apartment and she'd shown me the gargoyle, and how my first instinct was to call Johnny. He'd shown up, known who to call, and he'd stuck with us every step of the way through the entire ordeal. He was a playboy, sure, but he had a good heart.

And *damn*, he was easy on the eyes.

He angled his body toward me, and I could feel the increased intensity of his focus.

"I've wanted to sit here with you like this since the first time we met," he said.

My first instinct was to laugh at what had to be a line, but instead my heart bumped. There was sincerity behind his words, even if they were a little cheesy.

I cocked my head, narrowing my eyes and giving him a considering look. "That was, what, two years ago? By my estimation you haven't been too lonely since then."

He dipped his chin, a tiny acknowledgement. "Yes and no."

"It's just because I resisted your charms and you like the pursuit," I said.

"Oh, so you do find me charming?" He gave a low chuckle, but then shook his head. "It's more than that. You've got an edge, a rawness, that's rare. Lots of people try to come off as edgy, but you're the real thing."

It was my turn to laugh. "If you want edge, you should go after Lynnette. Unless, of course, you've already made that conquest."

He'd moved closer, his arm across the back of the sofa and lightly touching my shoulder blade. He set his wine glass down and then turned to me, his dark eyes drilling into mine.

"I'm not interested in Lynnette," he said.

He was leaning in, and he was close enough for me to feel the faint heat of his skin and the gentle current of his breaths.

For a moment I wavered. It would be so easy to give in, to enjoy a couple of hours of company in my now too-quiet house. But my mind jumped ahead to the emptiness I'd feel after Johnny made his exit.

I reached up and patted his cheek. "I don't kiss on the first date."

He sat back a little and gave me a bemused arch of his brow. "This is a date?"

"No, this is wine on the couch," I said. "A date would require us to, you know, actually leave the house."

"Ah, true." He bit his bottom lip and nodded once, then cocked his head, regarding me silently for a moment or two.

Just then, a fit of barking emanated from the kitchen. I set down my glass and jumped up. Loki had his front paws up on the back door, and he was looking through the window out into the yard. He gave a couple of high-pitched whines and scrabbled his nails against the wood.

"Whoa, Loki. Let's not nullify my security deposit," I said. I reached for the knob and let him out, thinking he needed to chase a squirrel out of the yard.

I watched him bound outside. It wasn't a squirrel that caught his attention. He stood a couple of feet away from the gargoyle, bouncing back and forth and letting out little yips.

The gargoyle swiped a stony paw out at him and he jumped back and then resumed his yipping. Fed up, the gargoyle yowled and then transformed into statue form and went still. Loki fell quiet, cocked his head, and then went up to sniff it.

I gaped. "How the hell did it find me here? How did it get away from Gregori?"

Johnny made a noise of surprise behind me.

"Looks like you've attracted another stray," he said. We watched the gargoyle for a few seconds, but it remained in its rigid form.

"She seems pretty comfortable out there."

I turned to him. "She?"

He nodded. "I captured some more data while we were at Gregori, and ran through it this afternoon. Definitely a she."

I shook my head, snorting a laugh. "A hellhound-doodle and a gargoyle. What's next, a tribe of pixies? A flock of fairies?"

I left the door cracked so Loki could come back in when he was ready. Johnny and I went back to the sofa and our wine, and I found the heat between us had mellowed a bit, which was fine by me. Enjoying another glass of wine, we chatted for a while about what had happened at Gregori Industries, and then he left.

A few minutes later my phone buzzed with an incoming message. It was Johnny.

Are you free for dinner on Friday?

A smile twitched at my lips. *Yes. Pick me up at 7.*

I locked up and turned off all the lights except for one table lamp and sat cross-legged on the sofa with Loki lounging on his side next to me. Stilling my thoughts, I turned my attention inward and searched out the *other*. The grave chill filled my core much more quickly this time, as if the reaper had been waiting for me to reach out to it. My head thumped and the shadows crowded in, sending smoky tendrils across my vision.

I unfocused my eyes, allowing myself to sink into the awareness of the soul of the reaper within me. I could feel it curling around in my mind, vying for control, but not powerful enough to take it while I was fully conscious.

Silently, I began to speak to it. I pictured the ghost house and felt the reaper take notice as the thumping in my head increased in tempo. It wanted us to return there. I pictured my brother's face, as he had looked in the vision of the vampire feeder den.

Give me more and I'll give you something in return, I tried to convey to it.

Again I pictured the ghost house.

The shadows danced and bled inward until my living room disappeared into darkness. I sucked in a sharp breath, disoriented. Then a scene began to take shape in the yellow and blue tones of the necro-vision. Treetops and rooftops and streets spread out below me, and the sensation of wind and unfamiliar movement caused my stomach to lurch.

I was flying through the night. The soft flapping of wings surrounded me. Minor demons. We were headed away from the residential streets toward the hills. I looked for landmarks but couldn't be sure where we were. One of the demons pulled ahead, and the rest of us followed, angling downward to what looked like a compound—a sprawling house surrounded by a high, solid fence.

Alighting on the branches of elm trees like a murder of crows, we had a view of a courtyard below. A figure emerged from a sliding glass door—I sensed the sharp predatory danger and tang of blood that told me it was a vamp, a rogue one. A handful of humans, slow moving and clumsy, followed the vamp.

The vamp tipped his head back and peered up at the starry sky. He inhaled deeply and then turned and beckoned to the humans. "Take in the night, shadows. Stretch your legs."

The humans—shadows, servants of vampires—looked around

with dazed expressions. One of them, a young man, tilted his face up, and my breath stilled.

It was Evan.

I tried to call his name, but the minor demon whose eyes the reaper and I were borrowing could only let out a faint squeal.

Then, it was as if a rubber band snapped against my brain, and the scene vanished.

My heart hammered. "No, wait, go back," I rasped. "I need to know *where.*"

But all I saw was my own living room. Loki was peering up at me, his pupils flickering dark red. A growl rumbled low in his throat.

"I need to know where he is," I repeated.

But the grave chill in my core receded. I half expected the reaper to pound against the inside of my skull, demanding that I take it to the ghost house. But instead, its anticipation bled through me like a black tide. I choked, feeling as if I were drowning. For a split second, the reaper's eagerness for the ghost house completely filled me and became my own. It was fast, but in that blink there was no Ella—I was a shell, a mere container for the reaper's desire.

My breath ragged, I gave my head a hard shake. Standing, I went to the bathroom and flipped the light on, suddenly filled with the need to see my own face in the mirror, to be able to look at myself and know that I *was* still myself.

I watched my reflection, staring into my own haunted eyes until my breathing returned to normal.

I called up the images from the vision, every detail of the

compound in the middle of nowhere. I had a bit of information—the place where Evan was being held. I had something to look for, something concrete to seek out. Now I just had to survive the reaper long enough to find it.

Look for the next book in the series:
Dark Harvest Magic **(Ella Grey Book Two)**

For updates on new releases, fun giveaways, and free books go here to join Jayne Faith's Insiders List: http://bit.ly/JoinJayne

For new release and sale alerts only,
text CCJFBOOKS to 24587.

Acknowledgments

I had more help on this book than any I've written to date, and this is the place where I get to say a giant THANK YOU everyone who played a part.

First, to the members of Jayne Faith's Reader Brigade: Your enthusiasm for my stories and support of my dream of writing full-time are simply amazing. I'm so lucky to have connected with each of you. Thank you for being so awesome and encouraging.

Huge props and deep gratitude to my editor Mary Novak, whose diligence, professionalism, and passion for story were absolutely critical in working out the kinks in this book. You are a gem, I'm so fortunate to have found you, and I can't wait to work with you on my next project.

Tia Bach, thank you for your excellent work on this and all of my previous books. Each time I reach the end of a new manuscript I'm grateful to have such a dependable proofreader to turn to.

Kim and the designers at Deranged Doctor Design, you have outdone yourselves on the projects I've brought to you. Thank you for your dependability and amazing cover art.

Rebecca Hamilton, thank you for your generous assist on the cover and for providing so many innovative ways to get my books into the hands of readers and take my career to the next level.

And last but most important, thank you Charlie for having such faith in me and cheering me on as I take this ride.